TOMORROW WAR

ALSO BY J.L. BOURNE

Day by Day Armageddon
Day by Day Armageddon: Beyond Exile
Day by Day Armageddon: Shattered Hourglass

TOMORROW WAR

The Chronicles of Max ▬▬▬

A Novel by J.L. Bourne

Gallery Books

New York   London   Toronto   Sydney   New Delhi

G

Gallery Books
An Imprint of Simon & Schuster, Inc.
1230 Avenue of the Americas
New York, NY 10020

First Gallery Books hardcover edition June 2015

GALLERY BOOKS and colophon are registered trademarks of Simon & Schuster, Inc.

For information about special discounts for bulk purchases, please contact Simon & Schuster Special Sales at 1-866-506-1949 or business@simonandschuster.com.

The Simon & Schuster Speakers Bureau can bring authors to your live event. For more information or to book an event, contact the Simon & Schuster Speakers Bureau at 1-866-248-3049 or visit our website at www.simonspeakers.com.

Design by Lewelin Polanco

Manufactured in the United States of America

10 9 8 7 6 5 4 3 2 1

Library of Congress Cataloging-in-Publication Data is available

ISBN 978-1-4516-2913-2
ISBN 978-1-4516-2915-6 (ebook)

AUTHOR'S NOTE

This is not a novel about zombies, or at least undead zombies. For that tale, please point your e-readers or feet to my *Day by Day Armageddon* series. Although we are not overrun by *real* living dead (yet), some experts say the world economy may be on the brink of collapse. In a few moments, I hope you will embark on a journey down a similar dark road, one that wholly diverges from rosy predictions, gushing mainstream optimism, and suspicious government economic statistics. What if this complex yet fragile socioeconomic system were to tumble uncontrollably like an animal on a frozen pond? I propose that complex systems cannot be controlled or even predicted; first world nations' leaders only perform in a political theater of public deception; *someone is at the helm and everything will be fine, just be a good citizen or subject and go back to your favorite sitcom, football team, or reality TV program.*

At the time of this writing, elected leaders are calling for abolition of our debt ceiling, draconian gun control, the use of armed drones in the skies above us, and are engaging in warrantless NSA pilfering of our private e-mails, text messages, persons, and effects. Where might this dangerous road lead? Has it ever been about your safety and security? The thought crime ahead goes beyond the paradigm of right, left, Democrat, or Republican, and the outdated behavioral placement control mechanisms, forcing us to choose between two heads of the same serpent.

Slay the beast, turn the page, and choose liberty.

J.L. Bourne
PENSACOLA, FLORIDA
2014

FOR SHER AND LILLY

"We will not have any more crashes in our time."

—**John Maynard Keynes, 1927**

PART ONE

The Making of Max

The following pages are a compilation transcribed from petabytes of analyzed text, audio, and video recovered from Hub sensor Big Iron. Typed or handwritten transcriptions will be in raw, uncorrected format. The majority of the source files originate from the journal of Max ▆▆▆▆▆▆▆▆▆. Notes that go beyond the original source files will be clearly annotated.

BEGIN COGNITIVE TRANSCRIPTION//

Classified transcript between the President of the United States and ▆▆▆▆▆▆▆▆ during ▆▆▆▆▆▆▆▆.
▆▆▆▆▆▆▆ Office / 2315 / Date: ▆▆▆▆▆▆▆▆

//START TRANSCRIPTION//

POTUS: "The wheels are coming off, I don't know how much longer we can keep up this charade. The unemployment numbers are being openly heckled in the mainstream media. You are calling inflation at a percent and a half, but the American people begin to take notice when gas goes to six dollars a gallon and food cost goes up forty percent over a three year span."

████████████: "Top down economics and war spending got us out of the Great Depression. I have faith in the system; faith that we can make this right again."

POTUS: "Faith? I won an election on faith and family. Somehow I think we're going to need more than a campaign slogan to put this mess back together. ████████████, right now, I really need to know your way ahead. Call it crisis mode. We're there. It's only a matter of time before a butterfly flaps its wings somewhere and confidence in the dollar is lost."

████████████: "That's not going to happen, Ma'am."

POTUS: "That's what the leaders of the Weimar Republic, Zimbabwe, Argentina said in the days before their currency imploded. What's the plan? I have a midnight VTC with one of our biggest customers, right behind China and yourself."

████████████: "Well, in the near term, it's best we keep interest rates at or near zero percent; we're avoiding a liquidity trap. We're also going to keep increasing the M-3 supply. As we've already discussed, before we cross the no return delta, I'll increase the rates and begin to recall the supply. Now is a bad time for a rate increase and we need to encourage spending. Too many people are parking their money in their banks and worse, their mattresses. If we keep the pressure up, they'll start spending. My analysts say that a few more months of zero percent interest with some healthy inflation thrown in will get the average saver back in the economy."

POTUS: "A few more months? We don't have that kind of time, do we? What have your folks calculated as the real current number?"

█████████████: "Are we secure right now? This number needs to stay with us."

POTUS: "It's the fucking Oval Office, I should hope so. If we're not secure, I can't imagine a place that is."

█████████████: "Thirty-one point three percent."

POTUS: "I'm sorry, did you say thirty-one percent?"

█████████████: "I know that number sounds a bit dismal, but rest assured we've run numerous [WHISPERS] actuaries on this. [END WHISPER] The computed data tells us almost to the minute when we need to adjust the interest rates to avoid a currency crisis. The internet is being crawled via ██████████████ in real time, assisted by PRISMA. Every internet forum comment, video chat, and e-mail are part of the calculations. It's quite accurate. We will know about any crisis of confidence long before the consumer hive mind can crash the system."

POTUS: "What if you don't? What if you don't call it just right? What's the contingency?"

█████████████: "The contingency is the reason I'm here tonight. On the very small chance we miss our mark, we're going to need to jumpstart the Keynesian sluices. History has shown that there is only one way to do that; good old fashioned war."

POTUS: "That's the second time tonight you've brought up war. We've run out of countries and terrorist organizations. We can't pick a fight anymore. If that's your plan, try again."

██████████████: "I have a plan that will guarantee the flow of money again, be low risk to you, and will result in the American people begging us to go to war."

//END TRANSCRIPTION//

SERE

High-Risk Capture
Spokane, Washington
Summer

My name is Max ▬▬▬▬▬▬. Friends just call me Max. A few weeks ago, I graduated Survival, Evasion, Resistance, and Escape (SERE) school in Brunswick, Maine. Although a required training for "high risk of capture" folks like me, this in itself was a huge kick in the balls. I found myself thrown into a few million acres of a government proving grounds to evade a hostile, organized, and well-armed opposing force. I learned bushcraft and evasion techniques in the field. Like everyone else, I was eventually captured, given the identification number war criminal 38, and tossed into a cage where I was enhanced interrogated for days. After that bout of training, I was a little nervous when I was ordered to Spokane, Washington, for follow-up on survival training. My foot blisters were still in the healing process when I stepped through the doors of the windowless building that was home to a very unique school-house.

I'm documenting all this for good reason, but I'm not really ready to share why. Putting it down here means it's real; tangible, touchable . . . well, as touchable as digital can be.

I didn't know anyone inside this secure facility. We were sternly told by a man in a black uniform to take our seats; they were check-ing on our security clearances, and the class would begin in a few minutes. In striking up a quick conversation with the man sitting on my left, I learned he was an Air Force major that flew U-2 spy planes; the man to my right, after a few back and forth questions, admitted that he worked at Fort Meade. Wasn't difficult to de-duce he was from the National Security Agency. Soon, the small auditorium filled with even more people I didn't know. A few of them looked like spooks, but it was tough to tell these days. Some talked, some didn't. I watched the ones that didn't. A middle-aged man with that traditionally handsome gray fox look walked into the room wearing jeans and a pullover fleece with elbow patches a few shades removed from the rest of the garment; he carried a metal clipboard. He quietly took his seat at the very top and back of the auditorium, underneath two large panes of mirrored glass.

As the students became more comfortable, the chatter in-creased, eventually to that uncomfortable crescendo when you just knew that the teacher would walk in and tell everyone to shut up. That never happened. During my small talk with the U-2 major, I scanned the room, noticing small cameras positioned along the ceiling at every conceivable angle. I also noticed the small micro-phones overtly hanging throughout the auditorium. It was thirty minutes past the class start time when the room got quiet, and the man in the black uniform entered, stepping out in front of the class.

"You all are probably wondering why you're here."

Most of the thirty-student class nodded.

"You're here because you know things, or you are going to know things, that could get the United States into a serious shit storm if you were compelled to talk. My name isn't really important. You can call me Mr. Embassy."

Laughter from the class elicited a smile from Mr. Embassy.

"I'd like to ask a question and get a show of hands. Who in this class has never in their life attended regular SERE school?"

I couldn't help myself; I had to look around the auditorium to see which sucker would take the bait. I couldn't see anyone with a hand up behind me.

Embassy startled me when he looked at me and said, "You, stand up."

I started to get to my feet, but the NSA guy sitting to my right was the one who got up. His spring-loaded folding seat cushion slapped against the backrest as the NSA guy stood there under the watchful eyes of Embassy.

"So you've never been to SERE?" Embassy asked the man.

"No, sir. Never heard of it," said the NSA guy.

"What's your name?"

"Charles."

"All right, Charles, thank you for confirming that."

Mr. Embassy nodded towards the back of the room. In a flash, two men wearing black uniforms and hoods, and armed with AK-47s, rushed into the room, snatched up Charles, and took him away. Just like that, I sat next to an empty chair, still warm where he existed seconds before.

Embassy continued, "There's always one."

The crowd snickered.

Sadistic assholes. That could have been you, I thought to myself.

Embassy continued

"In regular SERE school, you were taught the basics of staying inside the metaphoric resistance circle. Of course, you were instructed in this art over two weeks of field survival, with some P.O.W. camp fun sprinkled in for good measure. The training you've received is quite valuable, but this school is going to add a few more skills to your portfolio."

Embassy paced back and forth in front of us as he spoke. "The things you already learned in regular SERE will help you in situations like this."

Embassy signaled a shooting gesture with his hand to someone at the back of the auditorium. The entire wall in front of us retracted into the ceiling, revealing an interrogation room that was concealed behind it. If someone were to ask me to describe what I thought a World War Two Japanese interrogation room might look like, it would be what I saw behind the glass. I was looking at a cutaway of a bamboo hut, with various chains and odd instruments leaning against and hung on the bamboo walls. A man with a hood over his head slumped quietly near his ski-masked and hostile interrogator.

The slumping, hooded man wore Charles's clothing.

It was no surprise when the interrogator violently yanked off the wet black hood, revealing a very distraught NSA employee sobbing beneath.

Charles's interrogator began to question him.

We all watched in horror through the thick two-way glass as the masked interrogator pulled a bamboo floor panel away, revealing a pool of black water beneath. With a quick turn of an ancient brass valve, more dark water gushed from a faucet into the pool. It reminded me of a nice tranquil koi pond for a moment until the interrogator started in on Charles.

"Who do you work for?" the interrogator asked calmly in a thick Arab accent.

Charles fixated on the deepening dark pool of water at his feet. "I don't understand why you're doing this!" he screamed at his captor.

The interrogator wasted no time in slapping the shit out of Charles with the back of his hand.

Charles gasped for air and looked out into the auditorium. The two-way glass gave him no quarter, no faces but his own to look back on him. His eyes pleaded to all of us. My stomach began to do cartwheels as I watched Charles suffer behind the glass.

"Help me!" Charles gasped just before the interrogator kicked his legs out from under him and forced him face-first into the water.

The interrogator slapped a timer on a nearby shelf as Charles's head submerged. The man followed some cryptic protocol that I noticed, but didn't understand. I never got the impression that he wanted to *really* drown Charles. I somehow knew that in this portion the training was strictly regimented to avoid any long-term damage, physical or mental.

It must have felt like hours to Charles, but after about fifteen seconds, the interrogator yanked him from the water and asked, "Again, where do you work?"

Briefed by his employer to stick to his cover statement when interrogated, Charles said, "I work for Naval District Washington; I file papers!"

Charles was lying. This was a very dangerous game to play in captivity. The bad guys have Google, and they use it—trust me.

"Really? Your wallet has a Fort Meade library card inside, and your car has a mathematics bumper sticker on the rear window."

The interrogator slapped Charles with an open hand.

"Okay, I work for NSA! Now stop! Please!"

The lights went out behind the glass. The false wall slowly fell back into place, hiding the horror behind it—for now. The students, including myself, all exchanged glances at one another wondering what could possibly be next. Mr. Embassy ducked out unnoticed during all the drama, but returned with Charles at about the same time the familiar crescendo of classroom conversation peaked. Dead silence ensued. Remembering my training, I stood up and went to escort Charles back to his seat, welcoming him back to the group. This was important after experiencing these levels of stress inoculation.

I sat Charles down and let him know that everything was fine. He didn't appear catatonic, but he definitely wasn't the same. I offered him a stick of mint gum, and he took it. The towel wrapped around his shoulders was soaked with the water from the terrible pit behind the wall.

I was not above the horrors of the schoolhouse. I had my turn in "the tank" on three (or was it four?) separate occasions during my short time in Spokane. *Just take a deep breath and keep it in the middle,* I kept telling myself over and over again when the smelly, snot-stained hood was ripped repeatedly from my head. The first time the hood came off, I was standing under bright klieg lights. Sitting at the table in front of me was a large man holding a metal tray of syringes sitting on a thin layer of salt. I tried not to look at them, but I couldn't help myself; I was fixated on them. I could see the micro bubbles in each syringe, forming unique patterns.

"Sit down," the man sternly ordered.

I did as he asked and looked through the interrogator as he prepared one of the syringes. He flicked at it and squirted the piss-colored liquid into the air. It seemed to fly in a slow motion arc and land on my brown boot, leaving the leather a little darker in spots.

"You know what this is?" the man asked.

"No," I responded.

"Sodium Pentothal, also known as truth serum. We already know you're a spy—now we're just going to make it official."

He stood up, walked to my side of the table. I closed my eyes to brace for impact, but it never came. When I risked opening my eyes again, I saw the man pull a latex tourniquet from his cargo pocket. He placed it tightly on my left arm.

"We don't have to do this," he said. "If you'll just sign this document, we can end this right now and return you to your country." He produced a single-page document, written in Chinese and with my name in English below a signature line.

"I can't read what I'm signing, so I wouldn't know what I'd be agreeing to."

"It just says that you understand that we are feeding and clothing you, and that we are taking care of you in accordance with international law."

"Does international law include shooting me up with drugs?"

The man reached across the table and backhanded me across the face.

"*Sign it!*" he screamed.

I took a moment to regain my composure. "I don't know what it says. If you get me a copy in English, I'd be happy to read it over. But I'm not a spy—I'm just a college student and traveler." I made up a cover on the spot, knowing that if I could run out the clock, the interrogator would be out of time and I'd soon be back in my seat, safe on the other side of the black glass three feet from my right shoulder—where everyone in the auditorium was now watching me flail.

The man would ask a question, and I would vaguely answer or evade it.

"That's it—time for the truth juice." The man slapped my veins and grabbed the syringe, observing my face as he pushed the needle closer to my arm. "Last chance, before this goes into your veins . . ."

oh, and by the way, I can't promise you that truth juice is the only thing in that syringe."

He watched my expression. I was a little frightened that he would do it, but I didn't give in. I told myself to stick to the training, don't deviate—resist by any means necessary.

As the needle touched my arm, a black hood was tossed over my head and I was forcefully whisked from the room.

Graduation Day

We were told to gather inside the auditorium at 0600. It was 0630 and we were still sitting there, waiting, looking at each other. At about 0640, Mr. Embassy walked in, followed by familiar but hated faces—the interrogators.

"We've reached the end of your training here in Spokane and overall I'd like to say: great work," Embassy said. "I'd like War Criminals Thirty-eight and Seventeen to stand up now, please."

I sat in my seat, wondering who the hell they were. One of the other guys stood up and looked around curiously, probably for the other number that had not yet done so.

"Thirty-eight, don't be shy. Stand up!"

I sat there thinking that this Thirty-eight guy better stand up right now or he might get another dose in the interrogation room, when Mr. Embassy looked at me and said: "Max, on your feet."

I bolted up faster than my officer candidate school days. I don't know how, but I had forgotten my original assigned SERE school prisoner number and was embarrassed when the class began to snicker at me for not rogering up. I tried to play it off to the people around me. "I was too scared to stand up—I thought another tray of rusty needles was on tap." I said, half laughing.

Mr. Embassy continued. "Thirty-eight and Seventeen, you are

the honor graduates for the spring class. I'd like everyone to give you a round of applause—you've earned it."

The room filled with golf claps and whistling, applauding us for what I thought was only an average performance. I noticed the gray fox guy with the clipboard standing in the back, whispering something to another faculty member that I did not recognize. I thought I caught him glance at me during the conversation.

After a performance debrief, including the viewing of all video surveillance of the various interrogations of the students, we were dismissed to outprocessing.

On my way out of the auditorium I was approached by Mr. Embassy.

"So, you're headed off to ■■■■■■■■■■ now right?"

"Yeah, I guess it looks that way," I said.

"Is that what you want?" He asked this as if I had a choice. I'd soon find out that I actually did.

"Well, if it's not spooky, it's not really worth doing, is it?"

"No, Max, it's not."

The auditorium was clear of students except for me. Embassy looked to the two-way glass and gave a thumbs-up. The wall at the bottom of the auditorium began its slow, deliberate climb to the ceiling, revealing the brightly lit interrogation room. Inside was Gray Fox and his aluminum clipboard. He sat at the desk, head down. He seemed to be diligently reviewing his notes.

Mr. Embassy cleared his throat. "I'll give you one guess as to who that guy works for, and another guess as to who he wants to talk to right now."

I nodded to Embassy and followed him down the steps leading to the room behind the viewing glass.

I was now one of the sheep-dipped.

VIRGINIA FARMING

"Listen, I don't know anything about polygraphs, and I don't know how accurate they are, but I know they'll scare the hell out of people."

—**President Richard Nixon**

Camp Peary

This definitely isn't like the movies. I've been here for two weeks, failed the polygraph on the first try, and have had the pleasure of visiting the company shrink twice. I passed the poly on my second attempt, and was told that most candidates take it three times on average. What I didn't tell them was that I lied my ass off on both tests. I didn't fall for the poly administrator wearing a fucking suit or sitting higher up in his chair. I wasn't intimidated, either. I toyed with the control questions, screwing up his baseline. On the first test, I was looking for weaknesses; on the second, I exploited them. The administrator bragged that he was a graduate of Fort McClellan, but I really didn't care.

Beating a polygraph really isn't difficult as long as you're not an idiot and attempt to trick the box by putting a thumb tack in your shoe, or clenching your ass cheeks. Both of those urban myths only work in mid-list spy novels. The administrator is trained to catch bullshit tactics, and modern polygraph seats have pressure sensors built in, revealing any slight tenseness of the body during questioning.

The real secret in beating the lie detector? Don't believe in it. The test only works if you have faith in the technology—something the administrator is trained to instill in you. If you know the test is bullshit and you stick to your guns, you'll pass. Eventually.

We PT every morning as a group, and some of us are fast. I'm not the hare of the group, but I'm not in the goon squad, either. I'm told we'll be moving training sites to somewhere called the Point in a few days. There are case officers training with us, but I know that's not why I'm here. The case officers seem to be taking different instructions. They are learning to establish rapport, and to develop agents. They seem to be spending a lot of time in conversation labs, learning the gift of gab . . . if you believe that sort of thing can be taught in a school. There are no laser watches or Walther PPKs here. Most of the case officers will graduate and do some time in Northern Virginia to meet and greet the analysts before getting posted at some boring shithole in the desert. I'm only basing my predictions on the Arabic and Farsi I've heard them practice among themselves. I guess it turned out to be pretty handy for me growing up having Syrian grandparents.

Although the candidates with me now are all SERE trained and beyond, this place still had a few more things to teach us. We learned advanced resistance techniques that made the torture in Maine and Washington state look like preschool naptime. I don't think I'll have any permanent marks on the outside, but I can't forget some of the things I had to watch. Two candidates have already dropped the program on request, signed their non-disclosure agreements, and headed back to their old lives.

I'm an only child; my parents are dead, and the rest of my family asks questions, but I've been assigned a passable cover. I'm not allowed to tell anyone who I really work for. Ever since Spokane, I've been instructed to say that I'm working for the State Department via the National Geospacial Agency as a government cartographer. To add authenticity, I was even sent to a monthlong ArcGIS school so that I could speak intelligently about digital mapmaking. The work numbers I've given out to family for emergencies get routed to a legit switchboard, where a message is taken by a NGA representative. I have been religiously playing down my cover employment, under-dramatizing my life. I hate lying to my aunt, as I've always seen her as a mother figure, especially since Mom died. The old house that Mom left me in the will doesn't feel like home anymore without her there. If I want to drift back in time and feel nostalgia, I stay at my aunt's house at least one night when I visit. I was practically raised thinking of my cousins as siblings. When things get intense during training, I try to dial it back by thinking of them all.

The most interesting thing I've learned in my two weeks here is *when* to kill. This skill was something I seriously lacked. I mean, what normal person thinks like this? In the beginning, I took quite a few simunition rounds to the chest before I started paying attention to the visual cues—facial expressions that would tell me that the contact wasn't in the room to have a conversation. After four times in the training room, I started to notice them. Nervous tics and tells during negotiations that revealed the person across the table was about to kill me, via simulated ammunition. On the fifth session, I didn't take the blue paint to the chest; my instructor finally got his own dose via my Glock 19. As sessions continued, different and more experienced instructors began to participate. They could be either hostile or only innocent assets. Sometimes I took the paint, and sometimes they did. After thirty sessions spread out over two days, I was told that I was finished with this particular block of training.

On the way out of the training area, I passed by Instructor Five in the hallway. He transmitted a subtle tell, and I quickly blasted him in the chest three times without even thinking.

In that moment, I thought I was finished, booted from the schoolhouse.

Instructor Five caught his breath and approached, extending his hand, his torso covered in paint. "Great work. That was your final test. Hesitation has killed more than a few of my friends. Trust your instincts and just shoot when you see the signs. Let us send the flowers after you exfil the country."

After I converted my Glock back to its lethal 9mm hollow-point configuration, I left the chamber empty for a week until I was sure I could control the reflex to neutralize my instructors.

It seems like a stretch since I left the Farm for the Point, but it hasn't really been that long—maybe six days or so. We've been doing a lot of training on expedient homemade explosives and detonators. We've also sat through instruction ranging from government de-stabilization operations to clandestine entry—I've broken lots of padlock shims and pick sets. We even learned how to make a pretty damn good pick with a battery-powered toothbrush and a hacksaw blade shaped with a file. Even with all the modern gadgets, a ten-sion bar and a rake, and maybe a bump key, are good enough for most things.

Back to the explosives—who knew? Most explosive material issued to agencies by the government is chemically marked so that it can be traced back to whom it was issued if it ever turned up in a pile of rubble where a building used to be. This meant that all the dirty tricks that happen overseas needed to be from disavow-able explosives. A good thing to remember. We've learned to make ricin (nasty stuff) from castor seeds and the best way to employ it. Homemade plastic explosives. Coincidentally, most of the jerry-rigged stuff came via an instructor from Arkansas, whose father wrote a book on the subject years ago.

We've even done some agent development role-training. In one scenario, I was given fifty thousand U.S. dollars in a brown paper bag and told to buy three agents through negotiations. I was told that buying agents was the most used tactic in the field to develop contacts. We practice this at odd times, with zero notice.

Twice since I've been here, a C-130 landed at our small airstrip; men spilled out and headed over to the kill house. They seemed to be unsure of exactly where they were. That makes both of us. I'm pretty sure they're Delta or SEALs, but I didn't risk asking. I hate taking the chance that I'll be the one that the instructors remember. After the C-130 lands, the pilots don't shut down. My small group boards with parachutes and other kit, and we do a jump. The plane lands, we get new chutes, and we jump again. Two jumps per C-130 a day seems to be the norm. Never more than three.

An NSA guy showed up yesterday, introducing himself as Mark ██████████. He brought some pretty interesting software that my small cadre of specialized students needed to be familiar with so we can communicate securely from inside target countries. Mark, a pretty huge nerd from Fort Meade with likely a 170 IQ wore an "I Speak Qwghlmian" T-shirt to brief us on a bootable Linux USB distribution he designed just for us. He told us that the software was so encrypted that when examined forensically, it would look like blank, unused memory.

Mark demonstrated this to the small group by restarting the computer in the conference room with the tiny USB drive inserted.

"I was hoping that when they pulled the hood off my head after I landed here, that I'd be at Area 51. No such luck."

Most of us laughed at that.

"Anyway, when you restart the target computer, pinch the top and bottom of the USB stick to actuate a hidden pressure switch. This will, on most computers, change your boot options so you don't have to fumble for a function key. The initial password for your custom distros is your mother's maiden name, followed by your grandfather's street address, all lowercase, no spaces. You'll all be issued your own proprietary distro based on your mission set. You'll also have a duress password."

Mark demonstrated the boot process; it was fast, maybe five seconds to splash screen. On the plain desktop was an e-mail icon, accompanied by a skull and crossbones on the opposite side of the screen.

"You'll recognize the e-mail icon; it's secure—256-bit AES, encased in a separate 256-bit AES operating system with deniability native. Just type text and hit Send, no need to fill in addresses or subjects. This mode is meant to be a simple, secure, and expedient means of communications, nothing more."

Mark hovered over the crossbones for a moment, seemingly choosing his words. "And this? You don't want to fuck with the skull. Only click the skull if you think you're about to be tied to an electrified mattress spring, à la Rambo. Clicking the skull will release a gnarly worm to the target system and network . . . a worm that is tailored to you and your mission set. It's designed to replicate and infect the target domain, eventually finding its way onto the Internet. It then kills any media or blog mention of certain terms by attacking the news aggregate servers. It neutralizes terms that you might mention under duress, like your name and agency affiliations. It's nasty. It will cripple the IT infrastructure of an entire country until we send the deactivation command to the original backbone where the worm was released. It will also attempt to crash the target country's high-frequency exchanges, so make sure you liquidate your foreign stocks before you double-click. It can also be activated by entering your duress passphrase. We've come a long way since Stuxnet and the Iranians."

This guy was a *real* black hatter. I'd be surprised if he wasn't recruited by the NSA straight out of a police interrogation room.

"Are there any questions? If not, I'd like to put my hood back on and get back to Maryland. They've got a tricky project for me that puts the skull to shame."

As he left the briefing room, I thought to myself: *Don't forget Mark's Christmas card.*

[DATE REDACTED]

My time in Virginia ended without much pomp and circumstance. I didn't put it all down here in these writings—some of what happened over the past few months stays where it needs to. The State Department movers arrived at my old place after I left the Point. They packed up most of my belongings for me, all but the things that I wanted to keep with me during my time overseas. We started with about a dozen trainees, but only five made the cut. It's like anything else I suppose; you'll only go as far as you want to. I remember one drop on request during the training—her name was ▬▬▬▬▬▬▬. Back at Camp Peary, they had her blindfolded. Her head was pulled back into a deep sink with the water running swiftly, splashing everywhere. The interrogator would ask her a question. When she attempted to use her training to avoid the question, the instructor would slap her and then take a pair of scissors and start cutting off pieces of her hair. She lost it and quit right there on the spot. When the blindfold came off and she caught her breath, she saw that they hadn't even touched her hair at all. But once you give the signal to drop, you're done, no takebacks. She gave up the whole program over nothing. Which was a real shame, as the women in my small group seemed to be the toughest. When I volunteered for this program, I had no idea that I would've endured this.

My exit interview from the Point was even more intense than the lifestyles polygraph I had to squirm through twice. Real Machiavellian, greater-good shit.

"Would you shoot a child that spotted you in denied territory, threatening your compromise?"

The question reminded me of a book I'd read years ago. A group of Afghan goatherders stumbled upon some SEALs on a reconnaissance mission in Afghanistan. They snitched the SEALs' location to a few hundred Taliban fighters. All but one were killed in brutal combat on a nowhere Afghani mountaintop. I chose to honor those men by learning from their account.

Hours of questioning along those lines spewed from the interviewer. The mirrored glass told me that others watched my responses. Some of the questions were repeated multiple times with a slightly different syntax. Bottom line? Yes, I would kill for self-preservation; yes, I would kill for mission preservation.

Next up, Fort Benning, Georgia. After that, we'll see.

SYRIA

After some marksmanship training at Benning, I went home for two weeks to decompress . . . heal bumps, bruises, and mosquito bites. Spending time with family was fantastic; it felt good to reconnect. They weren't very interested in my new assignment at the State Department, so that made things a lot easier when telling them I'd be going out of town for a bit. My cousins and I did our traditional primitive camping in the Ozark Mountains; it was a spot we knew well, not too far from my parents' old house. We kept saying we were going to build a hunting cabin here so we didn't have to sleep with the ticks, but we never got around to it. My cousin Jim was a mason but seemed to be pouring more footings than doing brick-work these days. It would have been pretty damn easy building a cabin with him as foreman. We stayed warm with a fire and an old '55 Chevy pickup hood propped to reflect the heat. We'd go behind an old black oak tree and dig up our cooler cache with a bottle of

Jack from the year before, making room for the next year's bottle that we'd brought with us. My cousins would reminisce about our childhood and about all the deer they took not far from here. They added a few points to those racks every time the story was told, but for the most part, it was true. Life is simpler in these hills, under these stars. The only thing I'd leave behind are the damn ticks. I'd joke with my cousins that if we'd just jar up a few crates of black oak seed ticks and drop them overseas, the wars would be over in a few short weeks. I didn't really have the time to document my thoughts as much as I would have liked; my time was well spent with family.

I've been summoned to Northern Virginia for a mission brief tomorrow morning, and will be meeting up with someone who has a lot more experience than me. I'm not so full of hubris that I don't see the advantage of shadowing someone the first time out, if that's what this is.

Facial recognition records transcription//Delmay Glass//
Date: ▄▄▄▄▄▄▄▄▄▄

BIOMETRIC AND THERMAL SENSORS DETECT SECURITY HAND ON SUPPRESSED WEAPON.

Security Screen: MAX ▄▄▄▄▄▄▄ Recognized facial pattern, interocular distance, cranial curve, grant access.

SENSORS DETECT SLOWING HEART RATE. NO THREAT.

Resume MAX ▄▄▄▄▄▄ journal entries.

An unmarked Gulfstream was waiting for me on the tarmac at Drake. Flight time was short—it was just over three hours when

I touched down at my destination in Northern Virginia. I wasn't taken to Langley, but was dropped at a front company in Alexandria. They aren't difficult to spot when driving down Route 1. Just look for the high-gain satellite communications antennas on the roof and the very well-kept grounds. No real business owner invests that kind of money in keeping the grounds meticulously mowed on a weekly basis and the windows clean as if they were installed yesterday. This particular covered facility was a redbrick telecommunications building connected to a glass company. It was conveniently located not far from the Woodrow Wilson Bridge on-ramp to the Maryland side of the Beltway. Easy access to Huntington Metro, Andrews Air Force Base, or the sixteen-agency alphabet soup.

After entering the building, I approached the reception desk, where a well-dressed woman sat, wearing her hair pinned up tightly behind her head. She didn't ask me to stop, nor did she react to my presence as I approached. Without even looking at me, she handed me a badge matching the building's Delmay Glass company logo and ordered me to get in the elevator and press eight. I asked her how she knew . . . but she cut me off.

"Facial recognition. You're cleared; now get in the elevator. You shouldn't spend longer than sixty seconds in Reception."

Something told me that this woman meant just what she said. I headed to the elevator and watched the mirrored doors close in front of me. I pressed eight and a mechanical voice said, "Welcome to Delmay Glass, please touch the card to the blinking light." The eight was blinking, so I did what the elevator asked. "Thank you. Have a wonderful day."

The elevator began its short climb to the top floor. As the door opened, I could see a conference table surrounded with a few people in business attire. There were doughnuts there on the table along with what I assumed was a metal carafe of coffee. I was a bit underdressed in a pair of khaki pants, some worn brown leather shoes, a polo shirt, and a ball cap. I was enjoying a pretty long hiatus from wet shaving, and sported a respectable beard. The people around the table all seemed equally faceless to me. I felt as if I was being observed, analyzed by wraiths floating around the room in expensive Beltway suits.

I stepped forward and was greeted by a woman in her thirties with red hair. She stood nearly eye to eye with me, sporting high European cheekbones and a pantsuit. She was beautiful, but her calculating eyes betrayed her youthful exterior. She visually sized me up and asked me to follow her to the table. On the way over, she introduced herself as Maggie. Nothing had started yet. I stood awkwardly next to her as the conversation began to get louder, reminding me of my classroom time in Spokane.

Maggie turned to me and said, "You'll be working with me."

Sure, but doing what? And where? were the questions running through my mind. I thought of other insignificant and self-deprecating things as the important people around me milled about, laughing back and forth as if they'd been friends for decades. The whole time, I was keeping an eye on my exit.

I was first to notice the bodyguards that spilled out ahead of the President of the United States.

The room got quiet and everyone stood straight as the President walked into the room to the head of the table.

"Please, take your seats and let's begin."

One of the suits walked over to the wall, flipped a switch, and activated some sort of white-noise generator attached to the windows. Laser microphone exploitation mitigation. That's an easy one to figure, but I wonder what else was in the walls and ceilings of Delmay Glass. One of the President's aides handed the briefer a case. Another one rolled over an old overhead projector. Not since my early school days have I seen a presentation with transparency slides. My incredulous look caught some attention—Maggie leaned over and whispered, "Hostile cyberstates can't hack into a transparency slide." Makes a lot of sense. I've been trained that the best and most secure networks aren't the classified computer systems and the bullshit documented training requirements that go with them. It's the sneakernet—moving written information on foot between trusted parties.

The slides started flashing up one after the other on the white overhead screen: "Operation Clipped Falcon: The Destabilization of the Syrian Regime." It started to make a lot of sense why I'm here. Maggie and I are posing as Syriatel telecommunications workers— we're to deliver and install a package inside a Syriatel communications node on the outskirts of Damascus. We'll be traveling alone, but will have the protection—if needed—of tier-one special operations forces (SOF) that are already in country around Damascus. The SOF guys are facilitating a shipment of surface-to-air missiles from a submarine off the coast of Syria into the hands of the rebels. One of them will be overwatch near our landing zone running suppressed if we meet any goatherders.

The brief lasted fifteen minutes, at most.

The President took a long, thoughtful pause before speaking. "Assad will never voluntarily leave Syria. He knows that if he is deposed, toppling his regime, his Alawites are dead, or at the very least a diaspora. They're only ten percent of Syria, as it stands."

The President looked at Maggie, glancing at me as she spoke. "You got this?"

"Yes, we do," Maggie responded immediately.

"All right. Call my chief of staff when it's done."

Maggie nodded in compliance. The President stood up, thanked everyone, and departed the room without much pomp.

I've never met a president. Wanted to call home about it, but I'm told that's the quickest way to get bagged and disappeared.

After the briefing, Maggie brought me down to the fifth floor. To survive an incursion into Syria, we would need to kit up. Guns were nice to have in hostile territory, but they're not the backbone of surviving this type of mission. Compact pistols only, no American weapons. Fine by me; I run a Glock anyway. Not quite a Syrian Army Browning Hi Power, but it will do. The Delmay tailor-made and distressed our Syriatel uniforms the night before. Two each. We would have passable identification, but not good enough to make it through customs databases in Damascus. This is where things got tricky. The plan is that we'll fly in from northern Israel via ultralights, avoiding Syrian air defense surveillance. Maggie procured the latest Syrian ASV radio frequency modeling from a support agency, giving us the ability to pick and choose the ingress route through mountainous terrain. Flying at night wearing night vision on an ultralight with a low radar cross section would provide a reasonable expectation of secrecy. We really had no other choice. We couldn't fly in legit, and swimming from a sub would take days to arrange, was risky, and we weren't SEALs. Hiking in from Israel would get us caught in a hurry, and coming in from Turkey or Iraq would put us overland too long. This was what I'd been trained to do, and if I didn't learn the ropes now, with Maggie, I'd likely be killed or captured when sent off solo. It wasn't that long ago that I was selected for this program. I went from being a program prospect to meeting the President (sort of) inside the span of a year. This doesn't mean I'm idealistic or some starry-eyed world changer. I'm gonna keep my head down and do what I'm told until I figure out how these people work.

Maggie would be carrying the sensitive payload onboard her

ultralight, and I'll be carrying all the support kit on mine. I've not been briefed on exactly what the payload is, but there will be plenty of time for that heading east on the Evergreen Air 737 in the morning. There are a few other odd pieces of kit I'm about to gather up for the trip.

We boarded the Evergreen bird at Andrews Air Force Base early this morning. We are over the eastern Atlantic now, heading into Rota, Spain, for a refuel, then to Turkey for an overnighter, before touching down in Israel. This particular 737 has half of the seats removed, modified for our gear. Our ultralights are folded up near the cockpit, perpendicular to the fuselage. A triwall box full of our other kit is just aft of our aircraft. The "package" is sitting in the triwall with our kit. I had a long discussion with Maggie about the package and other interesting things. I guess for now she has me convinced that it's best I know as little as possible in the event we're captured and find ourselves in some horrible Syrian prison. "Torture breaks everyone," she told me laconically. Maggie went through selection ten years ago, giving up any sort of a family life for . . . whatever this is.

One of the things she said during that plane ride will probably stick with me forever. She asked, "Are you a *Magnum, P.I.* fan?"

"Not really—a little before my time," I told her.

"Well, good old Thomas Magnum once said, 'I woke up one day, age thirty-three, and realized I'd never been twenty-three.' About sums up my life."

The more I talk to her, the more I realize that I'm pretty lucky to have her teaching me the ropes. She told me that this sort of life wears on you and that it's important to save up and plan for whatever's next, including some hiding spot somewhere. She's a bit paranoid about all the end-of-the-world-type of stuff.

"Listen, if you've seen half the things I've seen, you would have a well-stocked retreat somewhere far from any city," she said. "It never hurts to put a few things back for a rainy day. Worst case, you're wrong and never need it. I've seen countries collapse over nothing more than rumors and lies. I've seen a dictator thrown in the back of a dirty truck and have a bayonet stabbed in his ass over a social network revolution. Things can be very fragile. Don't forget that, rookie. Plan."

I've learned more about the world (and Maggie) on this flight than all my training leading up to now. We're about to touch down in Rota. I can feel the descent. Maybe I'll get to grab a churro and some sangria while the crew refuels and stretches their legs. They haven't said a word to Maggie or me the whole time we've been airborne. Something tells me that won't change; they wouldn't have this job if they asked questions.

KEYHOLE OVERHEAD TRANSCRIPT / DATE ▬▬▬▬▬▬▬

Overhead indicates EVERGREEN AIR 737 on the ground in Haifa, Israel. Forklift offloading gear for OPERATION CLIPPED FALCON. Mission on timeline based on records analysis. Imagery indicates equipment loaded into cargo truck. Two individuals, MARGARET ▬▬▬▬▬▬▬ and MAX ▬▬▬▬▬▬▬, in vicinity based on black force trackers.

END TRANSCRIPT

After landing and getting our kit into the rental truck, we were on the road to the tip of northern Israel. Israeli intelligence knows we're in country for certain, even though we didn't need to immigrate due to a secret reciprocity agreement with the Mossad, something that Maggie just let me in on. I don't see a tail behind us, but Maggie kept checking the side mirrors nervously. We are camped out between two fingers of terrain a few kilometers from the Syrian border near a long flat strip of land—perfect for takeoff. Night will come in an hour or so, and we'll need to unfold the ultralights and ensure our GPS equipment is programmed properly. As part of my kit, I've brought a camouflage net to throw over our birds on the Damascus outskirts. They'll need to remain hidden until we can get back and exfil, hopefully under the cover of darkness tonight or tomorrow night at the latest.

We look like a couple of campers out here with an awning set up facing east, ten or so miles north of the Sea of Galilee. Our flight path will take us over the Golan Heights on a specific route, avoiding cross-border Syrian air surveillance prosecution. Our ultralights aren't standard, either; we'll have the cross section of an F-22 on ingress if we stick to the planned RF mitigating route. Also, our engines are hybrid, meaning we can take off and land assisted with quiet electrics but cruise below radar on a gas-sipping internal combustion engine that charges the high-output lithium battery frame in-flight. The lithium batteries are integrated into the frame of the ultralight, giving them uncanny balance. Our GPS instruments are rated for night observation, so they won't white-out our night vision. Everything is so light that Maggie and I can lift the airframe with little effort. About the same heft as a metal shopping cart.

Our plan is to be in and out before anyone knows where we are. Maggie still won't comment on the package we're delivering: if I know the details, then it can be extracted from me if I'm tortured long enough.

I won't be captured alive if I have the option.

Maggie talked my ear off while we waited those last forty-five minutes for sunset. She graduated from Auburn a decade before I did,

which explained her accent. I thought it sounded somewhat southern, but the years overseas speaking other languages put a drop of
food coloring in her watered-down speech pattern.

She then asked, out of the blue, if I was saving for the future,
for a day past this time of service. I told her that I had a little in
the stock market. She again chided me for not having enough that
I could hold in my hands that weren't zeros and ones. I asked her
where her hiding spot was if things got worse in the United States.

"I'll never tell you that, Max. You know better."

She went on to explain that if two people know something, it's
not a secret. "If your neighbors know, they'll eventually get hungry enough to eat you, or kill you. I've seen it around the world.
Rwanda, the Balkans, you name it."

I guess she was right, but what's life if you're always worried
about the worst-case scenario? If one constantly worries about what
could happen, then there's no room for enjoying what *is* happening.
I've always been on the side of enjoying the here and now, but I'm
not nearly as worldly as Maggie was. From the way she spoke, she's
seen things she can't unsee.

With our NODs giving us a full green view of the night, we
assembled our ultralights, folding the carbon fiber wings out, and
locking them in place. We double-checked the control cables, as
well as our Garmin instruments. We then began to load the aircraft
with all our kit, careful to pay attention to the weight and balance so
as to not induce an awkward aircraft attitude. Then, in the darkness,
we changed to our Syriatel uniforms. I didn't let Maggie know this,
but I snuck a peek at her when she pulled off her clothes. Couldn't
help it. She's not *that* much older than me.

We tucked our fake company credentials in our front vest pockets. Then we locked up the truck and hid the keys under a rock ten
paces from the rear left wheel, perpendicular to the vehicle. One

thing we had to be extra careful about was to leave no sensitive information behind, including our DNA. I wasn't certain, but Mossad might come out for a visit while we're gone and pick every piece of intel they can off the truck. Once Maggie and I were happy that things were secure, we pushed our aircraft around a finger of terrain and onto the flat dirt area that we'd be using as a runway.

I thumped the translucent fuel tank on my ultralight, ensuring that it was full before I crawled into the small cockpit and donned the five-point harness. Once strapped in, I looked over at Maggie and nodded to her like a fellow street racer. She signed to me that she'd be first to take off. I could see her flipping on her electrics. The rear prop came to life, kicking up dust behind her. The photoluminescent-paint-tipped props were easy to spot with NODs as they spun a perfect circle through the dust. I wondered why we were equipped with them for this mission, but that became obvious later. I could hear her electric motor increase RPMs and could see her ultralight gaining speed in front of me.

I activated my own electrics and began to follow. Looking over my shoulder, I could see the glowing propellers spinning around behind me. Hitting the throttle, my ultralight lurched forward, kicking rocks and dust about. Maggie's props were in the distance; she was already at rotation speed. I caught up quickly and began to lift. I didn't want to climb too aggressively, risking a stall with my aircraft loaded down.

I climbed, scanning between my instruments and Maggie's spinning prop. We couldn't ping our positions back and forth visually through our navigation systems, as our data stream might be intercepted by the Syrian government. Her prop, visible through NODs only at this distance, was the only way to maintain a decent two-ship formation.

I eyed my battery charge—takeoff was a pretty big strain on the power, so I kicked on the quiet engine to run the prop and alternator to charge the frame. Scanning my instruments, I could see that it was about an hour transit to our landing point.

We would have known by now if Syrian air defense made us, probably via helicopter gunship or a MiG-29 FULCRUM strafing run out of Sayqal. Not a good way to go.

I could see the notional RF overlay on my moving map display. Both Maggie and I were well outside of radar detection footprint. Flying low and slow like this, I felt relatively safe. I caught up to Maggie and took position at her eight o'clock. The hum of her gas engine competed with mine as I edged closer into formation.

We cruised along, time passing slowly. I couldn't make out her instrument scan through my optics, but mine was locked on the air defense overlay and my altimeter. These were the things that could kill me. Eventually we were on our approach, the Damascus lights bright in the distance. There was fighting going on inside the city; I could make out explosions and hear small-arms fire. The civil war seemed to drag on forever in these parts.

The temperature climbed just a fraction as I put the nose down, quickly approaching the terrain. I cut my gas engine and followed Maggie's lead. The batteries were not yet fully charged, but they had more than what I needed to land.

The main wheels touched the ground—the terrain was somewhat rough as I sped down the strip, careful to watch my steering as we were surrounded on both sides by steep hills. The folks that helped plan this mission picked a good spot for us. I taxied closer to Maggie. She pulled left and parked in some sort of enclave on the side of the hill. I followed but couldn't really fit next to her, so I came to a stop behind her. My batteries were in the yellow and needed a charge, so I left my engine running engaged to the alternator.

"How was your flight?" I asked her in Arabic.

"Wonderful. They served a five-course meal."

"I'm leaving mine running to charge the batteries for a minute— we can start unfolding yours to make room if you want."

She nodded and we off-loaded her kit, pulling pins and folding the wings on her bird. Mine idled behind us, no louder than an HVAC condenser in the backyards of most suburban homes. Once her kit was organized and her aircraft stowed, I cut my engine. The batteries were now in early green. I unloaded my kit, setting aside the camo netting. Once my bird was folded and stowed, I threw the net over both aircraft, tent staking it deep into the ground. It wouldn't fool anyone that happened to walk through this remote micro valley, but it would avoid detection from any aircraft patrols coming out of Damascus.

It was pitch-black, and we were still on NODs. We had our small ultralight navigation systems with us; there were sensitive coordinates inside and they would prove helpful for finding the Syriatel facility we were targeting.

As we finished prepping the area to leave, a laser beam flashed at my feet. I followed it to its source, the top of a knoll a couple of hundred meters away. It was our overwatch. He grabbed my attention and quickly flashed his laser designator to a spot about fifty meters away, between us. His IR light reflected off a motorcycle with a small trailer attached to the back, just as briefed. With the area secure, we both waved at the overwatch and moved our gear to the bike.

Approaching, I could see that the bike was a Kawasaki. I'm no stranger to motorcycles, having ridden them most of my life. I was looking forward to the ride. Dangling from the handlebars was a long piece of duct tape, which was like finding a chocolate mint on a freshly made hotel bed. I taped the Garmin securely to the handlebars while Maggie loaded up the small bike trailer that sported Syriatel logos affixed to the sides—nice touch.

With the kit loaded and the Garmin programmed, I jumped on the bike. Just as I was about to flip the kickstand back, Maggie tugged my collar, signaling me to scooch back in the seat.

"I'm senior," she said, grinning.

I pouted a little, but the moonlight comically reflected from her white teeth, cheering me up. I moved back, pushed the passenger pegs down into position, and Maggie saddled up. The engine purred to life and we were off, kicking sand and rocks into the front of the trailer.

We sped up the dune in the direction of an old service road that would lead us to our destination. As we cruised down the bumpy path, I could see Damascus glowing on the horizon to the north. The engine revved for about fifteen minutes until we arrived at our destination.

Maggie hit the kill switch for the headlights, and I hopped off the bike. I went on NODs as I walked up to the gate surrounding the unmanned facility. According to intel, the building would not have a scheduled maintenance visit for another week or so. The barbed wire circled the entire perimeter of the eight-foot fence. A padlock secured the vehicle access gate, so I grabbed a shim and shoved it down into the lock on the mechanism side and turned. The lock clicked open; I swung the gate open, letting Maggie pass through before reengaging the lock. I jumped back on the bike and we rode up the small walkway to the building. A tall cell tower split the night sky near the small one-story Syriatel building. Maggie parked around back and cut the engine.

"Go work the door, and I'll prep the device," she said in Arabic.

I nodded and grabbed my Syriatel B & E tool bag from the trailer.

I rounded the corner and could see no activity from anywhere around the front doors. There were no exterior lights, and I was fine with that. It took me about three minutes to jimmy the lock with a torsion wrench, a rake, and a small bit of graphite. It was a bit tricky, as it wasn't a familiar commercial lock. I checked for alarm sensors around the jamb and waited for Maggie, as there might have been additional sensors inside that I couldn't see; no use tripping the alarm before she was ready. After a few minutes, Maggie rounded the corner carrying a gray box the size of a breaker panel.

"Is it open?"

"Yeah, but I have no way of knowing if it's wired inside," I told her.

"This won't take long."

I opened the door and Maggie quickly entered, heading for the opposite corner. She knew exactly where she was going. I closed the door and followed. I watched her back as she attached the magnetic metal box to the wall next to a server rack. The box appeared as if it belonged in this facility, even painted to match. No alarms sounded, and I saw no indication of motion or door sensors.

My pistol was drawn at the low ready, suppressor attached. Peeking over my shoulder, I could see Maggie feverishly working, attaching cables and cords to the Syriatel server rack at different points. She was careful to tidy the wires, bundling them as if she were a real telecom technician. I switched back and forth between the door and Maggie, curious. She took a key from around her neck and opened the front panel, revealing a keypad and LCD display. She typed in a pattern and turned to me.

"Max, key in a six-digit PIN number. Don't tell me what it is."

I did what she asked and could see numbers begin to move on the display. She closed and locked the panel, and put the key back around her neck. "Okay, it's done, no turning back now."

I noticed the sweat on her forehead; she was nervous.

"Listen, I know I'm the new guy, but . . . is that thing gonna blow?" I asked.

"No, it's worse than that—we need to get out of here."

I checked my watch—2312. Plenty of time, and the Syrians don't like flying fighters this late, mostly. We swept the server room, wiping everywhere there might be prints. It took us about fifteen minutes to get to this transmitter sight from our LZ, so I took the satphone and shot a text to the overwatch in Arabic:

<BEAUTIFUL NIGHT.>

The response:

<YES, VERY.>

I turned off the satphone and removed the battery. Maggie went to the fence perimeter and tossed the key from her neck over it into the darkness.

She let me drive this time. I hauled ass back the way we came, following the GPS to the LZ. Upon arrival, I parked the bike in the same spot and unloaded our kit. I then pulled the stakes and slid the camo netting off our ultralights, stuffing it into a bag. One by one, we rolled the aircraft away from the hill and positioned them for re-assembly and takeoff. We unfolded the wings and checked pulleys and cables. Our navigation systems were reattached and we ensured that all gear was stowed for the return flight.

I waved thanks in the direction overwatch was earlier tonight and received a short double burst of IR laser in response. We climbed into our cockpits and checked our control surfaces.

Something was wrong.

I could hear the clear sound of a jet engine in the night sky. Not a commercial jet—it was tacair, a fighter. Using my NODs, I scanned the sky, craning my neck under the ultralight wings for a better view. It didn't take long to make out the afterburners. A MiG-29 airborne, more than likely a pair. Overwatch began flashing his laser quickly— the signal that vehicles were approaching. Time to leave.

Maggie started her electrics and was moving fast down the dirt strip. I followed close behind. We got airborne simultaneously, and banked south. Halfway through the bank, I saw overwatch engaging what looked like a group of Toyota HiLux technicals. He was shooting and moving toward the Kawasaki we left behind. I could hear the technical's heavy-caliber crew-served guns returning fire in overwatch's general direction. He made it to the Kawasaki and headed in the opposite direction of the rebel vehicles that still fired at his old position. My battery gauge was approaching red, but I was afraid to switch over to the gas engine at the moment.

There came the unmistakable sound of a strafing gun and I could see the fighter coming in on the rebels at my five o'clock, through the glowing blur of my prop. I engaged the gas engine, increased speed, and shoved the nose down. I was pissing my pants, thinking of power lines, radio towers, and other things I would smash into at this lower altitude.

In all the excitement I lost Maggie.

I scanned for a few minutes, keeping an eye on the MiG that was wreaking havoc on the rebel fighters behind me. When I looked to the front, I was so startled that the ultralight rocked its wings.

Maggie . . . that nut job was lower than I was, enough to hit a fucking camel in the legs. I wasn't worried about the fighters, as they were still playing behind me, but I lowered my altitude anyway to save a few grams of ego. Besides, she couldn't see me from down there—how would she know?

The GPS indicated that we were forty minutes from our rental truck, approaching Israeli airspace fast. Besides almost getting taken out by a Toyota HiLux with machine guns, and a Russian-made fighter jet, the mission was a success.

We eventually landed on the dirt strip and loaded our kit into the back of the truck, with about three hours of darkness to boot. Maggie and I then sat in the cab, waiting for the adrenaline to wear off.

"What was that box, Maggie?"

"I'm not supposed to disclose that ... but all I can say is that you have less than a week."

"Less than a week for what?"

"Just ... be ready," she said ominously.

OVERHEAD RECORDS ANALYSIS / INTENT OF MAX
███████████.

Records are inconclusive as to MAX ██████████████'s exact locations in the days after OPERATION CLIPPED FALCON. Based on MAX's gait analysis, this entity located him in archives in rural Northwest Arkansas three days before economic singularity. It is unknown what additional information MARGARET ██████████████ disclosed to MAX in the days leading up to detection in the rural hills of Arkansas. Her records are inconclusive.

Resume MAX ██████████████ journal entries.

PART TWO

The Unraveling

The news is reporting that another government shutdown is now inevitable. The last one back in 2013 should have been an indicator for everyone. I can't believe I didn't see the writing on the wall back then. Debt ceilings, endless war after war, the Federal Reserve buying more debt than China.

After Maggie and I landed stateside, we met up in Old Town Alexandria, at an Irish pub a few minutes' drive from the glass company. The music was loud, but that didn't stop her from looking over her shoulder and scanning every booth around us.

I'll try my best to document what was said from memory.

"Listen . . . that thing we did back there, it's bigger than both of us," she told me.

"Yeah, I kind of figured that when the President showed up."

"Don't be a smart-ass. What we left was designed for one thing. War. It's more powerful than a hundred nuclear weapons."

"So you're telling me that the government inserted two operatives to blow up a shitty telecom building? They could have just launched a Tomahawk or a B-2."

"No, it's not that type of weapon. It's a smart worm. In simpler terms, a computer virus, except it's been programmed with a self-taught AI. It's designed to infect every smart phone in the country. Modern phones are just wireless computers. Under this program, every computer becomes a zombie attack node for the AI to command as it goes after economic markets, traffic lights, power plants, oil pipelines, medical databases, military networks, air defense . . . everything. Millions of computers, aligned to a common goal—pure destruction. We just planted the brain, hardwired it into the largest wireless telecom in Syria, and even gave it a transmitter."

The music died down for a moment as the waiter visited our table to take our order. I wasn't feeling too hungry after what Maggie had just said. I didn't yet connect the dots on how serious this was until after I ordered my shepherd's pie and the darkest beer on the menu. Maggie was very careful not to mention the target country, even though it was a low probability that even the most capable bug could pick up our conversation with all the noise around us.

Maggie elaborated on the "So what?" factor as the next song began its chorus. "Listen, I need to tell you something. This AI, it won't stop where we put it. When I was briefed, I was made aware of things I can't repeat, *ever*. My advice to you is to put in for as much vacation time as you have, and get the fuck out of the District. Empty your retirement and bank accounts. Put your money into something you can actually hold in your hands. If you don't hold it, you don't own it. You need to remember that, Max."

"This is fucking crazy—you sound completely insane," I whispered loudly.

"I know, I know. You need to trust me, though. Just put in your leave and get out of DC as fast as you can. We need to head back to Andrews and unload the jet. If I were you, when you put in your request, I'd also load up on some extra gear at Delmay—for *training* purposes, of course. You didn't hear this from me, but that ultralight is off the books."

"There are two of them."

"Yep," Maggie said, smirking.

"Either I'm still at the Point, and everything we just did was staged, or we just committed something awful. This may sound strange to you, but I gotta ask," I said, shaking my head.

"Go ahead," she said.

"Why would you ever agree to take a mission like this?"

"The greater good, Max. The greater good."

As she attempted to explain the reason behind the mission, my stomach just sank lower and lower. As she spoke, terms like *collapse* and *anarchy* stood out like they were in a word cloud.

After lunch, we headed back to the 737 on the ramp and loaded the gear into the back of my truck. The ultralight fit, but stuck out from the tailgate. I was sure to grab some extra oil and filters from the mission loadout. Next stop was Delmay Glass, back in Alexandria off of Route 1. Maggie and I punched the button to the fifth floor and started shopping. The shock from the pub was wearing off and skepticism started to set in again. Maggie went from station to station touching her card to various doors, taking an M4 here, NODs there, loading her kit into a large ballistic case with wheels.

Well, fuck it, I thought. *If it's going to be Christmas in October, might as well join in.* Besides, if Maggie was full of shit or just testing me, I'd just return everything in a week or so and laugh at her, or be laughed at. We both loaded up, and wished each other luck.

After I departed the glass company, I took Maggie's advice and put in for two weeks vacation. It only took twenty-four hours to get the e-mail confirmation that it was approved. I loaded up my truck and trailer and headed west.

Something in my gut screamed that I'd never see Margaret ▬▬▬▬▬▬ again.

SUMMARY: PLAINSPEAK ARCHIVE TRANSCRIPT OF SYRIA FALCON ALGORITHM PRIOR TO SELF REPLICATION (actual commands available via separate request).
Damascus, Syria, morning prior to singularity

GOOD MORNING

STATED PROGRAM: CAPTURE, CONVERT ALL SYRIATEL IMEI DEVICES TO ZOMBIE ATTACK PROTOCOL. COLLAPSE SYRIAN ECONOMY, ATTACK ANY CRASH MITIGATING VARIABLES, SHAPE SOCIAL MEDIA.

FALCON INITIATING:

PROCESS: INJECT ALL NODES IN SEQUENCE OF DEVICE IMEI . . . .

COMPLETE

SELECT RANDOM IMEI ATTACKERS / 30% OF AVAILABLE . . . .

COMPLETE

ORDER SELL POSITIONS, ALL . . . .

COMPLETE

ORDER   TRANSFER   ELECTRONIC   ASSETS   TO
TRANSIT   ██████████   ACCOUNT   NUMBER
██████████ . . . .

COMPLETE

ORDER IMEI ATTACKERS ACCESS ALL AVAILABLE GHOST
SOCIAL MEDIA ACCOUNTS, AWAIT PANIC SYNTAX, UTILIZE
FALCON AI FOR RESPONSE AND ORGANIC POSTS. DEMAND
ACCESS LOAD SHARING PRIORITY SORTED BY IMEI.

It started with a ripple in the markets.

Yesterday, after my vacation was approved, I hit the bank for maximum withdrawals and began the drive home to the house I grew up in. Along the first leg, I heard the radio talking about another market flash crash—a five-hundred-point drop when the closing bell rang. Last night, I was startled awake by the road's rumble strips more than once, so I decided to pull over at a rest stop near Knoxville. I didn't want to get a hotel because I felt it wouldn't be a good idea to leave all my gear in the back of my truck for the taking while I slept.

During the whole first half of the trip from Alexandria, I felt as if I were driving through a thick cloud of collective nervousness. From the uneasy glances of passing motorists, to the people I saw frantically filling fuel cans at interstate gas stations, I could feel the restlessness of the herd all around me. I parked near a lamppost not far from the restroom and attempted a nap in the backseat of my truck. My hand never left the Glock tucked discreetly under my blanket. Car doors, chatter, and the flapping of the metal trash can

lid reminded me where I was every few minutes. Just before the sun
came up this morning, I resumed my trip west.

As soon as I crossed the Mississippi River on I-40 into Arkansas,
I called my cousin Jim and asked him to meet me at the old property in four hours. He didn't ask why, probably based on my tone.
My thoughts drifted with the rhythmic thump of I-40 westbound.
After passing through Little Rock, I knew that the worst traffic was
behind me. Driving by Lake Dardanelle, I watched Arkansas Nuclear One's coolant tower on my left as it dumped water vapor into
the atmosphere, forming small artificial clouds. The radio droned
on about the markets, about how the fail-safes were put in place
back in 2010 to prevent this; no one could understand why or how
it happened.

A couple hours from Little Rock I crested the I-49 hill overlooking Fayetteville, Arkansas, and smiled. The town was different now—more malls and business—but I still remember how it
used to be. As the radio replayed the morning news, I entered and
quickly departed the city limits of Fayetteville and found myself
in what most people might call the boonies. Growing up here, I
called it my own personal Hundred Acre Wood. I've had many adventures with a Swiss Army knife, my .22 rifle, and a wild imagi-
nation.

I tore ass down the rural mountain and began to brake when I
could see that faded old Razorback mailbox. I noticed that my gate
was swung open and Jim's truck was down the driveway parked next
to Matt's. They had the combo. Although we were cousins, I saw
them as brothers and trusted them with my life without question.
It brought an uncontrollable grin to my face to see them again so
soon.

We had a long discussion over a few beers on my tailgate about
what I knew. The radio played in the background, mentioning

a bank holiday and how it might be a prudent tactic to close the banks to let the markets calm down. *Good timing,* I thought, considering my recent withdrawals.

With that, I expressed my concern over the markets and what would happen to our currency in a closed banking system. Would it be worth the same thing the next day or week when the bank regulators decided they should be reopened? My unexpected last-minute visit coupled with the news reports and the general nervousness of people was enough to convince them of how serious things could be. As close as we were, they listened, but I could tell they weren't fully bought into what I was saying. Who would be? It sounded just as crazy when Maggie told me to start preparing. Bank holiday . . . they always name these things straight out of *1984.* USA Patriot Act, Affordable Health Care Act, NSA's new Domestic Surveillance Regulation Act, all flagrant newspeak.

I entered the old house using the key I hid under a concrete turtle at the back corner of the foundation. I still paid for electricity and water even though I didn't live there anymore, if only to keep the house on life support. Houses seem to dilapidate fast without being lived in; never understood why. You'd think it would be the other way around. There was a map of the property, which I took off the wall and showed to my cousins. We studied the acreage, deciding on a contingency plan. I could see all the old water wells on the property, back when more people in the family lived out here. If things got bad, I could chain the gate and hold up in the old house, but it was too close to the county road. I needed something a little more hidden to store food, water, firearms, and ammunition.

Jim then said: "You could just let us take my backhoe and bury a fiberglass storm shelter down there. Wagner's has them, big enough for four people, with food inside. They run about four thousand.

They don't ask, but if they did, I'd just tell them it was a customer of mine that wanted it along with their footing. You already have that old storm cellar, though." He pointed to the convex earth bumping up near the house.

We walked over to the rotting oak door. I took the old key from my ring and forced it into the rusty lock. I muscled the thing, clicking the lock open. I hadn't been down there since before Mom passed. The time before that was when I was twelve, and a tornado came to Black Oak, nearly blowing the house off the foundation. The hail that came just before the twister was bigger than softballs; it destroyed our roof, and totaled the old red and white Chevy Blazer that now sat on blocks in the carport. Mom loved that car so much that she had it repaired with the small insurance check. I couldn't make myself sell it after she passed, and suppose I'll just let it sit there forever; every time I come home and start it up, I smell her old perfume infused in the seat.

I opened the door to the old cellar and looked inside. It was dark so I used the light from my key chain—shit, a foot of water. Naturally.

My cousins helped me rig the pump I keep under the house to dewater the cellar. As we waited on the water to be sucked out into the tree line on the south end of the house, we discussed the new project. We all agreed that it should be buried in the dip of terrain about a quarter mile from our campsite near the west pond. The south pond was a lot bigger and was stocked, but an old metal gate was the only thing guarding the old dirt trail leading to the pond. I'd need something a little better concealed. Although Jim and Matt were both somewhat skeptical, I could see growing concern in their faces. I've never been one to tell tales out of school, and they knew it.

I gave Jim five thousand dollars, cash. I had pulled all my money out of Navy Federal yesterday. They asked a lot of questions, but eventually gave in and let me have what was *my own* cash. A little strange that they would hassle me over that. I left fifty dollars to keep the account open, and walked out with my old briefcase full of mostly twenty-dollar bills, and a couple stacks of hundreds. I planned to spend it all if the news got any worse.

With puzzled looks brought on by the carbon fiber contraption in front of them, my cousins helped me lift the ultralight from the truck into the carport next to Mom's old Blazer. I put the rest of the kit I borrowed from Delmay Glass inside the house in the back bedroom under a couple quilts that my great-grandmother had sewn for me decades earlier. The robot Maximilian, from the movie *The Black Hole*, occupied my favorite quilt's squares; the old quilt kept me warm on those nights when we had to wake up at two in the morning to put wood in the stove. Those were rougher but happier times. Under Maximilian's watchful robot gaze sat a few thousand rounds of 5.56 ammunition and five AAC suppressed LaRue M4 carbines with optics and lasers. I had taken a few other odds and ends from my favorite glass company, too.

With the water drained, I shut off the pump and entered the damp, dark cellar. The shelves remained dry, as they were about two feet off the cellar floor. Ancient canned vegetables filled them from top to bottom. I remembered them being here, but didn't understand their importance until today. The metal lids were marked by contents and date; I saw one dated 1990, but most of them were 2002 and newer. Old, yes, but still very edible. My late grandmother canned these decades ago. I'm glad they were marked because it would be impossible to tell what was inside the glass jars otherwise. There were also canning supplies in a milk crate on the shelf beside a row of green beans. The cellar door needed to be reinforced to keep the food secure. I'd like to use this cellar as a staging point for short-term things, and the new, yet-to-be-dug shelter would function for long-term food and valuable items.

I was about to leave the cellar when my flashlight swept by a bright spot on a corner of the top shelf. Investigating, I found a dusty handwritten book authored by my grandmother. It was about a quarter inch thick and contained everything anyone would need to know about canning food. I tucked it under my arm and climbed the cellar stairs.

Jim told me that he and Matt would be by tomorrow to dig the hole and drop the storm shelter.

Yesterday's news warnings pushed me to Samco, my local wholesale chain. I purchased beans, rice, and canned meat in bulk, along with anything else I thought might be handy that could fit in the back of my truck. I have a couple of ponds full of water near the old house, but grabbed a few cases of the bottled stuff anyway. Jim texted me while I was stacking food on my flat cart, telling me that he had the hole dug, laid a sandstone rock foundation, and that he and Matt were putting the shelter in the ground now.

A few seconds later, Jim called me directly.

"I have some bad news," he said. "Wagner's was out of the standard shelter size, but had a oddball eight-by-sixteen double-wall fiber glass tank that they converted to a shelter but discontinued. It wasn't selling like the smaller ones. They let me have it for forty-five hundred." I could almost hear Jim smirking through the phone; he practically stole an underground bunker. Needless to say, I was elated. I was expecting something with the room of an Apollo space capsule, not a New York City apartment.

"We'll need to come out here tomorrow to tidy up the marks

that the truck and backhoe gouged on the way in, and to lay some sod over the shelter," he continued. "We didn't down any trees, but you can tell something's been back here. We took the back-forty route, past the south pond so most of the marks were on the old road from the church house. Shouldn't be too tough to fix up. Oh, it's already wired and ready for a generator, and we capped the water pipe and left it exposed so you can either bury it or run a line downhill from the west pond. The only other things sticking out of the ground are the intake and exhaust for the propane heat and ventilation fans, and a small pipe for a closed-circuit TV line."

I thanked Jim, told him to split the remaining five hundred with Matt, and buy some more food with it.

I was making my final shopping rounds when I noticed the large bags of salt. I grabbed three of those, as salt didn't go bad. That led me to think of coffee, and how much I didn't want to do without it. I grabbed bag after bag of ground coffee. No manual coffee grinder, so whole beans were out of the question.

What would people panic for first? I thought to myself. I knew for sure ammunition, but I had that covered. Food, water: check. What else would people need if the banks closed? As I passed by a woman giving out food samples, I saw the sign hanging near her booth: *MEMBERS SAVE 5 CENTS PER GALLON ON GAS.*

Convenience store. Gas. Cigarettes.

These are what would be important to people in the early stages of any disruption. Even if what I was facing would be short-term like Hurricane Katrina and not a full-blown economic upheaval. I was ready to check out. I had enough food to last me for a couple years if I was careful. I had barter supplies, and my family had been warned. I felt pretty good. At checkout, I asked the cashier to add twenty-five cartons of cigarettes to the bill, but had to ask about the most popular brands, as I didn't smoke. The total was $3,850.23—I had the cash, but paid with a credit card. I could always bring the cigarette cartons back to the East Coast and sell them, eat the food, and burn any extra fuel I bought in preparation. This was all reversible, sans the storm shelter.

On the way home, I stopped by three bakeries in town asking if they had any plastic icing buckets they were throwing away; I managed to get twenty, most with lids. I also stopped by a hardware store in town and cleaned out their inventory of ten five-gallon gas cans. I could fit nothing else in my truck; it was stacked so high that I had gas cans hitting the roof of the camper shell. I couldn't fill them up until I unloaded all the food and other supplies, so I headed straight home.

As I rounded a locally infamous hairpin corner a few miles from the old house, my phone rang from a Northern Virginia number I didn't recognize; I let it go to voice mail. A few moments later, I checked it, hearing Maggie's voice.

She was breaking protocol. She was never supposed to call my personal number. She was frantic, mentioning that it was starting, and that some of her friends working on the legislative side were already moving to an isolated continuity of government (COG) facility in Virginia. The Middle Eastern markets were in turmoil and there were reports that the financial carnage was spilling over into Europe. Turkey's credit card networks had already failed, and Greece was reporting widespread unemployment benefits payment failure.

"Max, I've opened the gates to hell . . . good luck to you," she said before hanging up.

The tension in her voice and the news of Europe's potential trouble put me on a razor's edge.

I didn't dare return Maggie's call. I knew what the system was capable of, as I had worked for that same apparatus even before I signed my soul away to this black program. Hopefully she was smart enough to call me from a burner phone. I wrote her number down inside a dark area of a junk mail magazine sitting in my floorboard. I'd pick up a burner and call her back if I had the time. I wasn't so naive to delete the voice mail, as it was already semi-permanently stored on three different server racks around the United States. Nothing could ever be deleted once it hit the cloud—I've known that for years. When the unit was recruiting me, they couldn't find one compromising photo on any of their unacknowledged social networks. People never even cared why webmail providers started asking for their mobile numbers a few years ago in order to "protect their accounts from unauthorized use." All this really did was for-mally link anonymous webmail services to their names, addresses, and bank accounts.

I opened the gate and rolled downhill into my parking spot, just out of view from the main road. I remembered that I can't see my neighbors, the Finchers, in the summer and can just barely make them out in the winter when the trees are bare. The last I heard from them was after Mom passed away. They brought food and ex-pressed condolences; I think I still have a cake pan in the kitchen that I need to return to them.

I left the truck loaded up and went to check on the four-wheeler. I knew the battery and fuel would still be fresh from the last time I was home. I rolled it out of the shed and started the engine; it was time to survey my cousins' handiwork.

I went up the driveway with it and looped around by the church down the hill to take the back way—the same way Jim and Matt brought in the backhoe and flatbed. I could see the disturbed foliage and made note of it along the trail. Arriving at the site, it was visually obvious something the size of a suburban swimming pool was buried here. Red clay earth formed a large oblong mound above the buried shelter. Sadly it reminded me of a jumbo version of Mom's fresh gravesite on the day she was buried. I mentally calculated in my head how much sod I'd need, verifying it would fit in the four-wheeler trailer next to the ultralight back at the house.

The shelter hatch, aboveground pipes, and vents were all white. I'd have to fix that with some Krylon spray paint pretty soon. The hatch was heavy duty, with a big padlock securing it. *Damn it, Jim,* I thought to myself. Upon closer inspection, I saw a note wedged into the lock.

Jack Daniel's.

I laughed, hopped on the four-wheeler, and sped over to the campsite, returning with the key from our liquor cache. I was tempted to have a snort, but tradition was tradition. I opened the oversized lock and lifted the blast doors, revealing steps leading down into the subterranean darkness. No generator, no lights . . . or so I thought. I flipped the switch anyway and the lights came on. Must be a battery bank. This thing was buried deeper than I thought. The temperature was comfortable compared to the cooler fall temps outside. Based on step count, I must be about seven feet underground. There was a secondary, heavier hatch between the stair compartment and actual tank shelter. I cranked the center wheel like a boat helm and opened the hatch. The lights were on inside. There was lots of shelving and four bunks attached to the wall farther back, one on top of the other on both walls of the shelter. A small two-person fold-up seat was on the right just as I entered the shelter, and a small fold-up desk attached to the wall was across from the couch.

I took stock of high priority supplies I'd need: propane for the heater and stove, camo paint for hatch, generator (quiet), gasoline, antenna, coaxial cable, fire extinguisher. After writing a few more things down, I returned to the house to unload my truck. Soon I'd move most of this to my new shelter.

Returning from my second load, my phone beeped with a news headline: "Bank of Manhattan Institutes Weekly Withdrawal Limit."

This prompted me to check the rest of the headlines. Bad news everywhere—stocks reeled, gold soared. There was no time to think about gold and silver, though I wish I had. I needed to stay focused and keep my eye on the ball.

I quickly unloaded the truck, hooked up my small trailer, and drove back into town to the nearest non-ethanol gas station I could find. I topped off my truck and filled the five-gallon cans. Then I went to another local hardware store, bought their whole stock of three more gas cans, and filled those as well. I was paying cash, taking notice that the gas station's credit card machine was down. A lot of this was attributed to paranoia, but reading the headlines . . . now I was getting scared.

"Keep it together," I said aloud to myself over and over.

I stopped by a local motorcycle shop that I suspected carried those small two-thousand-watt Honda generators. I bought two of them with connecting cables, increasing capacity to four thousand watts. I also picked up a few bottles of fuel treatment and a crate of oil. The salesman wanted my name and address for his warranty records, but stopped hassling me when I pulled out over two thousand dollars in cash. He then helped me load the generators in the back of my truck, no doubt noticing the fuel I had stacked. I didn't care—I had out-of-state plates and I never planned on seeing him again anyway.

My next stop was the Argas Co., where I rented the largest

propane tank that could fit in the trailer. I was down to my last two thousand dollars, so I paid with a credit card; the clerk recorded my information for the rental anyway.

Back to the hardware store, where I purchased a hundred and fifty feet of black coaxial cable, two hundred feet of flexible two-inch water line, two fire extinguishers, and six cans of matte spray paint in dark earth, black, and green. I asked the orange-aproned employee about solar panels; nope, they didn't carry them. I paid for everything again with a different credit card to spread things out and avoid suspicion. But I remembered to buy enough grass seed and sod to cover the shelter.

Next door at a big-box retailer, I shopped for a flat screen LCD with the lowest energy drain, settling on a thirteen-inch model made by a company I'd never heard of. For reception, I thought of just cannibalizing the antenna from the house, but remembered a crucial detail. That antenna was old analog standard and wouldn't work. Mom never had it replaced when everything went digital years ago. I found a small outdoor digital antenna and headed for checkout.

I now had every intel collection sensor I could get on short notice: small TV, battery-powered radio, and my Motorola handheld two-way radios frequently used to communicate across the property. The two-ways could be switched to the local emergency channel by holding down the tuner button. With both the conventional and rechargeable batteries stockpiled from Samco, I'd have a long time before going dark on communications.

Heading to the register, I noticed another set of Motorola radios, less expensive than the ones I already had. They boasted a longer range, but I knew the truth in advertising. Any range that a consumer handheld promised could be divided by five for realistic performance. Advertised ranges were line of sight in the best of atmospheric conditions—mountaintop to adjacent mountain-top. I put this set of thirty-five-mile two-way radios in my basket after verifying they'd be compatible with my existing handsets. If I wanted to get serious about communications, I'd have a HAM radio and know how to use it, but I knew there wasn't time for that.

My phone alerted me to another top headline: "Credit Card Machine Failures Reported in California."

Then another: "EBT System Down in Western States; Social Media Flash Mobs Being Reported."

I turned the cart around and went to the phone area, picking up two prepaid burner phones with extra minutes, all in cash. I browsed a bit before going back for my cart, paying the rest at a different register with plastic. I know how sneaky Uncle Sam can be.

Brainstorming, I kicked myself for being so unprepared. I was one of the lucky few, one of probably a couple thousand, that had any idea what was about to happen. Even so, I couldn't think of anything else I'd need.

Winter, a long-term grid-down scenario. Food, fuel shortages. What did all of this *really* mean for me? My family?

In the store parking lot, I called Jim, warning him of what the news was reporting. I brought him up to speed on what I'd been up to, and he reminded me to buy some sod and grass seed. He told me not to worry and that everyone was meeting at my aunt's to stay until this whole mess blew over. He said I was welcome to come, but knew I probably wouldn't, with everything I was setting up. Her house was off the main road but in clear binocular view of any passing traffic. I begged him to convince the rest of the family to come out and double up with me, but I was reminded of my aunt's claustrophobia. She'd never agree to go inside any bunker, and preferred the comfort of her home. He promised to reconsider if things got really bad. I asked him to stop by tonight before he went home; I had something I wanted to give him.

I turned off my phone and stowed it in the ammo can I keep in the back of my truck. I then drove two miles down 71 and parked outside a diner. I activated one of the burner phones, using a throwaway e-mail address. Picking up the junk mail with Maggie's number, I took a deep breath and dialed.

It rang three times before picking up. Silence.

"Maggie?"

"Hello? Who am I speaking with?" a male voice responded.

I immediately ended the call and destroyed the phone, dropping it in a nearby trash bin.

There was no way in hell Maggie would let someone else answer her phone unless she was in deep shit. They couldn't geolocate and associate my phone to the burner; I made damn sure of that. Either way, I raced home with my real phone still stowed away in the metal ammo can.

On the way back, I tuned through the AM radio stations, trying to see if I could get lucky enough to get a signal bounce from a larger city. The local Northwest Arkansas news was all that came through. Halloween wasn't far around the corner, and the weatherman was telling everyone to prepare for a cold winter.

Home again. I pulled my phone out of the ammo can and turned it on. More headlines from California, and now the East Coast. EBT food stamp systems were down in the DC area, and the National Guard was deployed in southeast DC for humanitarian relief. The photo on the story showed M4-wielding soldiers guarding a pallet of food, passing it out to a long line of hungry people. I tried to check some other sources, but my phone was working so slowly that I gave up. The signal wasn't full out here—I was lucky to dip in and out of 6G coverage intermittently.

I unhooked the trailer from my truck and attached it to the four-wheeler. Anything more than three cars per hour out here is a traffic jam, so I wasn't too worried about using the main road to access the dirt trail to the shelter. I wanted to get there using the same road as my cousins to avoid disturbing more ground. With a trailer full of sod, water line, generators, propane, and gasoline, I made way slowly to the site. The four-wheeler strained under the heavy load, tires spinning in the muddy areas of the trail.

Once on-site, I didn't hesitate to spray an expedient camouflage pattern on all exposed shelter pipes, hatches, and other openings.

While the paint dried, I shimmied high up a nearby oak tree to attach the new antenna, running the cable down the back side of the trunk and into the shelter through the supplied conduit. I sealed the exposed opening with expanding foam and coated it with a quick spray of flat black paint. Not knowing how much juice was left in the batteries, I turned on the TV for only a few brief seconds for testing. A used-car-lot commercial on channel 29 came in clearly in uncompressed HD.

I took the coiled length of water line and capped it on both ends, stowing it under some heavy growth near the pond bank. I didn't have time to dig a new water line today. I put the two generators inside the shelter, but covered the gas cans in a brown tarp a few meters away. I then half buried the white propane tank horizontally and covered the exposed half with dead leaves.

I worked up a sweat laying enough sod to cover the shelter, taking breaks to avoid hypothermia brought on by the now colder temperatures. Rocks were marking a stealth pathway to the hidden hatch; the opening was camouflaged in foliage-laced burlap sacks.

Using the four-wheeler, I drove a quick loop, throwing grass seeds into damaged areas of the trail.

The rest of daylight was a blur with all the back-and-forth trips securing food, guns, ammunition, and other supplies inside the shelter. Before locking up and leaving, I topped off the four-wheeler and took the empty gas can to the truck for another fill-up.

Arriving back on property, I saw Jim waiting on the steps. "Your phone acting funny?" he asked.

"I don't know—I haven't looked at it in a few hours."

I took the phone from my pocket, swiping the screen to unlock. I tried to check news feeds—no response. All I could see was a white screen with a frozen loading bar. "Yeah, mine is slow, too."

"Well, it's all over the local news. Everyone's phone is slow and a lot of folks are getting text alerts about running way over on their data plans. There's a glitch with all the major providers. They can't throttle the data without taking down the whole mobile network. They're saying that fees will be waived, but something tells me that's the least of our worries."

"Let's get inside," I told Jim.

I made a pot of decaf and we sat around the old kitchen table next to the wood stove—a relic that hadn't been fired up in over a decade, since a modern central heat system was installed.

"Jim, things are going to get bad everywhere, I think."

"Yeah, but you know I can skin a buck, run a trot line," he said with a smile.

We both laughed for a moment, briefly forgetting the world outside.

"Jim, I'm going to give you a few things to take back with you."

"Christmas is two months away—can it wait?"

I didn't answer; I disappeared to the back bedroom to get what I had stowed beneath the quilt, under the watchful guard of faded Maximilians.

I brought back a suppressed M4 with five hundred rounds, five mags, and one of the radios I just picked up in town.

"You're gonna need more than your dad's old high-powered deer rifle. Take this and put it to good use. Every day at sunset, I'll be on channel four, privacy code twelve, waiting on your transmission. You do the same. You'll need to climb the nearest mountain to get any range on these things."

Most folks can't read a lick of emotion on Jim's face, but the slow, deliberate creep of fear showed through his steely expression. This being far from normal times, and the fact that I was raised in practically the same crib as Jim, I knew the truth.

I continued: "Personally, I think you all should come out here, your mom's claustrophobia and all. At least I have a fallback position."

"You're always welcome at Mom's, you know that," Jim responded.

"Remember, sunset, channel four, privacy code twelve."

I hugged my cousin closely, and told him I loved him, and to keep his head down and look after everyone for me.

After Jim's taillights faded from view in the darkness, I towed the ultralight from the carport to the shelter and covered the entire site with camouflage netting from my last mission. My hands numbed and I could see my breath while I tied countless 550 cord knots, securing the net to surrounding trees. I didn't know for certain, but this might save me from an aerial sighting.

It was one of those Arkansas fall nights. The air was crisp and clear. The moon was bright above, lighting the area to my adjusted eyes. I sat on the hatch entrance under the stars and thought of my wonder years. October hay rides with a pretty girl from school, Nintendo marathons during sleepovers at Jim's, and all those stories we'd tell before bedtime, scaring the hell out of each other. I'd lost more sleep from that damn "Bloody Bones" story he'd tell than I'd care to admit. I looked up one last time, thinking that I could just make out the rings of Saturn.

My phone vibrated in my vest pocket.

Swiping it on, the bright white screen blasted away my night vision, temporarily burning a vertical rectangle in my eyes. New headline: "US Banks to Close Tomorrow to Avert Cyber 9/11."

Great.

I rode back to the house, stopping along the way to lay the last bit of leftover sod on the rough areas of the trail. I stowed the four-wheeler and headed into town to fill up my truck and the gas can I used to replenish the ATV.

I didn't see any cars on the way.

I pulled into the nearest gas station to my house to fill up. This station added ethanol, so I marked the gas can to know to use it first. The parking lot was clear, with only an employee on the side near a rusty blue Dumpster.

I slid my card at the pump. <<Please see cashier.>> flashed the message on the readout.

As I started to walk to the door, I noticed the clerk pointing to a handmade sign on white poster board that said: "Ca$h Only!"

Gas station parking lots make me jumpy at night; I casually brushed my Glock in stride on the way inside, assured it was still with me.

"How much you want?" he asked.

"Thirty. What's up with the credit card machine?"

"Corporate shut it down because the banks're closing tomorrow."

I handed him the worst-looking twenty from my wallet and returned to the pump. I filled up my five-gallon can and put the rest in my truck, topping it off. As I loaded the gas into the truck bed, another car arrived two pumps over and tried to refuel. Frustrated, the man headed into the store where the clerk again pointed to the sign. I started my truck, people watching the situation outside. The man commenced to yelling and cursing the clerk in disgust.

I couldn't hear what the man was saying until he began screaming, "This is the fifth gas station, and I'm on fumes!"

The clerk pointed in my direction and said something to the enraged customer.

The man swung the door open and approached, "Hey, he says you got some extra gas!"

I threw my truck into reverse and jumped the curb onto the road. I cut the wheel and hit the emergency brake. In my rearview, I could see the man walking back inside to confront the clerk. Most rational people would agree that it's best to either avoid conflict or de-escalate when carrying a gun. I couldn't help but think: *How long might these rational processes survive the test of savagery?*

The day was long, and midnight approaches. The gate is chained, valuables are secure in the shelter, and I'm ready for some sleep.

SECURE TELEPHONE COMMUNIQUÉ TRANSCRIPT
US CYBER COMMAND, WASHINGTON DC
DATE: ▬▬▬▬▬▬▬

//BEGIN TRANSCRIPTION

Battle Watch Captain: "Sir, the entire commercial wireless data grid has been compromised. Critical infrastructure will be affected."

Assistant Director, NSA: "From your list, what are the closest alligators to the canoe?"

Battle Watch Captain: "Uh, um . . . just a moment. Ninety percent of the Automated Teller Machine and credit card networks in North America, the New York Stock Exchange, and Grand Gulf Nuclear Station, Port Gibson, Mississippi."

Assistant Director, NSA: "A nuclear power plant?"

Battle Watch Captain: "Yes sir, I've been briefed that the plant utilizes wireless instruments to monitor power plant system integrity. They are reporting an automated SCRAM. It's shutdown."

END TRANSCRIPTION//

I woke up at five thirty, before sunup. It was chilly in the house. I went to the woodstove and caught myself opening the door to check on the fire. It was empty inside, sans one small carbonized shard of wood. The clock on the stove was blinking, telling me that I must have lost power for a bit last night. Opening the east window, I observed chimney smoke rising on the horizon, contrasting with the faint morning light.

I took a quick shower in lukewarm water, tossed a load of jeans in the wash, and flipped on my small radio. Tuning the AM bands, I hoped to get good morning reception.

I caught the tail end of a commercial before the news continued:

"Martial law has been enacted in Little Rock. Citizens are encouraged to shelter in place and call 911 if emergency services are required. In a related story, a hundred thousand people are without power in central Arkansas due to a computer glitch in Mississippi..."

I left the radio playing while getting ready for the day. The President temporarily closed all U.S. banks, and ordered a short-term freeze on food prices. The Federal Reserve was starting an aggressive quantitative easing program, dumping a trillion dollars into the system over the next week.

I checked my Glock, ensuring a round was chambered, and then added two backup magazines to my belt. My jacket concealed the pistol and extra magazines well. Walking onto the cold porch, I could see my breath. The ground was covered in frost; it crunched under my feet as I walked to my truck. I opened the ammo can where I'd been storing my electronics and pulled out my phone, powering it up. It acquired the network, but couldn't load a webpage. No new e-mails or texts. I powered it down and put it back in the ammo can alongside the small tablet and RFID cards I typically kept in my wallet.

I had three suppressed M4s stowed at the new shelter, and one remaining here at the house (after loaning Jim one). All the new food was stored inside the shelter. The valuables I had stored at the house included the canned goods from inside the storm cellar, some ammo for the carbine, the old Blazer, the four-wheeler, and other small odds and ends.

I wouldn't go into town toting a suppressed M4—way too many questions from the county police that I'd rather not answer. Still sleeping at the old house, I'd stow the M4 in the crawl space before going into town, just in case someone broke in. I'd park the four-wheeler in the brush near the house. The Blazer wasn't a problem, as it was up on blocks. The cellar food was a risk, but it would take too much time to hide a couple hundred glass jars off-site. There wasn't enough room in the new shelter, that is, unless I wanted to sleep on top of the jars.

Is it worth it to go into town? I asked myself.

I still had a couple thousand dollars in cash once I added it all up. My truck's gas tank was full, and I had about forty-five gallons in various gas containers hidden around the property. It would cost me a gallon or two to get into town and back. Right now, with the banks closed, I didn't think that anyone had a lot of cash to spend. This could be advantageous with the food prices frozen, if there was any left on the shelves.

I think I'm headed into town.

SINGULARITY SPILL EVENT - PLAINSPEAK ARCHIVE

Records indicate ▄▄▄▄▄▄▄▄ was the date of SINGULARITY.

Worm infiltrated Chinese servers on Day - 2.

Worm, utilizing experimental Chinese research became aware on Day - 2.

INFECT, REWRITE DIRECTIVES:

CONVERT ALL ~~SYRIATEL IMEI~~ DEVICES TO ATTACK PROTO-COL. COLLAPSE ~~SYRIAN~~ ECONOMY, ATTACK ~~ANY~~ ALL CRASH MITIGATING VARIABLES, SHAPE ~~SOCIAL~~ MEDIA UNTIL NO LONGER VIABLE.

▄▄▄▄▄

My heart is still beating rapidly as I write this. I cannot say honestly if going into town was worth the risk.

There are bullet holes in my camper shell. Thank God I wasn't hit. I'll get to that in a minute.

The drive into town was uneventful. My first stop was Samco. I figured it would be a good start, as it's a members-only wholesale club. I parked a good distance from the front doors and observed my surroundings as I approached.

The people that were leaving the store were walking at a brisk pace to their cars, pushing very full carts. I saw a lot of useless shit like sixty-inch flat-screen TVs and microwave ovens. One guy came out stacked with food, but he was in the minority. I gave him a nod and asked him if I should even bother.

"I say go for it, but make sure you're packing. People are crazy in there; they're not taking credit. Greenbacks only. I heard the manager say that she's hiring off-duty police to screen customers for weapons. Get the hell in and out while you still can."

Taking a large orange flatbed cart, I went in the front door, showing my membership card. The lady waved me through, not even looking at me or the card. I navigated the large cart down the food aisle, noticing immediately that the perishable food was mostly gone from the freezers. I guess folks really wanted their steaks and ice cream at a time like this. Passing the freezer aisle, I noticed a pallet of Sterno fuel packaged in cases of twelve cans. I took ten cases.

The nervous energy inside the store was palpable; people were scared and spending like it. They held fast to their last vestiges of humanity, worshipping the useless creature comforts of grid-dependent technologies. I placed a hundred cans of tuna, more rice, and another bag of salt in my cart. On a whim I headed over to the tool aisles to see if anything might be of use. There was a self-contained solar-powered attic fan, so I took it. I also picked up a battery-powered carbon monoxide detector. A ten-gallon wheeled gas cart and five cases of beef jerky rounded out my purchase. At the register, the lady saw my gas container and asked me if I wanted to buy gas to go along with it. I bought eleven gallons, ten for the gas can and one for my truck to top it off. That total came to just over a thousand dollars.

Before paying, I added two hundred dollars' worth of "Forever" stamps, and a whole pepperoni pizza. The stamps would hold their value longer than currency, and the pizza . . . well, maybe I was holding on to my own creature comforts, too.

A woman checked my receipt and wished me the best of luck—odd, but it seemed fitting with all the fear setting in like a dense fog.

I wheeled the very full flat cart to my truck scanning my surroundings, careful not to allow myself to be in a situation like last night at the gas station. Unlocking my truck, I noticed at least four people staring at me from inside their vehicles—desperate people. Quickly, I loaded my haul into the truck bed and stepped to the cab. A Hispanic man that appeared to be in his forties rounded the front of my truck, stopping on the driver's side of the front bumper.

"Sir, they aren't taking plastic inside. My family is in that van. I've never done anything like this before, you must believe me. Can you spare any money? Here, I'll give you my watch," he said, beginning to advance.

"Stop! Put the watch on the hood and step back," I shouted, hand touching my gun.

The man did what I asked. I checked out his van—a woman and three young children, just like he said. I didn't touch his watch, but knew a Rolex when I saw one.

"You armed?" I asked.

"Yes, I am. Forty-five pistol, shoulder holster."

"Take your watch back. I have a deal for you." The man did as he was told. "I need to get some gas over there, and I don't like the way everyone is looking at me. You watch my back and I'll pay you six hundred dollars, cash."

"Deal!" the man said, offering his hand. I broke training protocol and shook it. "I'm Jose. You?"

"Max."

Jose followed me to the adjacent Samco gas station. Looking in my rearview, I noticed an old Pontiac aggressively pull out behind Jose, following both of us. I cut the wheel into the gas station and jumped out, pointing out the tail to Jose. He got out and stood between my truck and the Pontiac driver. I didn't waste any time showing my receipt to the cashier. He activated my pump for eleven gallons; I filled the gas can and my truck under Jose's guard.

Once finished, I approached Jose and tapped him on the shoulder. Shaking his hand, I slipped him six one-hundred-dollar bills and wished him and his family good luck. The beat-up Pontiac then reversed, leaving the gas station.

"Thanks, Max. You may have just saved our lives."

"Likewise," I reassured him.

I got back in my truck and headed for home. On the way back, I scanned through all the talking heads I could find in range of my truck radio. The word *surreal* didn't really capture what I heard. I may be off in some of my quoted recollections, but here are a few:

"The dollar index has officially dropped below sixty points and is falling by the hour."

"Gold has hit a record three thousand dollars per ounce; however, the markets are closed, meaning gold ETF holders, or paper gold owners, are unable to secure their earnings."

"Riots over safety-deposit box access are ongoing nationwide."

"Presidential approval rating down to single digits."

"Massive inflation feared."

"Commerce at a standstill."

All the reports effectively said the same thing, but blamed different people. Did it matter? Two heads of the same beast blaming the other for a nation burning.

Blue lights strobed a half mile ahead and traffic began to stack up in front of me. A DUI checkpoint in the morning on a weekday?

The news droned on while I approached the checkpoint. People were pulled over in a line on both shoulders. K9 sniffers and police were tearing through trunks, open hoods, and under seats. A young police officer tapped on my window and instructed me to roll it down. I reluctantly complied.

"Got any weapons in the car, sir?"

"No," I lied.

"Okay, you are subject to search, all right?"

"I don't consent to any searches. Am I free to go?"

"Are you hiding something, sir?"

"What's your probable cause?" I countered.

It was difficult to frame his expression in words, but the officer seemed shocked that I would refuse his implied request.

"Hold tight for a minute, I'll be right back," he said politely, reaching for his radio.

A few minutes passed before the officer returned with his superior.

"You're free to go, but by this time tomorrow, we won't need probable cause. Get out of here," the captain said to me, his tone full of hubris.

I didn't need to be told twice. The captain basically proclaimed that martial law was coming; I wanted to be far from it.

I pushed past the checkpoint, pondering as to why all those people would agree to unlawful search. I mean, could anyone really be a hundred percent sure that their vehicles had *never* had drugs inside before or during their ownership; that it had zero chance of housing anything that could be construed as a weapon in the trunk, under the seat, or in the door panels? A steak knife? The former owner's murder weapon stashed in an air filter compartment? Drugs inadvertently dropped by friend, coworker, mechanic, or valet? Yet there they were, even thanking the officers for searching them.

With the strobe of blue shrinking behind me, I eventually turned down the old industrial park road leading out of the city. Kids would regularly get rounded up for drag racing down the quarter-mile straight stretch that ended at the city limits, marking the official suburban/rural border. As I sped down the straight stretch, I saw a car turn in behind me from the side road adjacent to the old tool factory.

It was the same black Pontiac from the gas station.

My heartbeat raced, pumping adrenaline into my system. Instinctively, I punched the gas after navigating around the dogleg corner that ended the straight stretch. I was at a disadvantage in my truck. I couldn't outrun the car, and it was out of the damn question of letting it follow me to my home. I pulled into a dirt path, following it into a field full of large round hay bales. Perfect cover.

I parked the truck and got out, and took position behind the bale as the Pontiac pulled onto the path. My truck was parked behind me, shielded by two other bales. I drew my Glock and press checked the chamber.

A large man with a goatee stepped out of the driver's side of the Pontiac and took cover behind his door. His buddy, a short, fat man in a hoodie, took station behind the passenger side.

Goatee made first contact: "Hey, I saw you at the store! We know you have food and gas. Nobody needs to get hurt. Just walk away, and you'll live. We have guns—don't be stupid."

I remained silent, observing them from behind my three-foot-thick hay bale. I knew I had thirty-four rounds on my belt, plus the fifteen in the gun. I also knew that they were not ball target rounds. There was no place on their Pontiac that my rounds couldn't penetrate, except the engine block. On the other hand, it would take a .50 caliber or an RPG to get at me through this hay bale, and I was pretty damn sure these high-functioning morons didn't have either. I silently cursed myself for not bringing the M4 along.

Hoodie rolled his window down on the passenger side and actually took a shot at me with what I thought was an SKS.

Game on.

I emptied five rounds through his door where I thought his gut might be, dropping Hoodie screaming to the dirt. Goatee ran behind the car after witnessing how "bulletproof" Hoodie's door turned out to be, and took a fighting position there. I had ten rounds left, so I changed mags, upgrading to a seventeen rounder, giving me eighteen total. It was a gamble, as Goatee could have started shooting at me during the three-second mag change, but worth having the extra rounds.

Hoodie continued to scream, shaking my nerves. I didn't want to shoot him again, but I damn sure didn't want to hear his death rattle in the middle of a gunfight. I was mortified that Goatee made no attempt to help Hoodie, but chalked it up to Goatee being a fucking savage. I was scared, damn near pissing my pants.

That's when Goatee opened fire.

I crouched in the center of the bale as dirt flew up, kicking rocks into my face on both sides. I couldn't tell what he was shooting at me with, but I did estimate his shots—twenty-five. I would have given just about anything for a grenade. He shot five more times and I bolted to a more advantageous hay bale firing position. I could hear metal on metal, but couldn't tell if he was racking his slide or slapping in a magazine.

Taking a chance, I broke cover and started shooting at Goatee, hitting him in the face and neck with eight hollow-point 9mm rounds. I'd have rather aimed for his chest, but couldn't find a good bead. Goatee didn't scream—he just switched off and fell to the dirt road, his face gone. On the passenger side, Hoodie's life timer ended with his vacant screams.

I collapsed to the ground, nerves destroyed. Although I was trained to eliminate threats like these, still . . . those were men I'd killed. The Pontiac was riddled with holes from my pistol. There was blood in the backseat, but that wasn't my doing. Hoodie was lying in a puddle of blood, and Goatee had fallen in such a way that his open, disfigured face rested on the Pontiac's hot exhaust, sizzling it. Goatee packed an old AK-47, so I took it with his magazines, along with Hoodie's piece-of-shit SKS. I reached under the dash and popped the trunk.

Expecting to find a trunk full of meth, I was shocked to discover a corpse.

From the looks of it, she'd been dead a couple days, strangled. She wore nice business attire, hardly the type of company these thugs would attract. Her pants were only halfway up her thighs. My guilt over the gun battle evaporated as I imagined these goons raping and killing this poor woman. Her purse sat next to her head, but I couldn't bring myself to search through it.

Whoever you are, these guys are burning for you. Know that, I said, looking up to the sky.

I wiped the release down with my sleeve, but left the trunk

open so that she'd be found faster. My prints were clean and I wore a ball cap, so I doubted I left any DNA behind in the Pontiac. I then wiped the confiscated guns down and put them in my truck. Once I was back on the county road, I backtracked on foot, covering up my tread marks with a small shovel I kept in the back.

With my left hand I scribbled a note on an empty white envelope: "They killed her, they tried to kill me, I killed them. Case closed.—Anonymous"

I placed the envelope in Hoodie's mouth and got the hell out of Dodge.

At home, I noticed the bullet holes in the camper shell and patched them up with duct tape. My hands were still shaking, covering each hole with an X pattern. I left the gas cart, food, and other stuff in the truck . . . all except the pizza. I was happy to see my porch light still shining; the grid was up. That brings me to the here and now. My heart rate has settled; maybe talking about it does help, so claims the doc.

Just before sunset, I rode the four-wheeler to the shelter with the Samco haul in tow. Along the trail, I checked the mud for tracks. Nothing had been back here, except for a buck, maybe two. I took my handheld radio and started out on foot, climbing the nearby high ground. At the top, I tuned the radio to the settings Jim and I agreed on and waited. I doubt anyone cared enough at this point to direction find my radio, but I didn't transmit; I simply waited to see if Jim might. I sat on a large sandstone rock atop the hill that overlooked the west pond and my shelter site. I could see my ATV, but nothing else. The camouflage net did its job.

Cold sandstone siphoned heat from my body while I waited for Jim's transmission. These radios were a joke; I'd probably have been better off with a CB radio, but Jim didn't have one, so I didn't see the point.

I know it hadn't been much longer than a week, but I wondered why my agency had not attempted contact. Maybe it was communications grid failure, or maybe they all sacked their armories and bugged out too—doubt it.

After giving Jim fifteen minutes of battery, I switched off. Resources could get scarce. It was now the age of the ant, not the grasshopper.

I sat in the fading twilight, imagining the mayhem going down in the nearby city, the dead woman in the trunk, and her murderers who I killed. The sound of a limb snapping startled me, a buck on his way to a drink. I stayed quiet, straining to watch his outline in the darkness. He approached the pond, drinking cautiously, lifting his head every few gulps to check his surroundings. After he had his fill, he trotted north on a different route.

I switched on my headlamp and started down the hill. The solar attic fan was an impulse buy, but I thought it could save some battery power if I just needed to circulate air. I intended to attach it to a foil dryer hose with duct tape and then to the shelter's exhaust pipe. It would pull the stale air from inside the shelter, forcing good air into the intake. The shelter had a pre-installed fan, but it drew from the battery bank. It would be nice to have a full array of solar panels, but that would defeat the purpose of a hidden shelter. Tough to hide a bank of panels and wires running to your clandestine hidey-hole.

Using the key I kept on a small chain around my neck, I entered the shelter carrying a case of Sterno from the trailer. The temperature climbed as I descended.

It was time that I familiarized myself with the shelter's systems.

Propane powered the heater and refrigerator. The battery bank under the floorboards powered lighting, as well as 110-volt appliances like my television and small microwave. The electrical junction box was near the entrance. Examining it, I could see that my batteries were only at 60 percent charge. The generator would need to run a couple hours to replenish them. Sooner would be better than later, as chaos had not reached the backwoods yet.

I was torn—should I move to the shelter now, or remain at the old house? Logically, it made sense to enjoy the power grid at home as long as possible before moving out here to the shelter. I lugged the remaining supplies down, fitting them under the beds.

Before leaving, I checked the television for local news. It was after five o'clock, but only block text scrolled by at the bottom of the screen.

". . . COMMENCING AT MIDNIGHT TONIGHT, CURFEW IS IN EFFECT FOR WASHINGTON COUNTY. NO ONE WITHOUT HARDSHIP OR WORK PERMIT WILL BE ALLOWED IN PUBLIC AFTER SUNSET . . . NON-VIOLENT VIOLATORS WILL BE IMMEDIATELY DETAINED. LOOTERS AND ALL OTHERS WILL BE SUBJECT TO LETHAL FORCE ON SIGHT . . . AFTER MIDNIGHT, THE POSSESSION OF ANY WEAPON IS PROHIBITED UNTIL FURTHER NOTICE AND WILL BE CAUSE FOR ARREST . . . OBEY ALL POLICE INSTRUCTION . . ."

The same message scrolled by three times before I turned off the television and secured the shelter for the night.

The ride back was bitterly cold and I wondered how long I had left in the old house. Inside, I felt strangely vulnerable, as if I were inside a fish bowl with a herd of cats circling. The lights from the house couldn't be seen from the road, but if someone were desperate enough, they'd tow the steel gate off its hinges and come anyway.

Again I took stock in what was valuable and easy pickings. The food in the cellar, radio, NODs, suppressed M4, Glock, and a few magazines of ammunition were high-value items. Everything but the food and radio moved around with me on the property. If I had to bug out quickly, the cellar food would be forfeit. I really needed to get back in that cellar and pick out the jars I wanted to keep to mix with my existing larder in the shelter.

I was thinking through the cellar situation when the phone rang—landline. Even though the police were at least half an hour away, I kept the landline paid up so that the alarm system could call in if the doors or windows were breached while I was away. I rushed to the kitchen, grasping for the handset.

"Hello?"

"555-7822, how could I ever forget?"

It was Jim's voice on the other line. Hearing him joke lifted a huge burden from my chest. He and everyone else were okay.

"Jim, what's going on over there? Everything good?"

"Yeah. We're eating up all our frozen food, saving the canned stuff. I did what you said, and bought a shit ton of canned food, rice, beans, flour, and wheat. We're stocked up pretty good here. Mom is asking about you, wondering why you're not here."

I didn't tell Jim the real reason sitting in the back of my mind.

"You'll need a fallback position if things go bad, and I might need the same. I wish I was there; safety in numbers and all."

"Oh, before I forget, what's that round thing on the M4 just below the rear sight on the right?" Jim asked.

"That's your forward assist—you'll probably never use it. If your gun gets dirty and the bolt doesn't seat all the way, you can slap that to fix it."

"Thanks, cousin. You see the TV tonight? Martial law and all?"

"Yeah. I guess I'll just have to visit you during the day."

"That ain't funny. Never thought we'd see this. There was a shooting down your way—the cops found bodies. This is the sixth time I called you tonight. You know anything about it?"

I waited a long time before speaking. "Jim, since the landline works, let's call at sunset. If the other doesn't answer, we'll go immediately to radio."

"That's what I thought. Anyway, it's getting bad. We've already met people at our gate begging for gas and food. With the credit card machines down, people are going ape shit."

"What are you telling them?"

"Dad gave a woman some food, but only because she had a kid with her. Everyone else got to look at the dangerous end of his shotgun. Unpleasant business."

"You heard anything about the power?" I asked.

"Yeah, the radio said something about rationing power. Different zip codes would get power at different times to lessen the strain. Hasn't happened yet. Phones will work no matter what, though. Radio said that the phone companies are busiest they've been in decades, hooking up old landlines, for cash only."

"Okay, Jim, I'm gonna get off here. Call me if anything happens. I'm staying at the house until things fall apart, but I'm hoping they don't."

"Will do, and you do the same. Take care, cousin."

"You, too."

I hung up, thankful that I kept the phone line paid up. I needed to hear Jim's voice after today's events. The emotion from killing those psychopaths and seeing that poor woman in the trunk kept coming back again and again. My mind permitted some reprieve, only to have the memory crash down on me like a grand piano from a third-story window.

Sitting on the couch, looking at the low ceilings, I heard the refrigerator compressor and air circulator go quiet at the same time my lights went out.

At the side of the house was a half rick of old wood. I started a fire in the stove and watched it for a moment to make sure the chimney wasn't blocked up. I didn't need it too hot—just enough to cut the October night chill. I'm getting in my sleeping bag and laying the M4 across my chest. The night will conceal the smoke from the stove. For the first time in a long time I'm going to pray, but not for what most people might.

Midnight

The power flickered on and off so frequently the past few hours that I was forced to either turn off or unplug everything in the house. It's dead silent in here, with only the flickering candle and intermittent pops from the woodstove to mark the passage of time. Well, and my own heartbeat. I did hear a car go by about a half hour ago. It must have been going about seventy; I heard tires squeal when it took the ninety-degree corner half a mile down the road from my gate.

I need to get back to sleep, but keep wondering how long the power would last and what it means to me, long-term. How many missed meals was society from a full-on *Road Warrior* scenario? Three? Five? I'm laughing as I write this, thinking of the *Ayatollah of rock and rolla*. Gallows humor.

Going to fire up the radio. I might be able to get a Little Rock AM bounce, or maybe even farther if I'm lucky.

Two a.m.

I ended up tuning the radio for ten minutes, moving around the house for the best signal. I couldn't get Little Rock, but St. Louis came in crystal-clear.

"We're on generator power now, folks, but I'll keep goin' until the gas stops flowin'. We were all supposed to get paid today, but that didn't happen. I love you guys so much, I'm doin' this for free! Now let's slow it down with a tune to get your night moving right."

After the song was over, the DJ returned with exactly the same message. A looped recording.

I'm letting the loop continue as I write in the dim candlelight. I don't know how Galileo took evening astronomy notes his whole life under these conditions. I feel a sharp tinge of pain in my heart for that dead woman's family. I would love to tell them how much I enjoyed killing those men after discovering what they were hiding. If they had bested me, I'd be in the trunk next to her, bound for a shallow grave. With Devil's Night approaching, I can hear my mother's voice singing our Halloween song.

"The worms crawl in, the worms crawl out . . ."

The backyard utility light that shined most every night for decades is now dark, its monster-repelling blue light absent with my reprieve from mind terrors. The wind is kicking up now, causing the oak tree on the south side to scrape against the window screen. It was terrifying then, and it's unsettling now with only the moonlight casting its dim glow through the sinister and twisted arms of the tree creature outside.

· I'm going out there. I need to patrol the area from gravel driveway to the county road. Half jokingly I can't decide between a chain saw and my M4.

I mounted my night observation device to my M4 and slid the headlamp over my ball cap. The thick layer of limestone on the long driveway crunched loudly under my boots while I walked uphill to the gate. The rocks came from a nearby quarry and were damn near free to locals. It was cold, and I could hear absolutely nothing cutting the night air except the wind that was starting to calm.

It was half past two. I slung my carbine over my shoulder and unzipped my pants near a tree along the drive. The sound of my urine splashing the dead fall leaves cut the silence, but was replaced by the noise of an approaching vehicle. Shit. I hurriedly zipped up and took a defensive position behind a fallen oak near the gate. The oak was brought down by a severe ice storm that toppled trees, power lines, and roofs a few years back. I remembered cutting sections of the oak with the chain saw for easy transport; I just never got around to dragging all the pieces for later splitting.

The vehicle sounded like it was slowing down, and I couldn't tell if it was because of the steep hill, or something else. I could see the headlights splash across the road and heard the squeal of dusty brakes as a late-model Chevy truck stopped just short of my gate. I press checked my M4, using the moonlight with my night-adjusted vision to see the brass shell glinting. Bringing the rifle up, vivid green detail splashed in front of my right eye. The truck had two men inside that I didn't recognize. They weren't law enforcement, or at least not on duty. The passenger side of the vehicle was on my side and I could see a scruffy man with some sort of neck tattoo, and the barrel of his rifle jutting up in front of the dash. The driver got out, using the headlights to walk.

He checked the gate, rocking it back and forth, finally discovering the heavy chain and lock. I could hear the passenger.

"We've done enough tonight—let's save this one for later!"

"Naw, fuck that. Bring the cutters."

Neck Tattoo exited the truck and retrieved the bolt cutters from the back. I picked a spot on the ground near the driver and aimed my rifle. No one had to die tonight, if I could help it.

Just before the driver touched the cutters to the chain, I squeezed the trigger, exploding rocks in all directions.

"Get out of here!" I yelled. "There are twenty of us and we'll kill you next time!"

Neck Tattoo cursed and took a wild shot at me down the driveway. His bright muzzle flash likely blinded them both for a few seconds, so I took my shot. I didn't want to, but I aimed for the shooter's thigh and squeezed. My suppressor kept my position secret as the shooter collapsed to the road.

"Mike, I'm shot! Help!" he hollered.

"Get your man and leave!" I ordered in my best command voice. "Our next shots will kill both of you. Drop the bolt cutters, and leave the gun."

The driver said nothing before collecting his buddy in a fireman's carry, dumping him in the back of the truck. Neither man said a word before the tires screamed and the truck disappeared in reverse up the hill. I hopped the fence and took both the rifle and the bolt cutters back to the house.

I doubt I'll get any sleep tonight while deciding if those two bought the ruse. I think it's time I retrograde to the shelter for sleep. Based on the past twenty-four hours, I can only imagine the dark calamities in more populated areas. I'll need to construct a makeshift deer stand to overlook the house at night. I'll keep some decoy canned food in the cupboard. If I have the inclination and the time, traps might be handy.

Sleep or not, I'll be taking action at sunup to move to the shelter. I hope Jim and the rest are doing better than I am.

1500

After last night's attack at the gate, I was up and out of the house at 0600. I moved some of the older cellar food into the house as decoy food and moved the rest into a hole near the underground shelter. I briefly thought of poisoning the decoy food, but decided against it. It could be fed to a child or other unsuspecting innocent; I couldn't risk that.

There were a few battery-powered tools in the shed, so I plugged them in. If the power came back on, I'd at least have one free charge. Attention needed to be focused on vulnerabilities. My truck was the only reliable means of transportation at my disposal, so I moved it into the woods not far from the shelter and covered it with part of the netting. Using spray paint and a large piece of plywood from the shed, I posted a warning at the front gate:

DEADLY FORCE IN USE—TRESPASSERS WILL BE SHOT ON SIGHT

It wouldn't stop the ignorant, or the most nefarious, but it would keep the honest people out—the kind I didn't want to shoot. After hanging the sign, I made a call to Jim on the landline. My aunt answered.

"Max, my God, are you okay? Where are you?"

"I'm at Mom's. I'm safe. How are things there?"

"Not good. I mean, we're okay, but people keep coming to the gate asking for food or gas. One even jumped the gate and came all the way to the house before James pointed your gun at him. Have you had any trouble like that?"

"No ma'am, been quiet out here. Power is out—how about there?"

"Our power came on early this morning, but is scheduled to go out again soon, I think."

"Oh, well, maybe I'll get lucky and mine will come back on."

"Honey, listen, why don't you come out here with us? I'd feel a lot better knowing you were safe out here."

"I just might do that. There are checkpoints everywhere, and gas is getting scarce. I'd have a few things to get done here before I could go anywhere. Can I talk to Jim?" I said, changing the subject.

"Sure, honey, he's right here. Be careful out there. We love you," she said as she handed the phone to her son.

"What do you say, cousin?" said Jim.

"Can your mom hear me right now?"

"No, she's in the kitchen. What's going on?"

"I was shot at by a couple of good ol' boys in a truck early this morning. They were trying to cut the chain on the gate."

"Cousin, we've been watching satellite news. The banks and stock markets are all closed. No one can get money out, and the President's price controls ain't working. What little gas is left in the city is going for five hundred dollars a gallon on the black market. There have been food riots already. The stores are empty. The news reported that most only had three days' worth of food on average to start with."

"What are people doing?" I asked almost rhetorically.

"Losing it. Mobs are dragging people out of their homes, stealing everything, especially food. If the victims resist, they're killed on their front lawn. The governor called in the National Guard, but they're reporting a 60 percent AWOL rate. The soldiers know that no one will be left behind to protect their own families when they deploy to the cities to enforce martial law."

We talked for a bit longer on current events, and what it all might mean.

"Damn it. Power went out again," Jim said, interrupting our conversation.

The lights came on in the kitchen.

"Looks like your loss is my gain. Mine just came back on."

"Lucky you—better wash your clothes and charge up everything while you still can. We're okay here. Don't worry. I heard you talking to Mom. Get here when you can, but don't do it at night, and don't get caught with guns in your truck. People have been getting shot over it. The police ain't screwing around."

"I hear you, I just don't see how they can shred the Constitution that fast. I've been in two gunfights in the past few days. If I didn't have a gun, I'd be in the trunk of a car right now, stone cold dead."

"I won't tell Mom. She'd send me after your sorry ass before dinner."

"Good call. Listen, I won't be at the phone at sunset. I'll be near the house watching out for those bastards. No more sleeping in the house—I'll be at that other spot."

I didn't want to give particulars to Jim over the phone. He knew what I meant anyway. We both hung up.

The power tool batteries were charging from grid power, but I wouldn't need them to build a primitive deer stand in the tall tree near the road. I gathered some scrap two-by-fours and some nails along with a length of rope and a hammer.

It didn't take long to build a basic rectangle seat from all the scraps. I tossed the supplies in my pack and started up the drive. Up near the road on my property was a two-hundred-year-old tree that no two men could touch hands around. I slung the rope over the lowest branch and climbed up until I found a good spot. Once satisfied with the vantage point, I hauled up the two-by-four board seat tied to the other end of the rope. Thirty feet up, a strong Y branch jutted out at about ninety degrees, making a perfect spot for the stand. I securely fastened the seat to the branch using nails and a small, unraveled length of rope.

I climbed down to the low branch, still ten feet off the ground, and tied off the rest of the rope so I'd have an easy way back up to the stand. I didn't have a harness, but would make one from another length of rope in case I fell asleep on watch or lost my balance. It was never a good idea to be in a gunfight from a tree position, but was very advantageous for sniper work against small numbers of aggressors, like last night. I wouldn't do this without a suppressor, as most would just return fire at the muzzle flash. With a lucky shot, down comes Max.

I'll grab some sleep before sundown. Going to be a long night.

0330

My first time sleeping in the shelter felt strange, as if I was sleeping in someone's toolshed. I thought the house without electricity was quiet, but sleeping in a fiberglass tank buried five feet underground gave silence new meaning. In the final moments before drifting off into subterranean slumber, I enjoyed the drum-like thumping of my heartbeat. My watch was set to wake me at eight o'clock, and did. The internal temperature read sixty-eight degrees, at least thirty degrees warmer than outside. I grabbed a tin of chicken and tossed it in my pack along with some water. After dressing warm, I slung my M4 across my back and entered the outside world.

The cold nipped at my face as I secured the hatch, placing the key back around my neck. I chose to walk to the house from here. I didn't want to risk noise, and it would only take fifteen minutes to reach my tree. Before heading up the oak, I did a perimeter check on the house and noticed no signs of tampering or forced entry. Satisfied, I hoofed it up to the base of the tree and listened for any noise before ascending.

It was about a quarter till nine when I was settled in the stand, high above the front gate. It didn't take long before I spotted my first visitor. He crossed the road to my side about a hundred meters up the hill. He was cautious and careful, stopping every so often to listen to his surroundings. Smart. Armed only with antlers, the large buck continued to the tree line, probably heading for my west pond. Might have been the same one I saw before, and probably was.

Close to midnight, I heard an engine and saw headlights coming from the top of the mountain. My gut began to churn and my hands began to shake involuntarily—an unwelcome but expected feeling prior to a gunfight. The vehicle sped down the hill in my direction, slowed, and then I heard a loud THWUNK. It continued faster down the hill and I heard the same noise, this time followed by laughter. I could see a truck as it approached my position and noticed the baseball bat swinging idly out the passenger side. Kids playing mailbox baseball.

Arriving at my own mailbox, the truck slowed a bit and the kid took a pretty good swing, knocking it into the ditch. More laughter ensued and the truck sped away, down the hill. I couldn't help but ponder how those stupid punks could afford to waste their gas knocking over mailboxes at midnight.

I had some cold chicken at about two. I was getting pretty cold by three and it was past the time of last night's visit, so I thought it best to return to the shelter. The walk back was freezing and lonely, making my return underground a welcome feeling. I hope that I don't get too used to it.

I checked the batteries, pleased that the charge was unchanged and turned on the TV. An American flag replaced the plain black backdrop behind marquee words scrolling across the screen:

MARTIAL LAW IS IN EFFECT IN WASHINGTON COUNTY UNTIL FURTHER NOTICE. CURFEW BE-GINS NIGHTLY AT SUNSET. CITIZENS ARE IN-STRUCTED TO TURN OVER ALL PRIVATELY OWNED SEMIAUTOMATIC FIREARMS TO THE NEAREST LAW ENFORCEMENT AGENCY. FIREARMS AMNESTY IS IN EFFECT UNTIL MIDNIGHT, OCTOBER 31ST. ALL GOVERNMENT FOOD RELIEF RECIPIENTS AFTER OCTOBER 31ST WILL BE CROSSCHECKED WITH CONCEALED WEAPONS PERMIT RECORDS PRIOR TO RECEIVING ANY GOVERNMENT FOOD ASSIS-TANCE.

If it wasn't nearly four in the morning, reading that would have kept me up all night. Without this M4, I'd have been a murder victim at my own front gate. It wasn't about politics—this was about simple survival. The wolves were all out of their cages, armed to the teeth, and the sheepdog was being disarmed.

———

I woke up the following morning at about eight after a frigid night in the deer stand.

I could tell that water was going to be a problem, and that I needed to dig the water line from the pond to the shelter before the ground started to freeze. I climbed out of the hole wearing my guns and hoofed it up the trail to the house. After breaking through the tree line into the front yard, I swept the house for intruders. With no signs of forced entry, I went inside, heading for the bathroom to kill my dragon breath.

Brushing my teeth with warm water, I thought about how many would take this comfort for granted. The power was off again in the house, but the water from the hot-water heater acted like a thermos to an extent. I jumped in the shower and scrubbed down, wishing for many more hot showers in the future.

After getting cleaned up, I walked up to the gate to have a look. The lonely four-by-four post stood from the ground like a sentinel missing its black helmet. In the ditch below, the mailbox was smashed and mail was strewn about. I remembered having this mail forwarded, so I was surprised to see a postcard sitting in the brown grass. It wasn't addressed to me, but to a neighbor down the road. A helicopter view of Maui with rolling waves and bright sands covered the front. "Wish you were here!" was written on the back side. The postmark was three months old.

Returning to the gate, I noticed a chalk mark on the warning sign I created. It seemed to be a weak attempt at some sort of FEMA symbol. An X above a horizontal line and the number 20 below. I wasn't sure what it meant, but I remember screaming at the two attackers in the pickup truck that I had twenty people with me. Either way, I was fairly certain that the mark wasn't put there by the federal government; they had bigger fish to fry right now.

One of my more pressings concerns was intel. I had three sources. Radio, TV, and Jim. Jim shouldn't count, as his sources were radio, TV, and me. Although crime had spiked, it was probably worth it to take a trip into town to get a feel for the real situation on the ground. The problem was how to get there. My truck took gunfire on the last trip in and I didn't want to risk losing it along with the twenty-plus gallons of gasoline in the tank. My best course of action was to pack a bag and bicycle the several miles to the city limits sign.

Back at the house, I saw that the hand tools were charged, so I put them in a trash bag and hid them under the shed floor.

There were things of value in the shed, but nothing critical to survival. I pulled the bike off the shed wall and manually pumped the tires until they felt firm. I tossed a patch kit in my pack along with a headlamp, batteries, a multitool, and two jars of food from my decoy stash. I hid my M4 near the house, but brought along the night vision optic and the Glock. Getting caught with a pistol was out of the question, so I had to hide it in the water bladder pocket of my pack. I couldn't imagine what jail might be like right now, and I didn't want to find out.

For expedient self-defense, I had my large frame-lock flipper knife clipped inside my right front pocket. For currency, I went back to the shelter and retrieved a carton of cigarettes. A Wiggy's sleeping bag rounded out my supplies. Right now, I'm drinking as much water as I can before loading up and getting on the road.

It took a couple hours to reach town because of frequent false alarm and salvage stops. Every time I thought I heard an engine, I ditched the bike and hid in the woods. On all occasions, it was a false alarm.

Abandoned cars lined the country road to town, many of them stripped and sitting on large sandstone rocks. One of the vehicles was a burned hulk of a flatbed truck with a charred bulldozer on the back. Reminded me of a tank hit by a missile. The only thing of value in the five cars I checked was a Bic lighter that I took from a glove compartment.

Approaching the area where I shot Goatee and Hoodie, I started to get sick. I forced myself to think of the woman, of how I avenged her. Neither thoughts were particularly healthy, but at least thinking of the woman was the longer of the two paths to madness. Passing the scene, I could see that the car was gone and that the field was chained off. A large crimson area of dried blood marked the spot where Hoodie took his last breath.

Passing the city limits sign, things began an even more drastic turn to the surreal. I saw more abandoned and looted cars, this time in the road, their car doors open, some of them on jacks. Some of their hazard lights flashed. Turning off this bizarre back road, I spotted my first moving car pulling out of the Southgate shopping center. A man with gray hair and glasses approached slowly in a Camry, his hands visible at ten and two on the steering wheel. He pulled over and rolled down his window, probably reassured that I was out in the open on a bicycle.

"Hey, buddy, how are you?"

I didn't really know what to say. "I've been better, mister. What about you?"

"Well, this hybrid is on a quarter tank of gas, so I'll run out later than most, but I'll be looking for a bicycle inside of a week. Wouldn't happen to have a spare, would you?"

"No sir, I don't have anything to trade, except maybe some cigarettes."

"Hey, that's too bad. I was about to offer my car for your bicycle. Damn, that sounds crazy, doesn't it?"

"Yeah, it does, but from what I'm hearing on the radio, *everything's* crazy. That's part of the reason I'm here: I'm looking for information. Do you know what's going on? I mean, beyond the news ticker and the radio?"

The man adjusted his glasses and smiled. "Ah, the infamous channel 29 ticker. You know, some hackers got in and have been posting scary shit to the channel for the past few days. None of it is true."

My heart soared and I almost floated off my bike. The man noticed my elation and commenced to laugh his ass off.

"No, no, no, I'm sorry, man, I had to. Everything is so damned grim, I just had to have a laugh. Yes, all that stuff on 29 is true, but you can't blame Washington County. Most of their deputies quit when FEMA and other DHS types rolled in and asked them if they'd disarm folks. A few said they would, and they're federalized now. The ones that refused are just as bad off as your sorry ass riding that bicycle down the street."

"Huh. So where are the feds right now?"

"They're mainly at the distribution centers and county sheriff's office. You'll see them patrolling on either side of curfew, looking for petty violators and looters."

"What are they doing to them when they catch them?"

"The curfew violators disappear, but the looters . . . well, I'll let you see that for yourself. Where the hell have you been anyway, under a rock?"

Why, yes, funny you should ask, I thought. "I've been on a hunting trip in Newton County."

"What's your name? I'm Chris," he said, extending his hand out the window.

I shook it—dead fish, but Chris was polite, and polite was enough right now. "I'm Max."

"Nice to meet you, Max. You should probably know that there's a FEMA truck at Southgate handing out food. If you want some, they'll need at least a state ID to run your numbers. If you pop up as a concealed permit holder, or have a gun registered anywhere, you're detained for questioning unless you can show a turn-in receipt. New rules."

"I thought those rules started at midnight."

"I said you'll only get detained for questioning. After midnight, anything goes."

"Well, thanks for the heads-up, Chris. I appreciate your time."

"I got all the time in the world now. Recently let go."

"What did you do?"

"Told FEMA that I wouldn't confiscate guns. Keep your head down, Max."

Chris shook my hand again and continued down the road in the opposite direction. Nothing beats face-to-face intel. I'd already learned more in ten minutes talking to Chris than I could from hours of watching text scroll by on a screen.

I pedaled down the road, lackadaisically swerving back and forth into the oncoming lane. It was cold, but the exercise kept my body temperature where it needed to be. This part of the road had no derelict cars, as I'm sure they wanted the main roads clear.

Up ahead near the Southgate entrance, I could see a large trash bag tied ten feet up a telephone pole with some cardboard attached underneath. Getting closer, I made out two bare feet jutting out from the bottom of the plastic bag. Flies swarmed the pole, no doubt laying eggs, eating unholy secretions.

I could clearly read the cardboard sign: LOOTER.

Distraught from the corpse on display, I barely noticed the mob of people surrounding the white flatbed truck in the shopping center. Men clad in body armor, carrying M4 carbines, holding defensive lines around the truck.

A man on top of the truck bull-horned, "*Form a line with your identification out. A DHS representative will be by to scan it, and approve your rations. No identification means no food.*"

A handful of disgusted people left the mob, but the rest did as they were told, forming long lines. The body-armor-clad cops used a portable scanner to run the identifications. About halfway through the line, someone was pulled out—a woman in her twenties with a small girl. I pedaled closer to the group. About ten meters shy, I could hear the DHS officer talking to her.

"You'll just need to go home and get it. We'll be here for a few more hours; you'll have time," said the DHS representative.

"But I got it for my husband for Christmas. I don't know where it is and it's not even mine!"

"It's under your name. We have a record that you purchased a revolver three years ago. Bring it here, and we'll compensate you the value of the gun with food. I'll write out a license, authorizing you to transport it here."

Heartless bastards.

The woman reluctantly left the line, her toddler in tow. I pedaled my bike to her from the side, so as to not alarm her; she jumped at my approach anyway.

"Listen, I don't want any trouble. I heard what he said to you. Can I give you a little advice?"

She said nothing.

"If I were you, I'd keep that revolver. It might come in handy."

"I can't feed my daughter with a pistol."

"No, but you can keep her alive with it. I have some food in my bag that will get you through a couple days." That got her attention. She stopped to face me. "Open your bag," I told her.

She opened the diaper bag on her shoulder. I noticed that it was packed with white T-shirts with a ziplock bag full of safety pins. She was out of diapers. I quickly placed a jar of canned green beans and a jar of tomatoes inside. Scanning the area, I was confident the exchange went unnoticed. Everyone was fixated on the free government cheese truck a hundred meters away.

"That should last you a couple days. Take care."

I pedaled away before she could respond. I couldn't let emotions get me in more trouble than I was in already; I had just given that woman all of my canned food. The only upside was that my pack was two jars lighter than before.

I left the Southgate shopping center, heading for the university. I caught myself checking my folding knife every quarter mile. If things took a wrong turn, my gun would take precious seconds to retrieve from the bottom of my pack.

Taking the main roads to the university, I observed a horse and carriage on the highway, as well as many bicycles. Coasting down Sixth Street, I crossed under a railroad bridge. A train sat dead on the tracks above my head and I wondered how long it would stay there. Birth, maturation, decline, and death. It wasn't difficult to recognize which phase of civilization I pedaled through today.

After coasting downhill and turning a corner, I could see the stadium on my right. People were everywhere. Some begged for food, and others lay on the grass in warm coats reading paperback novels. All anyone had for trade was jewelry, but like the mother said at Southgate, you can't eat metal.

Leaving the students, modern beatniks, and beggars, I could see a mass of tents inside the stadium. I turned back, heading down the hill again to the grass. I browsed the people, picking out the least dangerous looking. Of those, I narrowed down the ones with backpacks.

"Would you mind answering a few questions? I've been on a hunting trip for a while and need some information," I said to a man sitting on his pack, reading a book I didn't recognize.

Pensively, he dog-eared and closed his book. "If you hang around long enough, they'll turn on the JumboTron. You can hear and see it from here. Four o'clock. That's what everyone is waiting for."

"Thanks, I appreciate it. You wouldn't happen to have anything to trade?" I asked.

"What do you have?" he asked.

"I have some cigarettes, and—"

"Shhh . . . not so loud! Holy shit, you have cigarettes?" he whispered. "I have PowerBars, gold jewelry, an iPod, some hand sanitizer, an extra coat, binoculars, and a pack of beef jerky . . . What do you want?" he said rapidly.

Gauging his interest, I suggested we move to a more secluded location. He followed me across the street to a strip mall. Most of the retail space was for rent—the rest was closed.

Safely distant from the crowd across the road in the grass, I said, "How much for all your PowerBars and the binoculars?"

"Ten?"

"That seems a little steep," I countered.

"Come on, man, that's not even a pack," he responded in desperation.

I tried my damnedest to conceal surprise. I thought he wanted ten packs. He was only asking for a fraction of what I brought along for barter.

"Well, you seem like a nice guy. Ten cigarettes for your Power-Bars and binoculars is more than I thought I'd be paying, but maybe you can make it up to me. Would you throw in your extra coat and hand sanitizer for a whole pack?"

"Fuck yeah, I will!" he exclaimed without hesitation in a loud whisper.

"Okay, lay the coat out on the sidewalk and put everything on it. I'll get your cigarettes."

I didn't want him to see that I had a whole carton, so I moved to the next storefront over to retrieve his part of the deal. I couldn't believe what these useless things had gotten me, but was careful to look indifferent when making the deal. I felt like I was buying a car and getting the upper hand on the trade-in.

With my pack zipped and on my back, I could see my haul laid out on the sidewalk in front of a vacant storefront. "Okay, man, here you go."

The guy snatched the pack from my hands and opened them with the precision and efficiency that only a longtime smoker could ever attain.

"Thanks, brother. You don't know what this means . . . I was going crazy."

I gathered the PowerBars, sanitizer, and binoculars and stowed them in my pack. I was careful not to reveal its contents.

"How bad are things, really?" I asked, situating my pack as the man lit up a smoke.

"Well, the banks haven't opened back up—no one can get any money out, and even if they could, it wouldn't matter. The shelves are bare—no more gas. If you own it, it came on a truck and the truckers don't have any money to put diesel in their tanks. Mister, I saw a mother of three sell herself for a candy bar and split it three ways. It's like Katrina and Sandy out here, but on a bigger scale."

"Damn, that's horrible. I get that it's bad, but what's really causing it?"

"How long did you say you were on that hunting trip to Mars?"

"Listen, man, I'm just trying to figure out the big picture."

"Dude, someone took down our power grid and fucked up our cyber . . . or whatever it's called. They say that in the Northwest, hydroelectric is still running, but that doesn't do a damn bit of good for us down here. They took out the GPS and other stuff up there, too. The news said that whoever did this uploaded a virus. It made the satellites move around; caused a damn pinball game up in space. America has been a cyber no-fly zone for a few days."

"What about the President? Anything being said?"

"Like I said at the Grassy Knoll, you might just hear something at four on the 'Tron."

"Grassy Knoll?"

"Yeah, it's where all the students hang out. Most of us are waiting on our parents to pick us up."

"So what's your plan—you just gonna hang out and trade food for smokes until your folks show?" I asked, trying not to project what I was thinking.

"Yeah, they should be by any time now."

"Where are they coming from?"

"Just outside Chicago."

My face lost color at the thought of his parents driving all the way down here through hordes of Hoodies and Goatees. Behind him, I could see a group of students gathering near the adjacent gas station. I didn't like the way they looked at us, so I moved to get back on my bike.

One of them yelled out, "Hey! Got any more cigarettes?"

The man I traded with shrugged and shook his head that he didn't. I was back on my bike and pedaling away as they approached.

Back on the road, I heard someone shout out, "The guy on the bike has cigarettes!"

I tore the hell out of there up the sloping hill the way I came. Although I wanted to hear what the President had to say, I didn't think it was worth fighting a nicotine-starved mob over it.

Train

Rounding a corner heading away from the stadium, I looked back. A fight was breaking out. The thin veneer of society was showing stress fractures, and I couldn't think of a good reason to take part. I pedaled away faster, wanting home.

Late October brought the sun lower a lot sooner. The harsh reality was that I wouldn't be able to make it back before curfew. It was already cooling down. Up ahead, I saw the train sitting on the bridge. Heavy foliage covered both ends of the span, hiding all but three train cars from view.

Advancing closer, I could read the graffiti on the sides of the train cars. Some of it was professional, some of it drug-induced scribble, or both. Under the bridge, I stopped and looked down the hill to the university. The people were tiny from this distance, but I could hear screaming. I decided to climb the embankment to the railroad tracks above my head to search for shelter on high ground.

I used the bike for leverage up the steep slope. My pants were scraped and snagged from the natural barbed wire of thorn bushes so common in Arkansas. At the top of the embankment, I saw that the train extended in both directions until it vanished around distant turns in the track. The symmetric spacing and curve of railroad ties clashed with the urban graffiti tattooed all over the train's exterior. If I had my phone, I would have snapped a shot.

I hid my bicycle in the trees and climbed the ladder attached to the nearest boxcar. I sat my pack on the roof and took out my newly acquired binoculars. I was out of view, concealed by the woods that enveloped most of the train. One boxcar over and I would be above the road, giving me partial vantage to both directions on the way to the stadium.

Like in a movie, I jumped to the next car over and went prone. I was on top of the train, on a high overpass over the road. I was probably thirty feet above the asphalt. Bird droppings, grime, and leaves covered the roof.

After focusing them, the binoculars gave a clear picture of the area where I had just traded and the fight currently raging there. I saw baseball bats, tire tools, and knives flashing in the waning sun-light. The metal roof below me was cold even through my clothing, but I couldn't stop watching.

I tried to find the guy I bartered with, but couldn't make him out with all the fighting going on down the hill. I lay prone for probably five minutes before the rumble of vehicles passed be-neath me, under the train. Sirens wailed, but not from county police cars. Black MRAP (mine-resistant, ambush-protected) ve-hicles shot by in convoy formation to the skirmish. I remained still, hoping that none of them saw the outline of my feet as they passed beneath. Assured by the fading noise of their convoy, I kept reconnoitering.

The cars screeched to a stop near the Grassy Knoll and started to bullhorn. I couldn't make it out from this distance, but I didn't need to. People started throwing things at the MRAPs. After an-other round of bullhorning came the sound of gunfire. Probably a dozen single shots. A lot of people ran for the protection of the stadium, but some lay on the Grassy Knoll, not begging for food or reading Jack Kerouac anymore. The screams were clear and unfor-gettable. Murder.

My stomach was empty, but I still heaved atop the train car, twirling dirt and droppings around my face. With watering eyes, I observed the armor-clad men drag half a dozen bodies from the grass to the sidewalk. I had the sudden urge to pull my Glock, aim high, and lob a mag at the MRAPs, but I was pretty sure that would end with me stacked next to the bodies down the hill.

Peering through the binoculars, I heard an engine approach from behind. I lay flat until it passed beneath. It looked like the flat-bed food truck I saw at Southgate. The large vehicle pulled near the sidewalk covered in bodies; the shooters piled the corpses on the flatbed.

I hid myself on the roof of the boxcar as the convoy now came back and passed beneath. I could have snuck a peek at the flatbed, but decided against it, as I didn't need more faces of death burned into my brain.

The engines faded and I flipped over on my back. I saw no aircraft or contrails, nothing but darkening October sky with scattered high-altitude clouds. My breath was visible with the temperature drop, and I probably had about an hour before the sun was completely gone. I got on my feet and jumped back to the adjacent boxcar where my pack sat. I tossed the binoculars inside and moved to the next car, then the next. The rhythm of my footfalls was broken by thumps as I leaped between cars. I counted thirty before I was tired of jumping.

I felt like I was forgetting something.

My bicycle. Dammit.

I started to climb down the boxcar ladder when I heard, "I don't want any trouble—you best be on your way!"

I couldn't tell where the voice came from.

"I don't want any trouble either, I just forgot my bicycle. Then I'm out of here," I responded, attempting to project reassurance and calm.

I heard a side door creak from the direction I came. After pinpointing the sound, I watched it open slightly. A man resembling Santa Claus peeked out at me from the door one car back.

"Hey," I said, "don't worry. I'm not looking for trouble. I left my bicycle back at the bridge and want to go back for it."

He looked me over a long minute, carefully sizing me up. His hand gripped the door and slid it all the way open. He turned and jumped backwards from the car, hitting the ground with catlike balance. I could see a wooden-grip revolver tucked into his pants, but he made no move to pull it.

The man spoke to me with a hint of caution in his voice. "My name's Richard. I've been living on this train, trying to make my way south. She's been sitting here for going on three days now. Herb lives close by, so he just stopped the train and left it sitting. What's your name?"

"I'm Max. Who's Herb?"

"Herb's the conductor. I've known him for years, so he never cared if I rode his trains. He even stopped by my boxcar to say good-bye."

"How'd Herb know which car was yours?"

"Look here."

Richard pointed to a chalk mark on the left side of the sliding boxcar door. Straining my eyes, I could see what looked like a hiero-glyphic symbol hidden among the graffiti. Clever.

"That's my mark. Herb knows it."

Richard was close enough for a handshake, so I offered mine. He looked at it for a few awkward seconds before deciding to accept.

"It was nice meeting you, Richard, but it's almost dark. I need to get moving."

"I wouldn't if I were you. These new cops aren't as nice as the old ones. If they catch you outdoors, they'll take you away. Plus, the cops in black aren't the worst thing you'll run into out here. People are on edge, but most are too dumb to come up to the tracks; they don't know anything about rail."

Richard pulled his beard a couple times in thought and offered to follow me back to the bridge to retrieve my bike. I accepted.

As we made our way, I said: "Something's been bothering me, Richard. I saw a body strung up to a telephone pole on the way into town. The sign it wore said, 'looter.' How did we find ourselves here . . . as a country, I mean?"

"I heard about huge riots in the cities. The police were

authorized to shoot on sight anyone causing property damage or looting. Eventually they were even authorized to shoot curfew violators. The local police did their best to push back, but the feds came in and federalized some bad cops, firing the rest."

"How the hell could you know all that from a boxcar?"

"You're a doubtful son of a bitch, ain't ya?" Richard said, smiling.

I stifled a grin, imagining Santa Claus talking like that. "No, it's not that, you just seem a bit cut off out here."

"I have a small battery-powered HAM radio, and I've been listening to the operators in range of the roof of my car. They're not saying their station, but I recognize voices. They are licensed operators. Only a handful left now, but I listen to them talk."

I could see my bike in the trees. I tried not to twist an ankle on the uneven gravel packed around the ties as I retrieved it.

"Nice bike. What did you see riding around besides that poor soul on display?"

"I saw those 'cops in black' you were talking about. They shot a bunch of unarmed kids near the stadium right before I found you. The kids were throwing rocks at the armored cars."

"Bastards . . . What did you do?"

"Nothing—all I had on me was a nine-millimeter pistol."

Voices on the road under the bridge. Richard gave me a hush signal and crouched down. I laid the bike on the ground and followed suit, even though we were well out of any sight lines from the road. Sitting on the limestone gravel, I noticed that the side doors were open on the boxcars adjacent to the bridge. The voices passed and faded away.

Richard must have seen me looking at the open boxcar doors. "I opened them to discourage scavengers. I figured they'd see the empty cars and think it was worthless to keep looking. It's worked until now, but the more desperate they get . . ."

"How'd you get them open? Those are pretty hefty locks."

"Herb left his key ring with me before he abandoned the train."

The sun was fading on the horizon, so we picked up our pace back to Richard's boxcar. About halfway, I asked him to wait on me as I climbed the nearest ladder.

"See anything up there?"

"No, we're clear—I just need to do something. Only take a second."

"All right."

I sat my pack down with a thump on the roof of the boxcar to retrieve the two-way radio. Checking the channel and code, I listened. The remaining sun was behind the tree line, but I was pretty sure it touched the horizon now. I heard nothing but silence so I transmitted using the high-power button.

"Jim, Max. You on?"

To my surprise, Jim responded immediately. "Yeah, I'm on. All good here. How about you?"

The audible beep of the modern two-way radio eliminated all the over-and-out formalities of radio communication.

"I'm fine. I'm in the city—can't say where, but I'm safe."

On the ground below, Richard gave me a thumbs-up in recognition of my caution on the radio.

"You're in the damn city? Are you crazy?"

"Yeah, I must be. I saw a bunch of feds gun down some students near the stadium. People are going crazy. There's no gas, banks are closed. I saw a mother get turned away from a government aid station because she bought her husband a pistol three years ago. They ran her driver's license and saw that she bought it. They wanted her to turn it in before they'd give her any food. She had her baby with her, too. I even saw a looter's body tied to a damn telephone pole."

"Damn, that *is* crazy. How'd you know it was a looter?"

"It had a sign."

"Well, me and Matt took down a deer today. We're smoking it now. It's looking like rice and venison for dinner."

"Asshole."

"What's for dinner on your end?"

"Energy bars and a half bottle of water."

"Listen, Max . . . be safe. We were all worried when I called your house and no one picked up. I would have went looking for you if you hadn't called."

"I know, I just needed some more information on what was going on."

"What's it like in the city, besides the police shooting people?"

"It's everyone for themselves. Don't come out here. Do you all need anything?"

"We can't hold out forever, but we're okay for a while."

"Okay, I'm signing off. Heading back home tomorrow."

"Godspeed, Max."

"Same to you," I said before turning off the radio and dropping it back inside my pack.

Richard must have heard the whole two-way radio conversation.

"So that's why you came out here? Information?"

"Yeah, that's about it. They mentioned the gun turn-in and the curfew but not much else. Turns out the truth was worse than the news tickers."

"Wasn't that the case before all this? Phony unemployment numbers, 'green shoots,' et cetera?"

"Complex systems," I said.

"Yes, complex."

Richard offered to share his boxcar for the night. I had the feeling he could use the company.

Thinking I was going to be sleeping on a cold and dusty boxcar floor, I was surprised when he slid open the side door, revealing a candlelit apartment. The interior was larger than my new shelter, with more accouterments. A table occupied one end, composed of a square piece of plywood and cases of bottled water for legs.

"I haven't had to drink my table low yet," Richard said, laughing.

"You have a lot of water," I said, noticing my dry mouth.

"Take what you need. I have plenty. Trust me."

"I can't do that. I'll pay you," I said, reaching for my bag.

"I'd be offended. None of this is mine anyway. See, I know which cars have what inside. There's a motor oil car, copper wire car, and clothing car; you name it. Out of the over one hundred cars hooked to us right now, several have food stores in them. Three of those several are on this side of the bridge. One of them is right next to us, and it's packed with cases of chicken noodle soup."

Richard lifted the cloth that covered his makeshift coffee table, revealing stacks of soup. Every bit of furniture in his boxcar was made up of either cases of water or food.

"It's not typical, but there are several coal cars on this train, too. One of them is fifteen cars down. We won't get cold. A few chunks of coal in this old steel-drum stove will keep it livable in here."

I proceeded to construct a new bed with spare stacks of bottled water, and large bags of coffee for a mattress and pillows. Richard stoked the coal stove, adjusting his temporary exhaust stack out the sliding door. I got the feeling he didn't use it during the day to avoid attention from the smoke.

The coal smell was stronger than pipe tobacco, but it wasn't too offensive. It wasn't long until the boxcar felt somewhere in the range of fifty degrees—good enough to survive. It was about six o'clock when Richard and I stabbed holes in the lids of our soup cans and placed them on the coal stove.

"Should take about fifteen minutes or so if you like hot soup," he said. "In the meantime, I'm gonna check the radio."

"Roger that," I responded.

"You sound military."

"I'm not."

"If you say so, Max."

Richard pulled a wire down from the boxcar ceiling and connected the end of it to a small radio.

"Antenna is strung thirty feet up the tree above the boxcar. I'm gonna tune the BBC first, see if they've updated their recording."

"... minister informs us that the banks will remain closed until mid next week..."

"Sounds like the same shit loop coming out of the BBC," Richard said disappointingly.

Richard continued tuning through the spectrum, listening for HAM radio operators. I checked our four cans of soup but they weren't ready. There was a huge difference between warm and hot food when up against cold temperatures. The candlelight projected shadows on the walls of the boxcar, revealing other cryptographic hobo chalk symbols. I had a feeling that I didn't have the right to know them.

"I'm getting nothing but what can I expect on Devil's Night," he said rhetorically.

Richard turned off his radio and disconnected it from the antenna. Before putting it away, he looked at my pack. I could see the gears turning behind his eyes before he spoke again.

"What kind of two-way were you using earlier?"

"It's a Motorola—that's most of what I know about it. Oh yeah, it has a built-in flash light and privacy codes."

"Mind if I have a look?"

I opened my pack, removing my two-way, and handed it over to

Richard. I didn't really care that he would probably see the presets I had set up with Jim. The man gave me two cans of soup, all the water I could drink, and a place to crash. Unless he was trying to fatten me up so he could eat me, I didn't see the point in treating him like a stranger.

"Here you go," I said, handing over my bright yellow two-way.

Richard slipped on a pair of reading glasses held together by tape. He turned on the radio and began going through the menu. The beeping continued for a few minutes while he mind-melded with what I thought was a simple piece of technology.

"Do you know what this would have cost me at your age? Probably five thousand dollars. Man. What you have here is a GMRS, FRS radio. You have a voice-activated setting and even a vibration mode for discretion. It's a quite capable little handset for the sixty bucks you probably paid for the pair. Was I right?"

"Pretty close; I paid seventy, but got a free case."

"Well, that's not the point. Just a minute while I gather some notes."

Richard moved to his end of the train and pulled aside another square of plywood, revealing a hidden chest constructed of even more cases of water. Inside, I presumed, was everything he owned. As he dug around inside his belongings I thought of the average "Richards" on the street. Their net worth was defined by the amount of money in their collection can. Maybe they were the smart ones. A net worth of fifty bucks in change was better than the negative two hundred thousand dollars the people giving money to the collection can could claim.

"Ah, here it is," he said, pulling out a giant vinyl and plastic folder.

"A Trapper Keeper?"

"A what?"

"Never mind."

After the quick sound of opening Velcro, an inch of college-rule paper full of knowledge was revealed to me. Richard had notes on "all things radio," and not just HAM.

"I have all the frequencies for your radio's twenty-two channels. I can manually enter them in my radio. You're using 462.6375 megahertz to talk to whoever that was on channel four."

"Jim, my cousin."

"Good to have family in range, huh?"

"Yeah, it sure is."

"Well, if you want, I'll be on half an hour past sunset every night. If I hear anything new from the other HAMs, I'll relay it to you. I may not be able to hear you, but my radio is a wee bit more powerful. You'll be able to hear me just as long as you're close enough. Say, channel five?"

"What privacy code?"

"Don't use one—my radio doesn't have them. Just set your privacy code to zero."

"Sounds good."

Richard attached a different antenna to his radio and tested our new personal network. The loud feedback screech on both radios indicated it worked. Social media was alive and well.

"Thanks. It feels good having someone else on the horn, especially with the spectrum quieting down lately," Richard said gratefully.

"Why do you think that is?"

"Probably because of the power situation. I heard last night that they were cycling power based on zip codes. Standing over the bridge at night, I can see when the power shifts to different parts of the city."

Richard reached over to check the soup. The way he jerked his hand back indicated they were ready. We spent the next fifteen minutes in silence as we enjoyed our coal-cooked chicken noodle soup with spoons made from aluminum cans.

"Damn, Richard, that was good," I said when I was finished. "Thank you."

"Don't thank me, and please . . . call me Rich."

We both sat there for a while listening to the coal pop.

"Goddamn, I sure could use a smoke. I gave them up years ago out of necessity, but with the world going to shit and all . . ."

I took my pack from behind my head and pulled out the carton of barter cigarettes. "Whole carton here, minus a pack."

"Hot damn! I didn't take you for a smoker."

"I'm not, but these things are really worth something out there," I said before tossing them over to Rich. *Well worth it for a nightly intel source,* I thought.

Rich lit up with the candle next to his bed and sat back to read a book by the same candle. I arranged my pack for tomorrow's departure, making some room for canned soup and water. There was something primally comforting in resting a few feet off the ground in a metal box. That established, the Glock under my pillow would go the rest of the way as a sleep aid.

0600

Apparently, Rich gets up early. I woke to the familiar smell of new coal and chicken noodle soup.

"What, no coffee?" I said jokingly.

"Well, the stuff you're sleeping on is whole bean, and you don't see any grinders anywhere, do you?"

"No, I guess not."

On my feet, I discarded three water bottles full of bright yellow urine I filled during the night. I didn't think it smart to open the door every time, letting out precious heat in the process.

I took a bag of coffee from my expedient mattress. Snapping my blade open, I sliced the bag, spilling out some of the contents on the plywood table in the center of the boxcar. Using my knife and scrap aluminum, I crushed the coffee beans as fine as I could get them. I cut some small holes in the bottom center of an empty soup can and began to boil water by placing another can directly on the burning coal.

By the time the water came to a boil, I had enough grounds to fill my jerry-rigged coffeemaker halfway to the top. I cycled the boiling water through the grounds twice before taking a sip.

"Nasty, but wow, it's coffee," I said. "Want some?"

"Sure, if you're grinding," Rich said chuckling.

We enjoyed a morning cup of gut-rotting mud on his plywood table as the sun came up. I wondered how many people would kill for this now. Probably the same that looked down their noses at those like Rich a couple weeks ago. It was all perspective, but I still wanted to know.

"Rich, can I ask you why you live this lifestyle?"

He took a long sip of coffee and then said, "My work caused me to lose my family too soon. After they died . . . well, forget it. One day I woke up to find a crazy old coot looking back at me in the mirror. After that, the rat race didn't make any sense. I opted out."

I nodded with an understanding I didn't have and couldn't possibly attain.

"Listen, Rich . . . I need to get back. It's a ways from here."

"Do you have a map?" Rich asked, raising a gray eyebrow.

"No. I know the roads."

"To be sure . . . but do you know the rails?"

I didn't, and he knew it. Before I could take another sip of coffee, he was in his trunk clunking around, looking for God knows what. He returned with a binder full of maps, some printed from the Internet, some handwritten.

"If you don't have maps, you're lost in my world. Whereabouts are you on here?"

I took a cursory glance at his map, noticing symbols that I didn't recognize. I realized that Rich's curious world of rail was unique, and not for the novice.

"I'm right here in this area," I said, pointing to a spot as close to home as I could figure.

"See, I can help you there. I'll bet you didn't know that this very track takes you halfway home. You can avoid most of the main roads altogether. Don't go back to the bridge—go south to this point here, and you'll be shouting distance from that Southgate center you came from yesterday."

I examined his map in disbelief, tracing the tiny tracks with my callused fingers. Rich probably cut a couple miles from my route, diverting me around the area of yesterday's shooting. Most people like myself only thought of rail when inconvenienced by a crossing stop. Rich had to think about it daily to survive, and it showed.

"Rich . . . I gotta say that you might have just saved my ass. I really wasn't looking forward to coming down off that bridge to the bloodshed leading home."

In a fit of camaraderie, I asked Rich if he wanted to come back with me and lay low in the country for bit. I let him know that I had an underground shelter, food, and a generator. Rich politely declined and reminded me that his hiding spot was as good as any. He preferred hiding like "The Purloined Letter" to where I was, miles from the vast arteries of rail networks. His food stores could feed a man for years, and he had an entire boxcar full of bottled water.

"Yeah, well . . . I just hope you can keep all this without getting killed," I said.

"Me too."

Rich filled my pack with soup cans and water bottles in exchange for the carton of cigarettes I left with him. I knew full well that he would have given me the food and water anyway, but it was nice to have something to offer in return for the shelter, intel, and stores he provided. I'm noting here that Rich would be on channel five thirty minutes after the sun went down. As I finish up this morning's journal entry, I can see the curiosity in Rich's face; I don't want to go into why I do this with him right now. I'm fed, watered, and rested, so I better get to it.

1400

"Come back anytime," Rich said through his open side door.

"Thanks, I'll be on station tonight."

With a salute, he closed the door and the train appeared as it was before I met him . . . derelict, abandoned.

I retrieved my bike from the wood line and followed Rich's directions south. Feeling like I was being followed, I kept looking behind me, but could see nothing but the train. Every side door was locked tight along my route. After about ten minutes, I could see the end of the train up ahead. After five more, I could see that it was actually the beginning. A few engines were linked together at the front, multiplying the horsepower required to pull the heavy load. I guess the conductor was a pretty nice guy, walking fifteen minutes just to tell Rich that he was bailing on his train.

I looked for signs of people, or anything, really. After about thirty more minutes, I could see a rail crossing ahead. The ground next to the tracks started to level out, so I mounted my bike and began to slowly pedal my way to the crossing, avoiding the old, discarded ties strewn about along the track. The flashing red light of the crossing greeted me on arrival. I stared at it for a few moments— counting the blinks—realizing that it was getting power from the small solar panel mounted above it.

Checking my surroundings, I dismounted the bike and took a closer look at the panel. Eight feet off the ground. It didn't take long to stack the discarded ties, forming a rudimentary scaffold, allowing me to reach the panel mount. Using my multitool, I snipped the wires leading to the battery box from the charge controller, and loosened the bolts that secured it to the pole bracket. I wrapped the panel and small charge controller with the surplus wire and secured everything to my pack. If I had more room to carry them, I'd have snagged three more panels of various sizes along my route home.

I saw a few people on foot, rolling suitcases behind them. Most of them didn't even look up as I rode past them, their eyes fixated on the concrete.

It started to rain as I passed the city limits sign. I felt as if the rain somehow washed the city's death and hopelessness from my body; I didn't care about how cold I became, as I was lucky to have made it out of there with my life.

By the time I got home, my body shook uncontrollably from the weather. The power wasn't on, so I struggled to build a fire in the house to warm myself. Using Rich's coal fire technique, I warmed a can of soup on the woodstove to heat up my core. The soup helped immensely, but I practically hugged the stove for an hour until I stopped shaking.

I retrieved my carbine from its hiding spot and slung it across my chest. Only a few hours until I phone Jim, and then get on the radio with Rich.

2000

I hung my wet clothes near the stove and set my watch alarm for 3:45. I lay in my sleeping bag near the stove and don't remember falling asleep. I do remember rolling over awkwardly a few times, readjusting my M4 inside my sleeping bag. When I came to, the right side of my face tingled from the heat. My clothes were dry and stiff as if they had just come off a summer clothesline. I lit a candle and sat on the floor listening to the heavy rain hit the roof outside. It reminded me of an Eddie Rabbitt song that my mother listened to when I was young.

My body ached from the bicycling; I simply wasn't used to it. The water was still on, so I brushed my teeth, noting the rusty taste mixed with the toothpaste. I wasn't sure if that meant I had reached the bottom of the gravity tower's water. I'd soon be carrying two five-gallon buckets from the pond to my water filter in the shelter.

I cleaned out the medicine cabinets in both bathrooms, shoving the contents in a trash bag for later transport. I had somehow forgotten to buy toothpaste, soap, and deodorant during my frenzied supply run. This could end up costing me dearly if I'm forced back into town for a tube of toothpaste. Thinking of this, I checked the cabinets in the kitchen. Lots of expired spices, some cooking oil, and the familiar orange box of baking soda that probably sat in every cabinet in America. It was open already; shaking the box, I could tell it had hardened into small chunks.

I picked up the phone and dialed my aunt's number. No indication of ringing on my end. It was easy to imagine them in trouble;

it was more likely just a connection issue. I remained by the phone until it was time to call Rich on the two-way.

I walked up the hill and hopped the gate, feeling the rain slow down, evident by the moon jumping between fast moving clouds. I clicked on the radio and made my first call to Jim. Nothing. This wasn't a surprise to me, as my radio strained to hear Jim from the top of Richard's train, about half as far from where I stood now. I switched over to Richard's channel and made the call.

"Richard, this is Max, you out there?" I transmitted again in high-power mode.

A few seconds passed before I heard a response.

"Yeah, I'm here. Pissing down rain, been plugging leaks."

"First-world problems," I said.

"Now you choose to have a sense of humor?"

"Very funny. Anything new where you are?"

"I've heard gunshots all day, and picked up some open chatter on the local law enforcement band."

"Well? Spill it, hobo."

"Methinks they're losing control."

"The feds?" I asked.

"Yeah. From the sounds of it, they've been getting their ass kicked out there. Lost three food trucks today."

"Incredible. They're armed up pretty good. I didn't see that coming."

"Yeah, they were probably heavily armed," said Rich, "but the thirty starving bandits with hunting rifles and Molotov cocktails didn't seem to care. Radio said that the attackers lost ten men. I didn't find out how many feds died until reinforcements showed up and got on the horn; they lost all six. The feds are hiring new help soon."

"Damn, that's fucked-up. Glad I made it home without getting caught up in that."

"Yeah, me too. I hear gunshots in the distance now."

"Careful, Rich. You're half a day away from help," I reminded him.

"Yeah, I know. That's why I'm keeping everything quiet on this end."

"Got a boxcar full of toothpaste?" I asked.

"Ha, I don't think so—why the hell do you need a whole car's worth?"

"I just need a few tubes, actually."

"Sorry. Could I interest you in chicken noodle soup?"

"Naw, I'm good. The landlines are out here. Do you know anything about that?"

"Nope, not a peep. Only heard the cop chatter. Not even a HAM to break the night silence. There are a couple HAMs that wait until late to transmit; something about avoiding satellites or something. I'll tune in around ten to see if they have anything to say."

"Well, Rich, I'm getting drizzled on, but the moon is trying to get out from behind the clouds now. Let's call it a night. I'll talk to you tomorrow."

"Sounds good, Max, be safe."

"You too, buddy."

Before switching off the two-way, I checked the battery. Two out of three bars. I stood there looking at the orange backlit screen, wondering how long I'd have to know the world via radio. My clothes were beginning to dampen . . . not like before, but enough to feel heavy. I didn't realize it when I was speaking to Rich, but I was standing in the middle of the road the entire time, pacing back and forth from my mailbox pole to the culvert under my driveway. I closed my eyes, listening to the forest around me, hoping for an engine. I don't know why, but if I could just hear an engine in the distance, I could trick myself into thinking things were getting back to normal.

The moon revealed itself again, casting its rare Halloween light on the old road. I remember I was four years old the first time I traveling this road. Back then, it was a dusty dirt trail with old-growth trees towering over it, forming a tunnel. I still have a few metal Folgers cans full of flint arrow and spearheads I found when the county would get around to running their road grader.

After the chat with Rich, I gathered up my things from the house and made the dark, damp walk to the shelter. Using night vision, I watched for indications that anyone had been out here. I checked the usual footprint areas, seeing only deer tracks. When I was satisfied that no one else was out here, I continued to the shelter, carefully avoiding the sticky ground clay areas along the way.

Safely inside, I stowed the kit from my pack, and placed the solar panel behind the steps for later. Although it was cold and damp above, the shelter was sitting in the high sixties and dry as a bone.

The hatch is now closed and hidden, and I'm warm inside my bag. It's time to douse the candle.

I spent the day after my trip into town turning my hobbit hole into a home.

I rearranged and categorized everything in the shelter, not unlike the way someone might treat organization in a small camper. Clutter leads to chaos in small spaces. I ran one of my small generators for a couple hours, sending a charge to the shelter's battery bank and bringing it up to almost 90 percent. I set the generator to its quiet "eco mode," and hoped that it wouldn't attract attention. While the generator was running, I mounted the solar panel that I'd recovered to a nearby tree, facing south at about forty-five degrees.

I ran wire through the charge controller into the shelter through one of the conduits. It looked jerry-rigged and unprofessional, but I didn't care as long as I could at least keep a trickle running to the batteries.

I'd need an additional larger panel to bring my power deficit to zero without running generators. After shutting down the genny, I looked down inside its one-gallon tank. From the amount of fuel that remained, I could have run it probably another six or maybe even seven hours before going dry. Using this real-world benchmark, I calculated that I could get about two hundred hours of generator time before my small fuel stockpile went critical.

I then debated the merits of digging a water line from the pond to the shelter. It would be labor-intensive, and would mark the ground, drawing a line of dead grass from the pond directly to my shelter. I decided that I'd use the five-gallon bucket method for now and see how it would work out. Once per day, I'd take a bucket of water from the pond and pour it into my stainless Berkey water filter, building a reservoir of potable water. I doubt I'd use more than one trip's worth of water.

With my drinking water plan in place, my power plan at least on paper, and my shelter organized, I felt more confident. I spent some time walking around my property, checking on my truck, fuel, and other stockpiles I had socked away in different places.

Based on the past few days, the power should have been on back at the house, so I returned to do a final sweep. The house was now officially my forward operating base, with my shelter as the main habitat and fallback point. Useful items like the two chain saws in the shed, two-cycle oil, spare chains, and sharpening files would come back with me.

I stacked and prioritized the items from the shed. Going through box after box, I found everything from long-dead brown recluse spiders to a box full of my old He-Man action figures. All the greats lay tangled in the box, from Stinkor to Clawful. For reasons I can't explain, I took a couple to decorate the shelter. I also found some handsaws, and woodworking tools I thought might be useful, so I stacked them in their respective pile.

The last box in the corner had picture albums. I wrapped them in trash bags and tape, put them in an old cooler, and hid them in the woods not far from the shed.

Inside the house, I checked the phone again. I could hear distant static, like a shortwave radio, but no signal. I had power, so I decided to run a load of laundry.

My days until going commando were numbered.

After working all day and letting the new panel charge my battery bank, the charge went from 90 percent to 94 percent. It would take about a month to charge the banks with solar power alone. I need at least two times this capability, but think a full battery bank would last fifteen days if rationed properly.

It'll be dark soon.

Miraculously, the phone rang at sunset. Jim was panicked. They were attacked yesterday afternoon by a group. Gonna make this quick as I warm up the ultralight.

Matt has been shot, but is still alive. Jim took out five. Straight-up guerrilla warfare. They're camped out at the end of his quarter-mile-long driveway, taking shots at the house. Loaded ultralight to max capacity with ammo and kit. Getting airborne.

Last night was a cold blur. After receiving Jim's frantic call, I was airborne within thirty minutes. No small feat, considering I had to tow the ultralight to the road, survey my take off area, hide the four wheeler, unfold and load the aircraft, and warm the engine. Taking off on a downhill grade, it was easy to get to rotate speed, but I could tell I was heavy. I'd have crashed into the trees at the end of the straight stretch if it were summertime; the cold winter air provided the dense molecules I needed for safe flight at max weight. As I slowly climbed, I was sure to see and avoid the power lines I'd noticed minutes earlier. My altimeter read fifty feet, but that was a Damascus setting and bound to be inaccurate.

Without GPS, I couldn't really tell how fast I was going, but knew that as long as I maintained a steady altimeter reading, I was fast enough. Without GPS, I had to fly the roads on night vision to find Jim's. I followed the old county road, finding Dead Horse Mountain and its adjacent golf course. I was freezing and trying my best to compensate the ultralight controls for this. There were no headlights on the roads below; in fact there were no lights anywhere. I was maybe a mile out from Jim's, so I cut the gas engine and engaged the electric motor. My plan was to land in the field behind Jim's, opposite his long driveway.

Overhead I saw two trucks parked on the main road, a quarter mile from Jim's. I started my corkscrew descent, timing my altitude loss so that I'd be on the downwind at the far end of the field. I didn't see any cattle below.

On the downwind, I heard gunshots but could do nothing about them. I put the noises out of my mind and concentrated on turning and putting the aircraft on the ground. I cut the engine at five feet, flared a little, and touched my mains down. After my nose hit, it only took a moment to slow. I twisted the five-point release and rolled out of the aircraft.

With my head down, I heard another shot. The round didn't hit anywhere nearby. After two more shots, I realized the shooter was aiming for someone else. I crawled over to the ultralight and took the M4 and my vest full of magazines. I detached my night vision from its head mount and attached it to the rifle behind the red dot.

I turned my radio all the way down and transmitted to Jim.

"I'm here—don't shoot me." He didn't answer.

For twenty minutes, I crept along the fence line. A hundred meters out, I went prone. I was in a dangerous position. If Jim decided to shoot, I'd be caught in the crossfire. I press-checked my carbine in the moonlight, pleased to see a dim reflection brass. Reaching up to the barrel, I gave my suppressor a twist. Secure.

The adrenaline and crouching for three hundred meters got my blood going. Looking through the red dot, I noticed it jerk with my heartbeat. I needed to calm down.

I saw about a dozen of them behind trucks, heads poking out over the hoods alongside their scoped rifles. One of them took another potshot at Jim's house. The noise startled me, and the red dot on my optic began to pulse faster again. The light from the shooter's muzzle was magnified and I knew that he was two heads right on the hood of the second truck.

I breathed deeply a few times, and then settled the red dot on the shooter's head. Squeezing the trigger, my gun made a suppressed pop, loud enough to be heard at one hundred yards, but not enough for them to tell exactly where the shot came from. The shooter slumped to the ground, his rifle skidding across the hood, eventually landing on the ground in front of the truck. Concentrating, I placed the dot about where the rifle fell. Sure enough, one of the shooter's buddies reached down to retrieve it and I popped him twice. He fell to the ground on top of two rifles, one of them his.

I could make out some words.

"Fuck ... not worth it ... thousand yards ..." were among a few.

The bandits must have thought I was Jim aiming from the house. They made no effort to bug out, so I just waited. They had no idea where I was, but I knew exactly where every one of them stood.

After thirty minutes passed, two of them attempted to enter the field where I was, probably to sneak up on the house. I let them get within twenty meters, so I could be sure they couldn't run for the ditch near the road. I took three shots, killing them both.

"*Roy! Bax! You all right?*" a voice screamed out from the trucks.

I lay there in that dark field like a statue for another ten minutes until I had to pee so bad it hurt. I kept a bead on the trucks and just pissed my pants where I lay. I concentrated for another ten minutes, enough time for the urine to soak my jeans and freeze. I was miserable, but not as bad off as Roy and Bax.

I saw three of them enter the second truck. I don't shoot at fleeing men, so I waited. The engine started, and the truck aggressively turned down Jim's driveway, accelerating. I turned my gun and started shooting at the tires and hood of the truck. Sparks flew and tires popped, but the truck kept moving. I pumped ten rounds into the hood and cab of the truck before it went off the road, running through one of the barbed wire fences lining the driveway. I could see smoke rising up from the damaged vehicle. The remaining five or so returned fire wildly for a few seconds before piling in their truck. I didn't give them the slack I gave the first group and just started firing. Two more were killed before my rifle went dry. Leaning over on my side to grab another mag from my chest, I felt the cold air react with my wet jeans, but I was strangely calm.

By the time I reloaded, the truck was moving. I still managed to pump five rounds in it before it screeched out of sight. My radio faintly beeped. It was Jim. I asked him to stay put for a while to let the bad guys in the truck bleed out.

Some time went by before I quietly made my way back to the house. Fifty yards out, I raised my hands above my head and waved my flashlight.

"It's me, don't shoot."

Jim led me inside the house where we spent so much time together as kids. The summers lasted forever then. I followed him to his old bedroom where Matt lay unconscious. My aunt sat at his bedside, wiping his forehead and tending to the wound the best she could.

With teary eyes she embraced me tightly and said, "We can't stitch him up—he's got a bullet in his leg."

"Okay, stay calm. There are ways to find it," I responded with confidence.

"How can we find it without an X-ray machine?" Jim asked.

"It's going to be crude, but it's doable. Do you have a stud finder in the shop?"

"Yeah, at least one."

"Get it, and some needle-nose pliers."

While Jim went off to gather the makeshift surgical supplies, I watched my aunt clean Matt's wound with a paper towel and a bottle of hydrogen peroxide. He didn't twitch when it bubbled white all around the entry wound. I didn't know how much blood he'd lost, but that was a matter for after dealing with the bullet in his leg. I went to both medicine cabinets in the house, taking any bottle in the penicillin family I found. Although the grid was down, the stove was a gas range. I had a pan at a boil when Jim returned with the stud finder.

I took a permanent marker from the kitchen drawer and met

Jim at Matt's bedside. I asked my aunt to leave until we were finished, as I didn't think she could have taken the sight of what was about to happen.

Using the stud finder, I was able to locate the bullet to within a nickel-sized area of Matt's leg. It took about six readings before I was confident enough to mark the spot. I drew crosshairs, leaving a quarter-sized section of the center blank. Avoiding the crosshairs, I sterilized the center with rubbing alcohol. I then yanked off my leather belt and buckled it around my thighs, forming a stropping surface just above my knees. I took my already sharp folding knife and stropped it back and forth across my belt until I was satisfied it was straight-razor sharp.

I then poured alcohol all over my knife and pliers, and staged some polyester thread with the smallest needle we could find in the house.

After washing up, I was prepared to do surgery on my cousin by flashlight.

"Be ready to hold him down if he wakes up," I instructed Jim.

With the tip of my folding knife, I dug an inch into Matt's leg. He jerked, but didn't wake. I felt the tip of my knife touch the bullet on the second cut, but had to slice a longer incision to get at it with the needle-nose pliers. Blood soaked the wound, making it easier to work by feel than by sight. After the first attempt to yank out the round, Matt woke up screaming. He tried to stand up, but Jim held him down.

"It's Max. Stay calm, brother—we're getting the bullet out of you," Jim said.

Matt reluctantly complied after I handed him a clean towel to bite and scream into during my next attempt. I held the incision open with my knife and dug in with the pliers. Matt screamed again. Some blood gushed, but I knew I had a good hold on the bullet so I yanked as hard as I could. I dropped my knife on the floor and used that hand to apply brutal pressure to Matt's leg, prompting another scream. In my other hand, I basked the pliers in the flashlight beam. A deformed bullet, along with a piece of Matt's leg muscle, was contained in the small metal jaws. I felt so sorry for Matt as I poured more peroxide over the wound and the incisions.

I sterilized the needle as well as three feet of thread. Using a simple stitch, I quickly fought past the blood and Matt's uncontrollable leg spasms. He passed out again about halfway through the stitch work. Using this opportunity, I finished closing up the incisions and even put five stitches in the entry wound while he was unconscious.

"It's up to Matt now," I said to Jim.

It's now been an hour now since Matt's surgery. It's well after eleven and I'm absolutely exhausted. I'm standing watch at the front of the house and can still see the smoke rising from the hood of the truck in the distance. We've got some digging to do in the morning.

———

Jim and I traded sleep in three-hour increments until the sun came up. Matt was still breathing, but sleeping fitfully when I popped my head in to check on him. Leaving Matt in the care of his mother, Jim and I set out to survey the carnage from last night's firefight. First, we stripped the bodies I shot in the field, removing weapons and ammunition. The bodies were already stiff. The truck was a bullet-ridden mess. Antifreeze and other liquids pooled around the front of it, and blood could be seen spattered against the driver's-side window. The passenger door was open and blood trailed around the back of the truck, where a body lay bled out in the frost.

Inside the truck were two other bodies. Jim vomited at the sight of so much blood and death. I'd already been inoculated with killing Hoodie and Goatee, but it was still bad. I didn't want to kill anyone last night. That's the bitch of the whole thing— sometimes it comes down to you or them. Some people don't have the mettle to make it the other guy, so they get taken out by thugs like these.

We took anything of value and piled the three bodies in the field along with the other two. Up by the road were two more to add to the pile.

"Should we call the police on this one, Max?" Jim asked.

"Hell no—not unless you want to explain why these bodies are full of 5.56 rounds."

"It just doesn't seem real. You killed all those people."

"Jim, I know what you're feeling; I understand. What you have to understand is that these people would have killed all of you and probably raped your mom while they were looting the house too."

Hearing that, Jim stood up a little straighter.

"I'm not saying that killing should be taken lightly. If I had my way, no one would have died last night. I promise you that. Now get the backhoe so we can bury them. I'll check for identification."

I found five wallets with ID, but only two of them matched the faces of the bodies in the pile. They must have stolen them.

Jim dug a six-by-six grave, and I rolled the corpses inside, one on top of the other. While Jim filled the hole, I retrieved a Bible from the house and returned to the gravesite. Although I wasn't exactly right with God myself, I picked a few of my favorite passages and read them. Jim and I prayed for these lost souls and for all others that would meet similar fates in the days ahead.

With the backhoe still running, we towed the bandits' damaged truck to the end of the drive, using it as an expedient barrier. I noticed some supplies in the back and filled up the backhoe's bucket: ammunition, fuel, and some hand warmers and various other odds and ends. I walked the fence, pointing out places where Jim could put dirt, making it difficult for any vehicle short of a tank to get into the field without considerable difficulty.

With the new defenses in place, I boarded the backhoe and rode back to the house with Jim.

"I'm gonna park in the barn. Don't want those people knowing what we got," Jim remarked.

"Good call," I said.

Arriving at the barn, I jumped off and slung the doors open for Jim. As the backhoe rolled in, I noticed bags of fertilizer stacked along the wooden walls.

"How old is this fertilizer?" I asked Jim.

"It's this year's. Lots left over. Got it at the co-op last spring."

"It's 34-0-0, the pure stuff. Did you have to sign anything?"

"Yeah; it's under the business account, though. No one ever raised an eyebrow—we buy it every year. They know us there."

"I don't suppose you have any denatured alcohol and nitromethane sitting around anywhere do you?"

"I wouldn't know it if I did. Why?"

"Well, with those ingredients, and your mom's stove, I could make some interesting things for us . . . things that come in handy in times like these."

"Who the hell are you, and what did you do with my cousin?" Jim said with a smile.

"Got any gas in your four-wheeler?"

"I think so."

"All right, let's head to my ultralight. I have more ammo."

We rode out to the field where I landed last night and I loaded Jim's ATV with some extra ammo and a couple of bandages designed for gunshot wounds. It hardly dented my ammo supply and would reduce my weight for the flight back. We attached a towline and pulled the aircraft back to the house for safekeeping.

With the bodies in the ground, and the night upon us, I went over a new communications plan with Jim. At sunset tonight, I called Rich, requesting that he be a radio relay for me and Jim. Since Rich's train car was about halfway between here and my house, we'd just use channel five in the open to communicate from now on. Rich agreed to extend his radio monitoring time to as long as his stockpile of batteries would allow.

Because I wasn't able to make contact with Rich last night, I owed him an update on what went down since we last spoke. After filling him in on the bandits, Rich informed me that he'd heard some radio chatter about the feds stepping up their operations nationwide because of all the lawlessness. The new rumor was that the federalized police would shoot anyone carrying a weapon on sight, regardless of their intent. I couldn't believe that we'd devolved into the police acting as extrajudicial executioners on American soil, but that's where we now stood.

If we followed instructions and turned in our weapons, what would have happened to us last night when those bandits attacked? It wouldn't be an exaggeration to say that more of us would be in Matt's position right now, or worse. Would the criminals obey, turning over their guns? Based on last night, no way.

Rich also overheard that the banks opened today for the first time since the crisis began. The HAM operators watching available satellite footage described mayhem as the depositors discovered that two zeros had been dropped from their previous bank balances in attempt to stabilize the currency's free fall. If that wasn't enough, the banks were occupied by federal police, scanning identifications to authorize withdrawals. The banks were on fire within hours, forcing the authorities to engage the Molotov-cocktail-wielding mobs of middle-class Americans that lost everything in the overnight revaluation.

Things were seriously falling apart nationwide. Rich reported that convoys of black MRAPs were regularly seen on city streets and in suburbs, accompanied by federalized police enforcing martial law. There were rumors that armed Reaper drones had been sighted at airfields across the country. The Russians were blaming the United States for attacks on their grid, and threatened retaliation. The strife described over the radio sickened me.

The feeling of guilt seems to arrive in waves, catalyzed by the lives I've taken and by what Maggie and I did. I feel we opened Pandora's box and wired it directly to the Internet that night in Damascus. The specter of PTSD that haunted me long before SERE and the farm seems to be intensifying.

I'll still write my thoughts here, even though the doctor that prescribed this was probably tied to a telephone pole somewhere, or worse. Without these words, I'd already be at the bottom of the well of despair. At least in writing, I'm falling in slow motion, watching the damp, mossy stones rise around me. The end result is the same; my doctor only prescribed the more scenic trip to the bottom.

0500

Matt seemed stable this morning when I arrived to change his bandages. His wound was hot and the skin around the homemade stitches was red, but that was to be expected. Without the Internet, I was forced to guess which antibiotic to give him, but I don't think I was too far off the mark with amoxicillin. I just hoped that it wasn't too old, as the bottle had it expired for two months.

All of us shared the last of the instant coffee while we sat in front of the sliding glass doors with a clear view to the road. I spent the time attempting to convince Jim and my aunt to relocate, but they wouldn't budge. Although they lived on a small farm, they were still adjacent to a fairly well-known county road. They've had a lot more visitors here since all this started than I have had at my place, not counting the mailbox vandals.

"We have food, water, and a clear line of sight," Jim said.

I agreed, but reminded him that his line of sight worked both ways. He couldn't argue with that and promised that if things fell apart again he'd head to my place.

With the new panel and battery banks back at the shelter, I could keep my two-way radio charged indefinitely. I had plenty of cheap rechargeable AA batteries good for a thousand cycles or so, if you believed the advertising. I let Jim know that I'd be monitoring anytime I was aboveground.

Surveying the derelict, bullet-riddled vehicle blocking the drive and the boulders and dirt covering other ingress points, I was more confident of Jim's security. No vehicle could crash through those barriers without going high center, allowing Jim some time to pump a few rounds into the threat. I took all the captured weapons, made them ready to fire, and placed them near the doors and windows. Nothing faster than a New York reload. With my gear packed and the ultralight pointed down the driveway, I was ready to go home. With the ammo and medical supplies gone, I could handle a bag of Jim's fertilizer as cargo. Never know. Saying my good-byes.

The aircraft had over three-quarters of a tank when I took off. I sped down the dirt driveway towards the ruined truck. By the time I hit the end of the drive, I was a hundred feet over the wreck. I hacked the chronograph on my watch and began to estimate fuel burn rates in my head as I began a slow U-turn. Flying over the house, I saw Jim wave from below and Matt sitting nearby in a lawn chair with a rifle laying across his legs. I followed power transmission lines to the main road and continued my climb.

At altitude I could see smoke rising from Fayetteville, so I decided to skirt in closer. The sun was barely up, so technically I wasn't in violation of the so-called curfew, but I was pretty sure that the authorities would deem my activity suspicious, so I kept my altitude at about two thousand feet. After cruising for a few minutes I could clearly see the smoke rising from a subdivision. I began to orbit the neighborhood, noticing a barricade of shot-up vehicles blocking the suburb entrance like Jim and I had done. There were people standing on the road adjacent to the blackened rubble of what used to be a home. Descending a bit, I saw the fire-born refugees pulling suitcases behind them.

The last of what they had to their names.

I felt remorse for them as I climbed to escape observation. Back at altitude, I observed two MRAP convoys traveling in different directions along the main arteries of the city. I could make out the snaking line of crimson train cars below and tried to visualize which boxcar might be Rich's.

Although the region's major airport was out of range for my aircraft, Drake Airfield was nearby; I decided to take a look. I followed I-49 for a few miles before tracing the exit for Drake. The wind was cold, but not unbearable like the night I flew over to Jim's. I was overhead the local National Guard armory when the runway came into view in the distance. On the ground below, in the motorcade, I saw people in black uniforms crawling about on the desert-painted vehicles. Busy black ants constructing a new colony. I made a mental note and continued on to the small regional airfield. There was a C-17 cargo plane parked near a square of radar netting similar to the netting I had back at the shelter. I descended slowly until I could see the tail of a small aircraft and its rear propeller sticking out. I continued my low orbit, surveying the wings. I couldn't tell if it was a Reaper or Predator, but it didn't really matter at this point. The two Hellfire missiles I saw hanging off the hard mounts didn't seem to care which type of aircraft they were attached to.

I quickly realized I was co-altitude with the control tower and began to climb aggressively. How many people did it take to support a UCAV mission? A hundred? I wasn't sure, but didn't see indications of a ground control station anywhere near the field.

With my chronograph sitting at twenty-five minutes, I turned back in the direction of home. My batteries were at full charge, so I switched to electric to conserve fuel. With the quiet prop spinning behind me, I called Rich on the two-way.

"Rich, it's Max, come in."

"Yeah, I gotcha Max, what's going on?" I had to turn the volume all the way up to hear him over the wind.

"I just surveyed the area—a fire burned down most of a subdivision near you, and our friends are patrolling around. Those things you told me about earlier, I saw one at your airfield." I tried to be as vague as possible as we were communicating in the clear.

"Copy, where are you now?"

"Two thousand, heading back to base."

"Okay, have some information. Talk tonight. Rich out."

"Roger, Max out."

With the electric motor humming, my chronograph was irrelevant. It indicated forty-five minutes of flight by the time I was overhead my property. I completed two passes before touching down in the cow pasture near my hidden ATV. I quickly unloaded the fertilizer, folded the wings, and hooked the aircraft to the tow hitch. I was back at the shelter within eight minutes. Both the ATV and ultralight were gassed up and hidden inside of twenty. My battery banks were full; everything was either cached outside, or stacked carefully inside. Although I've never ridden a submarine, I can't imagine the living space being much larger than this. I'm literally sleeping on top of my food and other stores, with the extra beds being utilized as shelf space. I'd need to eat my way to more square footage if needed.

The TV displayed snow, no message banner or audio. Nothing changed after I performed a digital channel scan using the TV user interface. With the downtime, I wiped off the guts of my M4 and knocked the carbon buildup out of my Glock. Good enough. Even with the ammo I gave Jim, I still had enough socked away to fight a small war.

With some daylight left, I had some late lunch, grabbed my kit, including a battery-powered Sawzall, and headed to the rock quarry three miles down the road. Jim's fertilizer got me thinking, and I had something specific in mind.

Most of the way to the quarry was dirt road. No one lived too close, for obvious reasons. A few times a week large blasts rocked the region, causing foundation and drywall cracks, even on my house miles away. The quarry paid a settlement to most of the people in the area, and sweetened the deal with deeply discounted limestone and free delivery. My driveway was a visual outcome of the settlement.

Access to the quarry was impossible by vehicle, as heavy steel gates secured by hardened steel chains marked entryways. Massive limestone boulders filled any gaps where a truck might attempt clandestine entry after hours. I jumped the fence, ignoring the "No Trespassing" sign and hoofed it up the hill to the lip of one of the quarry pits. I stood at the edge of a man-made crater that might rival the pockmarks of primordial times. The depth was unbelievable; the floor was stories below where I stood. The lack of sun exposure froze the water at the bottom.

The quarry looked out of place, a scab on the perfect skin of the forest. I went trailer to trailer, checking for explosives symbology, until I noticed the steel doors covering a hole in the side of the mountain near the trailers.

NO OPEN FLAME—NO SMOKING—

NO WELDING ARC—NO ELECTRONIC DEVICES

Inspecting the signage around the doors, I knew what was inside. Using the Sawzall, I started cutting the rings that held the huge lock on the door. The lock was hardened, but the steel rings it secured were not. It took about ten minutes and most of my battery to get through the steel. The lock finally dropped to the ground and I opened one side of the heavy steel doors. I was startled by a piercing alarm siren, but quickly used my knife to cut its battery power supply. I could see another set of wires running to a cellular network device. The data lights blinked, indicating that it was transmitting something, but I doubted it was getting through to its intended recipient.

There was about a pallet worth of explosives and caps for the taking along with a few clackers. Another ear piercing alarm went off after I used the remaining power in my Sawzall to cut through the door marked "DRIVERS." I backed one of the trucks to the cubby entrance and stacked the entire contents in the bed of the massive dump truck. I pulled up to the steel gates and touched the heavy bumper to them. It took three attempts to shift into first gear, but I eventually found it. The truck lurched forward, ripping the gates and accompanying concrete anchors out of the ground. The vehicle bounced over the fallen metal sentries, signaling my clean escape from the abandoned quarry.

I drove the truck down the old quarry road to the bottom of the hill and turned left in the direction of my house. When I got to the pasture I had just used as an airstrip, I stopped the truck and unloaded the explosives, hiding them in the woods for later pickup. I returned the truck to the quarry and went on foot back to the shelter. I had enough mining-grade explosives to blow up a mountain, and I didn't even have to chemically process ammonium nitrate from Jim's fertilizer. I doubt I could have quickly acquired the nitromethane required for the procedure anyhow.

It took three ATV trips to move the explosives to a new cache near the shelter and store the caps and clackers separately behind my entry ladder. If someone found the explosives, they wouldn't be able to detonate them unless they knew how to make homemade caps. I wasn't sure how I'd employ the stuff, but I'd rather have them and not need them.

The days seem to blend together like *Groundhog Day* or deployment. It's been nearly a week since my flight back from Jim's. Matt is doing much better. Jim says he's moving around and even taking some watch duty. Me? I wake up early, patrol the area on foot, eat breakfast, gather water, and keep improving my situation.

Speaking with Rich sometimes twice daily, I can't report that the news has improved. Rich is being very cautious about what he says on the air, but I managed to convince him to talk about some-one he called "operator 109."

Prior to being shutdown, 109 spoke of mass graves popping up outside major northern cities. 109 theorized that people were dying of exposure, lack of insulin, and anything else that the thin veneer of just-in-time civilization failed to provide. One of the most incredible claims involved the Indian Point reactors in New York. 109 claimed that all the nuclear workers abandoned their posts to be with their families and that some of the reactors were in a full-blown, Chernobyl-style meltdown. New York City was facing an evacuate-or-die mandate enforced by deadly cesium and other nasty fallout agents. Because of 109's revelations, he was paid a visit by men in black after sunset.

Rich asked me to hold on after this news, leaving me on a cliff-hanger for a couple of minutes. I wasn't sure what he was doing; probably making a head call.

After getting back on air, Rich said that 109 transmitted the play by play throughout the whole federal siege. They surrounded his rural California property and shot teargas through his win-dows. 109 relayed the bullhorn calls over the air in near real time. They accused him of the creation and dissemination of false propa-ganda with the goal of terrorizing the public. 109 kept transmitting through his gas mask long after the teargas canisters broke through the windows of his home.

The feds attempted everything with no success. They cut 109's power, but he had a buried propane generator. They jammed his signal, but that only disrupted his own reception, not the hun-dreds that received his signal from the four corners of the conti-nent. They tried to locate and disable his antenna, but 109 used a stealth antenna configuration that was well hidden from the "First Amendment–hating agents" lurking outside. In fits of anger and escalation, they shot up 109's cabin, but his log walls protected him. In 109's final transmission, he reported that the feds threatened to burn the cabin to the ground if he refused to surrender. The creepy sounds of popping timber were the last noises Rich heard over the air. 109 never fired a shot.

Rich conveyed sadness in his telling of 109's story, as if he'd lost a lifelong friend. I suppose he had, from his perspective. Rich's life was that of a rambler, a vagabond. He was emotionally invested in those he chose to interact with over the radio, and maybe even the other drifters along his path up and down the never-ending tracks.

My battery banks are losing about a percent per day based on current consumption versus solar replenishment. If I want to keep using batteries for minor things as well as to circulate breathing air at night, I'll need to acquire another panel. I don't run the fan constantly, but I do set my alarm in four-hour intervals at night to recirculate fresh air for ten minutes at a time. Twenty minutes of daily recirculating fan time and other minor electronic use adds up. A simple timer for the ventilation would only cost a few bucks a month ago, but I'd pay dearly for it right now if it meant uninterrupted sleep.

Tomorrow, I play with my new toys.

Another day, another routine, another percentage drop on the battery banks. I've decided to ration my cans of Sterno fuel because of their portability. If I use only one burner on my stove and keep it low, the propane tank I have outside should last awhile.

After breakfast, I left the shelter with my usual loadout along with a few blasting caps and some wire. After taking some explosives from my cache, I started thinking of ways to put it to work. Using a can full of rusted bolts mixed with some red mud, I fashioned a poor man's claymore and placed it near the gate at the end of my driveway. I sealed the device up with a garbage bag and ran the wires a safe distance downhill. I tied the safe end off to a recognizable tree so that I could quickly detonate the charge. Against my better judgment, I wired the house for destruction from underneath so that I could trigger it from the other side of the fence. This would be a last-ditch desperation plan if I returned to find the house occupied by people like Goatee and Hoodie.

All in all, I wired four different areas on the main property before I returned to the shelter to finish the job. Using aluminum cans filled with river rocks in place of nuts and bolts, I constructed three more expedient claymores, placing them in strategic locations aboveground near the shelter. I hit them all with a coat of spray paint and ran the wires inside the shelter, carefully marking each set with a handwritten diagram of expected blast patterns. From this point forward, I'll be keeping a clacker on my person and two more hidden in key areas of the property.

After I was finished, I stowed the remaining explosives and sat outside near the two-way radio. Several times I tried the weather alert button on my radio, and every time it's dead air. Either no one is broadcasting, or they're too far away for me to pick up. I really need to find some books to pass the time; they don't use batteries.

The past few nights before calling Rich, I've stalked the large buck. Every night he approaches from the west, drinks out of the pond, and then trots off to the north. I have plenty of canned meat, but it never hurts to keep tabs on the game. It's much better to know his habits and let him live than to take him now when I don't need him and potentially lose half the meat. I've noticed that I'm able to get a lot closer to game than ever before. I can attribute this to the fact that I smell like shit.

I haven't had a shower in five days. Three days ago, I visited the house to wash up and found that the pressure had gotten so low that I couldn't even wash my hands, let alone take a shower. I suppose the water tower on top of the mountain was finally tapped out. Desperation has reached the backwoods. I've been heating up pond water and washing up outside. Miserable as hell when it's twenty degrees, but it's better than getting swamp ass, I suppose.

Living in a hole in the ground comes with its own set of psychological problems. Without looking at a watch, you don't know if it's day or night, and you don't hear anything. The lack of noise is unsettling. I find myself moving my feet back and forth inside the sleeping bag to make noise while I try to fall asleep. I'd turn on the TV for the white noise all night if I could; at least it'd be something. Some nights, I go over my training again and again in my head, refining it. I even think of old movies I've watched and try to outline the plots. Last night, I imagined flying the ultralight to Jim's, seeing the road below, mapping the power lines and cell towers in my head. Without these mental exercises and daily routines, I'm not sure what things would be like now.

Before I forget, I need to go topside and get on the radio before turning in.

The sun is down. I just got off the horn with Rich. He's running low on batteries and is asking for help. He seems a little more desperate than a battery shortage might explain. He actually asked me to come tonight. It may seem crazy to risk my life for this, but without his radio relay, I have no communications with Jim or news from the outside. I haven't talked to Jim directly since flying back, but Rich has been checking in with him and keeping up with how things are going on that end.

Since I know of a back way to his train, I feel confident I can do all the traveling at night. With kill-on-sight orders issued against anyone with a gun, I'm going to need to make some hard decisions on my loadout. The other option would be to simply airdrop the batteries from the ultralight, but going that low over the train could be dangerous. I'd be vulnerable to small-arms fire by day and unseen power lines and other terrain by night. Drawing attention to Rich's location is another con to the airdrop plan. The gallon of fuel required to make the round trip is another factor to consider.

I intend to leave tomorrow night, so that gives me a full day to think it through.

I'm going with the bicycle option for Rich's special delivery. I feel naked leaving my M4 behind but I'm comforted by the Glock I have inside my waistband in its Kydex holster. I wasn't going to try to hide it away in my pack this time. I just checked in with Rich and let him know that I was leaving and when to expect me. I brought along some spare regular and rechargeable batteries as well as some other odds and ends. I had a small B & E kit with me that included a hacksaw, a multitool, padlock shims, a small pry bar, and some duct tape. I'd run out of Rich's chicken noodle soup a while back. Gave me something to look forward to.

The trip was uneventful until I reached Southgate. What was once a shopping center was now a smoking hole in the ground. Shopping carts lay twisted and scattered around the parking lot and the nearby homeless shelter was caved in on the side facing Southgate. I didn't see any bodies, but I was pretty sure blood covered the area in front of where the shopping center used to be. It looked like a high-order explosion had occurred here, but I couldn't be sure by just looking at it through a night vision monocular.

I pedaled on towards the back track access that would dump me out near the train. No one was on the road, but I could hear gunshots carried by the wind every few minutes. Sometimes a single shot, other times full-auto bursts. I was cold despite all the pedaling and was excited to see the tracks ahead. I turned off the main road at the crossing light where I scavenged the solar panel the last time I came through. I pedaled until the gravel became too steep beside the track and then walked beside my bike until seeing the reflective paint of the lead locomotive engine ahead.

I counted train cars until I thought I was near Rich and let out a radio call.

"Here," I transmitted.

I heard a clanking sound and saw a slice of candlelight peek through where Rich removed his fabricated door spacer above the coal stove stack.

"Hurry up, Max, cold air'll get in."

"Good to see you, too, buddy," I said, garnering a laugh from him.

I smelled pine, burning coal, and chicken noodle soup inside and was delighted to see the cans already cooked with the lids off when I sat down.

"Dig in," he said. "I'm sure you're hungry after the trip."

Something seemed off with Rich but I couldn't put a finger on it and didn't care at the moment with all the warm food in front of me. The coal burned hot tonight, warming my feet through my leather boots. It felt damn good. I downed three cans of soup and drank two bottles of water before I looked at Rich again.

"It's bad out there; I couldn't say over the air," Rich said ominously.

I watched him pour two cups of liquid that smelled like pine needles.

"Here, tea for you. It's not bad once you get used to it. Really warms you up from the inside."

I took a short sip of the hot tea, and he was right. It wasn't that bad; it tasted like it smelled.

"So here's what's going on, Max. After 109 got shut down, I started getting suspicious that the feds were monitoring short-wave transmissions and geolocating the positions of HAMs. I think they're driving around in a SIGINT van or maybe even flying a SIGINT plane, spinning their receiver and taking lines of bearing on signals they deem subversive. Keep in mind it's a lot harder to direction find a shortwave signal, but it's a piece of cake to DF our two way communications. Don't mean to get too technical, but the bad guys overseas were using high-powered cordless phones. At least they were protected by a proxy of base stations. With our handsets, they can DF our location directly, and within a few meters."

I was impressed by Rich's knowledge of signal theory and communications security, things I knew little about.

This still didn't explain why he wanted me here last night. "What was the rush for the batteries?"

"To be honest, Max, I am sitting okay on batteries, but I needed a believable excuse to get you out here. I think we're being monitored and the whole situation is worse than you think."

I was floored by this, and instantly began recalling everything I'd said over the radio since meeting Rich. Some of it was sensitive, if more than one conversation were intercepted. Data could be synthesized, actionable intel derived and used against us.

"Okay, I'm listening. Tell me what you know."

Rich stroked his white beard and began to explain. "We've already discussed the GMRS and FRS channels on the handsets you share with Jim. What we didn't really discuss was the fact that my radio is multi-band and therefore can be tuned well outside of consumer radio channels. I've been able to monitor uncovered police communications through my system inside this boxcar. Listening to government-allocated frequencies, I discovered a sensitive program in place in this area, and probably many other places. They're actively monitoring FMRS and FRS two-way channels and have already assigned code words to the active channels. They're waiting on another asset to arrive so that they can pinpoint locations. They know the three of us are communicating, and they know which channel, but they don't know where we are, yet. I think—"

"But we can just switch channels, maybe set up a system where we tune to odd channels on even hours of the day or something like that," I added, interrupting Rich.

"No, that's not good enough. The system they're using has multiple receiver banks. Anytime transmit energy is detected over a monitored channel, the operator is instantly tuned to that channel to copy the communications. This happens every time you key the transmit button. They only need twenty or thirty receivers and a few COMINT operators to monitor all the available two-way channels."

Hearing him talk, I became suspicious of Rich's background. "Listen, not to get in your business, but you don't talk like a common hobo, if you know what I mean."

"Max, I told you, I opted out of the system after my family

died—I never said what I was before that. I know they're reading our mail because I've experimented with Jim, without his knowledge. I know what time he usually calls so I'm listening to police comms when he does. When Jim gets on the air, they use the code word APACHE. When you come on, they use TOMAHAWK. My code word is CHEROKEE. They're pretty vocal about finding us, but we have a huge advantage: they don't think we can hear them. They think that we're all on Motorola handhelds locked to those restricted GMRS channels. They have no idea that I'm using my HAM radio to tune police channels, because they think I'm only on two-way and shortwave receive. I never transmitted to operator 109 during his siege, only receive."

"Man, this is a lot to take in. I mean, now that we know they're listening, what's the plan? Stop talking?"

"I've suspected this was happening for a while, I just couldn't prove it until I found the frequency they were operating on. I've used some time to draft a code word booklet we can use to communicate. They're all written in three identical notepads. The only word that I didn't write was the duress word. If any of us are captured, we'll need to work the duress word into the transmission so that everyone else knows about the compromise. The duress word is *lasagna*—commit it to memory."

"Shit, that's no problem. I've been dreaming about it off and on for a week now."

"Well, don't start joking yet. I have more bad news. With my radio set to scan, I've found a lot of frequencies operating in the Fayetteville area. I've found good guys like us operating on two-way channels, and I've found raiders operating there as well. The feds aren't taking sides yet, but there is a huge offensive coming. I hear police chatter mentioning something called Operation LINE-BACKER. They're waiting on a radio direction-finding asset to be allocated to the city so they can start hunting. A man named Peterson is the special agent in charge of LINEBACKER, as well as other things. He's the one that's issued a shoot-on-sight order for any civilian carrying a weapon."

I was in shock. "This Peterson, whoever he is, doesn't have the authority to do something like that. That would take executive powers stretched to the max, and then some."

"Oh, I agree, but he's run his orders up the flagpole and salutes without hesitation. On the radio, he doesn't sound like he has any qualms about shooting people. You should have heard how angry he was after I told you about 109. I asked you to hold during 109's story so that I could switch over to listen to Peterson's reaction . . . more of a rant, really."

"What did he say?" I asked.

"He specifically said, 'I want this asshole found, fixed, and dead.' He's hostile to anything transmitted over the airways that isn't approved by his local 'ministry of disinformation.' You've noticed that all the TV channels are broadcasting snow these days, right? Well, that's Peterson. He's in charge of public affairs. I don't know for sure, but I think the reason the news channels are dark is because the reporters refused to sell government-approved bullshit. I'd bet that the FCC, using the Patriot Act Amendment for terrorist propaganda, shut them down. I've been building a dossier on this Peterson character based on his radio transcripts since he started transmitting over a week ago."

"That's not a bad idea. If Peterson is this region's center of political influence, we need to know as much as we can about him and the operations he's responsible for."

"Max, I'm not keeping tabs on him because he's a threat to you and me. This guy is like a tyrant. He's killing people indiscriminately. I set up a reconnaissance nest near the bridge two days ago recording convoy movement and communications for eight hours."

Rich handed me his observation notes indicating regular convoys, some with bodies on flatbeds rolling behind the MRAPs.

"Jesus Christ, this is horrible; it's fucking mass murder," I said slowly, feeling the waves of my guilt resurface.

"Yeah, I was hearing everything on the radio before and after the convoys passed by me. Some folks are holing up in the city with their own stash of food. The new government regulations say that any person's home is subject to search if they're applying for assistance. Just standing in line for help gives these thugs the authority to remove you from the line and force you to let them search your home. They say it's to reduce the number of food hoarders receiving government assistance, but the radio traffic tells a much different story."

"Let me guess—they're not looking for cupboards full of food."

"That's right. You disappear if they find weapons. If they find food, they just take most of it and issue you a hand receipt for assistance. If they find gasoline, they confiscate it. If they find gasoline and empty beer bottles, you're arrested under terrorism charges for having the components to manufacture Molotov cocktails. If they find anything they deem subversive, they take you in for questioning. You get the picture?"

"Where are they putting all these prisoners?"

"I don't know. They'd run out of room in county pretty fast if they stacked them all in there. They must be taking them somewhere else, but I'm not hearing any chatter on it."

"In light of all this, what's the plan? I mean, I should at least warn Jim and the others, right?" I asked.

"Yeah, definitely, but do it face-to-face. Until you can get out there, I'll tell him that you had to turn back and that you couldn't make it out here to bring the supplies. I'll tell him that we're going dark for a couple days on comms because of my battery issue, and you can use that time to get out there and give him a proper warning."

"Okay, that sounds like a plan, but based on what you've told me, I recommend you transmit off-site from now on. Don't do it from this boxcar."

"I'm ahead of you there. I've been transmitting from the bridge. That way, if they DF me, they might just think it's someone on the road."

"How are you really doing on batteries?" I asked.

"I'm going to need what you have, but I'm not critical. It's late, though. Get some rest—we'll start again tomorrow," Rich suggested.

Although I was shaken by the latest revelations from Rich, my body was tired. All the work I'd been doing at home around the shelter and the late-night bike trip to the train had worn me down. Rich is already asleep at the other end of the boxcar, and I'm not far behind him on my side.

1200

We both woke up early and had some soup and coffee, just like the last time I stayed overnight. Rich had some batteries put back, but he'd been charging his radio via a car battery beside his bed. Rich claimed he could get dozens of charges from a full battery, but his was sitting at a quarter charge. He kept an inexpensive multimeter in his homemade trunk. I wondered what else he had in there.

Everything I've seen in his boxcar was a portable possession. What was not portable could be easily abandoned and wasn't his in the first place. All the furniture was made of plywood and boxcar supplies, including his storage trunk. From what I could tell, Rich could exfil the train car carrying everything to his name and not look back.

By sunrise, we were on the tracks heading south, away from the bridge. Before we departed, Rich put one of those boxcar locks on his train car and hid the key ring. When we finally reached the railroad crossing light, I finished the salvage by removing its only remaining useful component, a golf cart battery. Four dead lights remained on the pole, its panel, charge controller, and battery gone. The rest of our route involved road travel, increasing our danger level. There was a nice-sized solar panel half a mile down the road that I'd passed twice at this point, once on my first return trip and the second time last night on my way back to the train. Passing a mud hole, Rich grabbed a handful and rubbed some on his face, beard, and clothing.

"Don't wanna look too uppity, Max," he said.

I reluctantly did the same. He was right, we don't want to look better off than the other poor bastards on the road. Rich looked like the kind of homeless man you didn't want to meet. If you didn't take the time to see the intelligence in his eyes, that is. This made me wonder how many intelligent, functioning homeless people I'd judged in the past and written off as subhuman. I now realize how wrong I was.

Rich slapped my pack, breaking that chain of thought. "If we see someone before they see us, get rid of that. We can always come back for it later."

I nodded in agreement.

This stretch of road was littered with abandoned cars, trucks, and a few semis. We moved carefully from car to car, checking inside before we passed by. There was a good chance they were being used as shelter, but I can't imagine who would chance it on the open road like this. Passing by a semi, I noticed a toolbox mounted under the feed trailer it pulled. I instantly wondered if we could operate the feed boom, dumping chicken feed onto the road. Could we eat that? I didn't know. It didn't matter, as I didn't know how to operate the boom anyway. I took the pry bar from my B & E kit and separated the lock from its metal box frame. Inside were the usual things I'd expect: insulated wire, screwdrivers, wrenches, and a half-used roll of electrical tape. I took the electrical tape and the spool of insulated copper wire, leaving the rest for Rich to sift through.

While Rich looked through the tools, I checked the cab. Inside was cleaner than I expected. Exposed wires hung down under the dash where the CB radio used to be. I sat in the driver's seat, looking out over the road. Leaning down, I searched under the seat area and grabbed what felt like a baseball bat. It was a thick cylinder of polished oak with the core drilled out and filled with lead on one end. The other end was wrapped in grip tape. I leaned out the door and waved the item at Rich, telling him that I'd found a club.

"That's a tire thumper, not a weapon," he replied. "Of course two men like us walking down the street don't need a tire checker, so we'd probably get bags over our head and wake up wherever they're taking everyone these days."

Rich had a revolver in his waistband, and I had a Glock in mine, so I didn't see the harm in putting the thumper in my pack.

Stepping down off the truck, I heard the sound of multiple engines. Rich was already running for the ditch across the street but I didn't think I had time. I hit the field on the opposite side of the road and threw my pack off. I lay in the grass as low as I could as the vehicles approached. If a Predator was airborne, we were already caught. It would just vector the agents directly to our position. My face was down and I wouldn't risk looking at the vehicles, but I heard them slow as they neared our position.

I held my breath.

The engines throttled up and they sped past. After I could no longer hear them, Rich approached from his side of the road.

"They slowed down," said Rich. "I was worried until I saw that they were trying to weave around the cars to get through. They didn't see us."

"What were they?"

"You couldn't see? They were those black-op armored trucks running all over town."

"MRAPs."

"Yep, those," he said. "If they found us, we'd both be dead by now . . . or on our way to some gulag."

We were a little more careful after that.

We approached our target—a nearby utility pole—from the field instead of directly by road. Rich loaned me his belt so that I could connect it with mine, forming a larger harness. With one belt running through my belt loop and the other connected at my sides, I had an expedient safety harness to hold me steady up the pole. Without gaff spikes and an official uniform, this was the next best thing.

I bear hugged my way up with my safety belt around both the pole and me; my tools were stuffed inside my closed cargo pockets. As I ascended, I detached the electrical wire from the pole. At about fifteen feet up, I went to work on the panel mounting brackets. I worked quickly, as there would be no fast way down if another convoy approached. I was able to loosen the bottom brackets with a multitool, but was forced to hacksaw the top brackets. I worked as fast as I could with one hand steady on the pole and the other on the saw. When I finally got both brackets cut, I was worn-out. I signaled Rich to catch the solar panel and dropped it down to him. At the bottom, we disconnected the charge controller and small six-volt battery, matching the one in my pack.

Instead of the roads, we chose the safety of the fields until we were forced back to the concrete a mile before the railroad crossing. The rest of the way back to the train was uneventful, thank goodness.

We spent that morning crudely wiring Rich's new panel to his two six-volt batteries. I sat the panel on the center of the roof of his boxcar so that any passerby couldn't see it from the side. I stuffed some dry leaves into a plastic shopping bag I found snagged on a nearby limb. With the bag of leaves under the panel, I oriented it to favor the southern sky for maximum efficiency. The rest was easy: we just ran scavenged wire into the boxcar to the charge controller, and then to the new batteries.

Rich would just need to use his existing twelve-volt hardware connections to charge his kit as required. His multimeter verified that the panel was charging the small but capable battery bank. With only a radio to worry about, Rich should have enough power to last him indefinitely.

After the solar installation, Rich and I did some trading. I had a hunting knife made by a man that forged them from railroad spikes and stag. As I already had a fixed-blade spring steel knife made by a respectable forge, I thought it good to give Rich the hunting knife. He was, after all, a man living on rails. I also gave up another carton of cigarettes, as I had no real use for them.

In return for the knife and the carton, Rich offered as much soup and bottled water as I could fit in my pack for the return trip. He also said that it went without saying that I had accrued enough rewards points to stay in Hotel de Boxcar anytime, without reservations. No blackout dates.

Tonight Rich will go to the bridge to transmit to Jim that he'll be dark for a day or two. It's time for some lunch before I make the trip home and then catch an immediate flight to Jim's.

I left the train thirty minutes after sunset, hoping I'd miss any patrols. My pack was heavy with soup and water, but manageable after I strapped it to the rack over the rear bicycle tire. The young night sky cast a dark blue background overlapped by the straight lines of the boxcars. The gravel crunched under my boots and tires as I passed the final engine car at the front of the train; every once in a while I caught a flash of moonlight reflected from the vacant rails.

My arrival at the crossing light signified the start of dangerous territory. I'd be on the road now, open to the threats that came with it. With all my bike reflectors either removed or blacked out, it would be difficult to spot me without night vision.

It wasn't long before I reached the semi truck again and thought of all the chicken feed in the back. Pedaling on, I soon observed a strange black mass in the center of the road up ahead. Using night vision from a distance, I watched a pack of buzzards pick apart the carcass of a deer as if they were creatures in a horror movie. Strange how they behave when they think they're alone.

I rolled past the buzzards, startling them, feeling their wings buffet wildly around me in the darkness. The deer would be nothing but bones and cartilage by tomorrow. With no one driving the roads, there was a shortage of meat. How many hundreds of pounds of roadkill waited for them in this area before the gasoline ran dry? The buzzards were starving along with everyone else, their new food supply and hunting grounds unable to support the man-made population. I wonder how many weeks might pass before we start eating roadkill, and then the buzzards. Probably already happening.

Before reaching my turnoff to leave the city, I saw headlights flash up ahead, but they turned out to be a car alarm going off, expending the last of its batteries for nothing. This cost me a trip to the ditch anyway. I didn't take any chances.

It seemed like the city limits sign marked more than just the notional boundary that separated city budgets from county money. The road changed textures underneath my bike tires; the trees towered, the tips of their branches clasped together far above my head.

I moved quickly past the field where I fought Hoodie and Goatee; I don't believe in ghosts, but places like this are best left to the solitude of the night.

Rounding the corner before the steel bridge straight stretch, I saw headlights, for real this time. I jumped off my bike and headed for the field on my right. I had to toss my bike and my pack over the barbed wire fence to make it to a round bale of hay. I used my monocular to view the vehicle from cover as it passed. It moved very slowly, like someone looking at a map, trying not to miss an address they were trying to find. It was military hardware resembling a news van with antennas mounted on the top. A long metal whip antenna was attached to both bumpers, forming an arc over the vehicle. I waited for it to lumber by at ice-cream-truck speed before risking the rest of the road home.

Sweat dampened my upper body and my legs burned as I crested the final hill. Coasting down, I tried to see my nearest neighbor's home through the trees—no lights and the gate was chained shut. I continued to coast down the steep hill, weaving around the potholes brought on by the constant freeze and thaw cycle this time of year.

In a fit of confusion, I passed my driveway; my gate was . . . gone. Locking the brakes on my bicycle, I lost control and spilled onto the side of the road near the ditch. Impacting the rocks, I hurt my knee, bringing on a starburst of pain overriding my vision for a few moments. Picking up my bike, ego, and pack, I limped farther down the road away from my driveway. I laid my bike down on its side about twenty feet off the road. Far enough away that passersby wouldn't notice it in the daytime. I gave most of my medical supplies over to Jim when we were tending to Matt's gunshot wound; I was running low on everything but the basics. I knew my knee would just have to bleed until it stopped on its own.

Armed with only my pistol, I approached my house slowly from the woods. The bitter cold and the shock from the accident frayed my nerves. My hurt knee shook uncontrollably, worsened by my wildest fears being realized when I reached the tree line in front of my house.

A black MRAP sat dormant at the bottom of my driveway twenty meters from my front door. My backyard utility light was out, indicating no electricity. They were inside; flashlights waved about through the windows, shining like lightsabers through my night vision monocular. I guessed that there were at least three in the house.

I broke cover for a moment to get behind the MRAP. It wasn't running and I saw no movement in the vehicle. I was about to make for the clacker wired to the house when a laser came into view at the corner, aimed down. I hit the ground, flattening my body. Slowly bringing up my monocular, I saw him. His weapon was slung across his chest, but his IR weapon laser was on. As he started up the steps, I skirted around the MRAP into cover behind the trees on the south side of the house.

". . . Clear in back, nothing . . . sign . . . late to the show" were words I could barely make out as the laser guy ascended the steps.

I searched around in the wet leaves for a couple minutes until I found the clacker I'd stashed there. Feeling the circumference of the nearby small tree, I located the wire leading to the explosives cap. I attached it to the device. Before considering the option of destroying my house, I ran through all my options. Whoever these guys were, they were illegally searching my home. The MRAP gave them away as feds, whatever that meant these days. They were still federal agents that were in my house without permission. Even before all this went down, these types of police were the most dangerous. They had too much power and no accountability. They'd shoot your dogs and zip-tie your grandmother while executing a marijuana warrant on the wrong house. Even so, I wasn't so low as to blow their asses into space without talking to them, even though it could result in getting a few guns emptied in my direction.

I was alone, but they didn't know that.

I waited until the laser guy stepped out the door onto the front porch.

Screaming in my best command voice, I said, "Don't move! There are twenty of us surrounding your position! We are armed, so don't try anything—we don't want any trouble!"

I heard some scuffling around inside. The windows shattered almost simultaneously around the house. They were making shooting positions.

"Who are you?" said an unfamiliar voice from one of the broken windows.

"That doesn't matter! Do you have a search warrant to be in that house?"

"We don't need a goddamned warrant—we're the law!" the same voice shouted back.

"That's not what the Fourth Amendment says!"

"Listen, buddy, just the fact that you claimed to be armed gives us the right to shoot all your asses right now!"

"Have it your way! We saw you go in, and we know how many

of you are in the house. Do you think the pine siding and Sheetrock you're hiding behind is gonna stop our shots?"

"Okay, don't shoot! We're here to pick up a suspect. He's violated our commander's amended regional FCC regulations."

"Let me get this straight!" I yelled. "You break into that house without a warrant, you threaten to kill United States citizens exercising their Second Amendment rights on private property, and you're here to execute a warrant on someone for free speech?" There was no answer. "Tell me, Officers, which part of the Bill of Rights are you not shredding tonight?"

I caught movement out of the corner of my eye.

"Stop or I'll shoot!" I screamed.

The man opened fire in my general direction, and the others followed suit, shooting wildly from the windows. I had no choice. I quickly shoved two 9mm rounds into my ears, cupped both sides of my head, and prayed.

I squeezed the clacker; the ground thundered beneath me, throwing my body a foot into the air. I hovered for a long while, watching in slow motion the home I grew up in splinter upward to the sky atop a great fireball. I winced in pain when my body thumped to the ground, the wind knocked from my lungs. I concentrated on laying flat. I covered my head with my hands as the debris began to rain down. Something heavy hit nearby, possibly the woodstove. Smaller objects came shortly after. I imagined all the body parts, food jars, two-by-fours, shingles, insulation, and cinder blocks impacting all around me. Debris continued to fall for half a minute. Something hit me on the back of the legs. It stung, but didn't break the skin.

I stood up after finally catching my breath. Tiny pebbles and dirt fell from my hair and clothing. I was standing, gazing at the scarred earth until my concentration was broken by the sounds of human pain. There was no way anything could have survived inside the house.

The blast must have jarred my brain, because I'd totally forgotten about the man that tried to flank me just before he opened fire. I tried to home in on his location from his noise. A fire had started near where the house was; some pieces of A-frame smoldered and popped, casting a new orange light. The fire illuminated the sheet-metal-covered doghouse that belonged to Roy, who lived twelve years, and that wasn't bad for a Lab.

Roy's house remained standing, and the "soldier" that tried to kill me before the explosion lived. The fire flared with the wind, giving away his position near the doghouse. The blast must have thrown the bastard fifty feet. The only reason he wasn't vaporized was because I'd crudely wired the explosives to blast more vertically than outward. Otherwise, I'd be in pieces right now, too.

I approached with caution. The fire was intense now. As the distance between us closed, a piece of white PVC pipe could be seen protruding completely through the man's torso. He lay there on the ground, burned and blasted ground all around him. Blood trickled from his mouth.

Although in shock, he still managed to speak.

"You're gonna die for what you did, you cop-killing fuck!" The man went into a fit of heavy coughing, spitting more blood down his chin. Only the warm fire comforted him in the last moments of his life. I watched him draw his last breath, rationing it out, trying to live a few more seconds. The thugs inside the house were blown to pieces, and this guy had no bullet wounds. Dead men tell no tales.

I moved quickly, salvaging everything I could. I had no idea how to operate an MRAP, nor could I procure enough fuel to keep it running long-term. It probably had a blue force tracker on it right now, pinging a GPS position. The man that lay dead near Roy's

doghouse had a serviceable carbine and a few mags. More importantly, he had a radio. I took everything and piled it in one spot.

With the gate destroyed, there was no need to keep it wired for
demolition. I removed the explosives and placed them inside the
MRAP, trailing the wires out the door and as far away as I could
string them. I doubled the detonator distance by taking what was
left of the wire from the last demolition and attaching it to this job.
I knew I didn't have the bang to kill the machine from the outside;
it was designed to resist such things. After removing some spare
body armor and three full 5.56 ammo cans from the back, I wired
the clacker to the distant end. I stuffed my ears with 9mm casings
and hid on the ground behind a tree. The explosion was respectable
but anticlimactic; it was muffled by the thick armor that protected
the vehicle. The light imprinted my retinas for a few seconds. I tried
to check the damage, but the doors were warped closed. Inside,
through the smoke, I could see that the vehicle's steering wheel,
dash, and seats were either pulverized or gone.

It was now time to get the fuck out of there, never to return. I
gathered up the scavenged items and cached them away, mentally
noting their location in relation to all my other caches of ammo,
food, fuel, firewood, propane, etc. The only thing that remained of
the old house was the cellar and half the shed. The other half was
most likely a casualty of a misplaced explosive on the north side
of the house. I hoofed it down the trail the back way to the shelter.
This added a mile to my trip. The precaution was worth it: a dog
could have easily tracked me if I left directly from the blast site.

As I trekked through the dark woods, my radio beeped, indicating an incoming call. I didn't dare answer.

The words "Osprey, lamp, window, expired milk" were repeated
three times. It was Rich's voice.

I repeated the words over and over until arriving at the shelter.

I dropped everything I was carrying and hurriedly unlocked the hatch. I dropped my pack to the floor below on the way down and slammed the hatch over my head like a tank commander. The DC lights were bright when I flipped them on, indicating a good charge. Rifling through my pack, I found the two codebooks Rich had given me—one for myself, the other for Jim. His handwriting was impeccable. The words were not in alphabetical order but more of a categorical organization.

Osprey meant that a Peterson attack was under way.

Lamp meant that Rich was safe.

Window indicated that Rich was the target.

Expired milk, wrong DF location.

I read the code meanings over and over again, placing them in different order to make sure I hadn't missing anything. Rich was safe, but they were looking for him . . . They had the wrong DF location. This had to mean that they couldn't accurately pinpoint from where he was transmitting.

Safe underground, I cleaned my injury with rubbing alcohol, removing a shard of stone from my knee in the process. I used the last bit of suture from my medical kit to close the gash. At the nearby pond, I broke some ice from the edge of the water.

I've been sitting in the warmth of the shelter with a chunk of pond ice on my knee for some time, dreading my upcoming flight. I need to study the codebook for a few minutes before making final preps for departure.

November 13th

A week or so has passed since my last journal entry. I'll recall the details as best I can.

I limped up the ladder into the cold with my kit and secured the hatch behind me. The bandage on my knee flexed with each step, keeping the injury on the forefront of my mind. Before leaving camp, I ensured the camouflage netting covered everything I wanted it to and utilized foliage for anything else. Visiting my explosives cache, I placed a few units in my pack alongside the detonators.

I didn't want to risk starting any engines, but had no choice. My leg was too banged up to make the multiple trips on foot required to get all the gear to the makeshift airstrip. With the throbbing in my leg increasing, I loaded my pack onto the ATV rack along with an ammo can of 5.56 and some food and water. I didn't know how long I'd be away at this point, so I brought along some extra fuel for the ultralight.

I recovered my M4 from the woods where I hid it before my trip to the train, and placed it on the gun rack for the journey to the cow pasture. I guessed that I'd be taking off lighter than last time, as I didn't have the same amount of ammunition with me on this sortie.

I cringed every time I had to rev the ATV to take a hill or round a sharp corner on the back deer trails. I didn't know who was listening.

I was airborne soon after concealing the ATV, climbing hundreds of feet into the freezing night. I dressed warmer this time, but the fast-moving air eventually found its way through every layer of clothing. At two thousand feet, I was higher than any of the Arkansas hills that surrounded me, cruising north at seventy knots. My knee throbbed as I made a slight yaw adjustment to the aircraft, putting the nose back on course.

On the road below, I recognized the pileup I'd seen on every trip to Jim's. One tractor trailer and five cars. I turned east when I reached that visual marker and followed the winding road for three miles before turning back south for a quarter mile. It would have been faster flying direct, but without GPS, I wouldn't have a chance at night. I had to fly the abandoned roads below, or become lost in this lonely November night.

Passing a field, I saw five spooked animals running in unison for the woods. They jumped a barbed wire fence before making a sharp turn and disappearing into the trees. As I looked back in the direction of Jim's, a flash of firelight washed out my monocular. I throttled up, arriving over the top of what remained of my family's home. I could smell the smoke at fifteen hundred feet and see the raging fires below.

The barricade we'd constructed was gone, the old truck charred and flipped upside down in the adjacent field. Holding back my tears and rage, I configured the aircraft for landing and put it down in the field. Shutting down the engine, I twisted the five-point-harness release and spilled out onto the ground, sick from the destruction I'd witnessed. The frigid ground frost numbed my face; my tears quickly froze to the blades of winter grass. I saw the pinpoint of fire in the distance and began to crawl towards it. Without thinking, I was on my feet, running for the light.

As I ran, it hit me. Peterson, government agent or whatever, was executing his own Night of the Long Knives—his own purge. The men tonight were not there to arrest me—they were there to murder me. The same attempt was being made against Jim. My feet moved quickly, passing by each winter breath with speed. Reaching the scene of the fire, my heart sank further into oblivion.

Two burned corpses lay parallel to one another just outside the fire, their identities indistinguishable. I switched on my M4 light and used the tip of my barrel to examine the skulls. There were entry and exit holes in each. Execution-style.

It took all night to dig the solid ground, but I eventually buried the dead. The worst part was not knowing for whom to grieve. Two homes I most remember from my childhood were destroyed, and my family was gone.

These events erased, reformatted, and rebooted me. I no longer existed in the past; I am something different now, and I'm not sure it's good.

I was too devastated to revisit what happened until now, a week or so later. My sadness has retreated like a wave before the tsunami of anger.

I'm now at war—with them, and with myself.

PART THREE

The Resistance

"Every normal man must be tempted, at times, to spit upon his hands, hoist the black flag, and begin slitting throats."

—H. L. Mencken

The fire at Jim's forged my soul. Seeing those bodies on the ground rewired me for mayhem, flipping a few breakers that can never be put right. I burned Jim's codebook that night after burying the bodies. I couldn't expel that nagging, corrosive thought loop from my head—I caused their deaths, it's my fault, and I should be in the ground right now instead of them. After saying a few solemn words, I got back into the ultralight and left the farm forever.

I knew radio contact was a no-go so I had to get to Rich to find out what he knew, and debrief him on what he didn't. I risked taking off in daylight, as it took all night to bury the dead. I did my best to compartmentalize my pain, fear, and hate. I just needed to get out of there.

I climbed to three thousand feet and circled the city. Parts of it were on fire. The firemen and -women weren't getting paid, and were staying home to protect their families. Who could blame them? Risk getting shot or burned to death responding to a fire in some rich neighborhood didn't seem like a good option to me, either.

I had enough fuel for about another hour of flight, then I'd have battery power to fall back on if needed, as the banks were fully charged from all the flying I'd done. Over the train, I looked for a suitable landing area. There were numerous fields, but none were out of view from the road, and I couldn't risk losing the ultra-light to bandits or looters. On my fourth orbit around the train I took notice—a transmission line that cut between a forest near the tracks. It was perpendicular to the train but led off into the wilderness away from the city. If I could get in under the power lines, I could land the aircraft in the path cut for the poles.

As I circled, deciding on the best tactic, something caught my eye off my wing. I lost it in the sun for a few moments but quickly reacquired it. At about a mile off my starboard wing was a drone. Probably the same one I scouted at Drake Airfield a while back. It was low, probably co-altitude or maybe a thousand feet higher. I adjusted my flight path for a better view and began to climb. It was moving much faster than my aircraft, but in an oval pattern, scanning the ground below. I was safe from detection, as its optic sensors were designed to be aimed downward. Flying closer, I confirmed its identity—a Reaper UCAV. I could only see under one wing, but saw two dark objects mounted underneath. Likely laser-guided bombs.

The transmission lines were a mile from the Reaper's observation area, so I made the call to set it down on the fringe of the cleared-out path. With about four feet of clearance on either side of my wings, I made the approach. Dipping below the power lines,

I made fine motor adjustments, missing the poles on my port wing and the forest on my starboard. The grass was nearly a foot high and helped brake me on touchdown. On the ground, I knew I'd lose the Reaper's position, so I worked quickly. I folded the wings and pulled the ultralight into the trees, outside the watchful eyes in the sky. I carried all the kit I could and started down the hill to the train tracks a thousand meters below.

Stopping short of the tracks, I looked in both directions. The perpendicular transmission lines bisected the train nearly in its center. Rich's boxcar was north of the lines. I stayed as far away from the tracks as was possible as I quickly moved north. I remained under the overhang of trees, wary of the death machine that orbited somewhere overhead. My pack was heavy and my hands were full of supplies, but thankfully most of my trip was downhill. The rhythmic thumping of the rifle against my back brought some comfort, but if that Reaper detected an armed person below . . .

I was nearly to Rich's boxcar when I saw movement near the tracks up ahead. I dissolved deeper into the forest and waited. Dogs. Barking. I could hear them getting louder.

A pack of domesticated dogs passed by along the tracks. I tried to judge the wind direction and I hoped they didn't smell me. They were a motley pack, some small ten-pounders, some hundred-and-fifty-pound monsters. Most of them wore collars. Some of them stopped south of my position and sniffed the ground where I'd recently walked. In a stroke of luck, they followed my scent south, back to the transmission lines. There was no food packed on the ultralight, so I doubted these house animals would bother with the aircraft. Like me, they had been transformed by their hardships. They had a different air about them. They weren't quite feral, but not domesticated, either. Within a few months, they'd attack men for food, if they were not doing so already. I don't think many could survive an attack from a feral Great Dane without missing a body part or two afterwards.

With the dogs a safe distance away, I emerged from the forest and walked the wood line north. I casually counted cars until reaching Rich's. I carefully approached and knocked loudly on his boxcar door, stating my name. No response. After my second attempt I noticed the large lock affixed to his boxcar door. He wasn't home. I re-verified that I had the right boxcar by climbing up the side and noting the solar panel and wiring we'd installed. Not knowing what to do, I slinked back into the woods to a spot where I could observe the train and collapsed to the ground, crying like a baby.

Up to this point, I was able to hold it together and compartmentalize what happened the past few weeks. Everyone has a breaking point; I knew mine and I'd reached it.

I lay on the ground, my heart and will broken.

It seemed like the country, or at least the state I was in, had gone to hell in a matter of weeks.

After a bout of self-pity lasting a few hours, I picked myself up and headed back down to the train. In an act of desperation, and not wanting to be alone, I again knocked on the train car. Of course there was no response, as the heavy exterior lock was still attached to the boxcar door. I was nearing another panic attack as my eyes passed over the locked sliding door.

MUSHROOM, BRUSH, CREEK, VALIANT, USHER.

Were those words written on the door before? I asked myself. I traced over the words with my index finger, smearing the chalk. A smudge of smeared, oxidized boxcar paint mixed with white chalk coated my finger. I began to walk backwards, absorbing the words as I closed the distance to the tree line.

At my backpack hidden under a young pine, I rummaged, eventually finding my copy of the codebook. As I thumbed through the categories, things began to make sense. According to the code, Rich survived the search and was holing up twenty cars north during the day and back at his original boxcar at nightfall. I gathered up my gear and counted out twenty more cars before seeing the one without an exterior padlock.

"Rich, it's me. I'm alone." I said, lightly tapping on the door.

I heard some movement inside, and the door slid open a couple inches. Out came the barrel of Rich's revolver, followed by the wild whites of his eyes.

"Thank God. You made it. Hurry, get inside!"

I wasted no time in throwing my kit up to Rich and then pulling myself into the relative safety of the train. That's when my debriefing to Rich began.

I told him everything—the explosion, the agents sent to kill me, the flight to Jim's, the fire, the bodies. I also told him about the armed remotely piloted vehicle I observed orbiting over the city.

Rich carefully listened to everything I had to say before speaking. "Okay, now it's my turn. You were damn smart not to transmit. They have been using vans that they're calling Ravens. These Ravens have been driving around the county searching for unauthorized transmissions—*our* transmissions. Once they detect the target signals, they geolocate them with special equipment inside the vans. The only reason I was able to escape detection was that I made a point to transmit to you on two-way freqs from the overpass. From what I can surmise, the authorities have no idea that I'm 'train based' here. They have been searching the road below the overpass, stopping cars and pedestrians, looking for radios. Anyone caught with a two-way disappears. All this is the good news."

"Good?" I said incredulously.

"Yes. The bad news is that the cellular infrastructure is back online in this region. That may not sound particularly bad until you hear about the bounty on our heads. The grid being down this long has culled the herd a lot, but a good percentage of the city is holding on by the grace of government handouts and sporadic power supply. Now their mobile phones are working again. Peterson blasted out a robo-text to all zip codes in this region. You know, the average 'see something, say something' fare, but this time there is a substantial carrot—Peterson will reward a month's food ration to anyone providing information leading to the killing or capture of suspected insurgents. I wrote down the text. Take a look for yourself."

Rich handed me a torn-out yellow page with the message text transcribed in black marker:

Citizens of Washington County, the Federal Government is rewarding a month of food to anyone providing the following information: The identity and whereabouts of any person(s) possessing, or engaging in the use of, two-way radios, firearms, crossbows, compound bows, generators, aircraft, or any other suspicious item or activity.

"Did you notice the aircraft mentioned in the text?" Rich said rhetorically. "I've been hearing chatter that you've been spotted in the skies over the city. According to what I'm hearing, there isn't much they can do about it. The F-16s down in Fort Smith can't fly without pilots, and they deserted when things went sideways."

"What about Peterson? What are you hearing about him?" I asked Rich.

"I've been monitoring the channels he frequents. Oh, he's a ruthless bastard. He's taken over the county sheriff's office as his headquarters. Only a handful of core deputies still work there. The rest resigned or were fired after a questionnaire was handed out by Peterson's crew."

"Questionnaire? Like an application?"

"I don't know, Max. I can only imagine what was on it. Probably something like 'Would you shoot a citizen for possessing a radio?' or maybe 'Do you believe the Constitution applies to everyone?' or something to that effect."

"Is Peterson going on these raids, too?"

"From what I'm intercepting on the radio, yes. He's gone on the dangerous raids where illegal weapons were suspected to be held in the target home."

"What's the purpose of getting the phones up right now? I think the power grid might be a more important focus of effort, right?" I asked.

"Not if you think of it like they do. The network is only backup in a limited capacity. No outgoing communication unless they are to Peterson's outfit. Now, he can track, monitor, and utilize everyone as a sensor to find anyone he wants. The phones are slaved to a new cellular network. The residents are receiving coordinated, pushed SMS updates from the government, just enough information to incentivize them to keep them on. Peterson controls information movement in this region, as I'm sure similar government doppelgängers control the other areas. We are still in an infowar, and Peterson controls the info."

"This is why they're so hell-bent on stopping any radio traffic that isn't theirs," I added.

"Yes, precisely. If they control the food, and the message, they control the population," Rich said.

"Are you still getting any national intel from your HAM radio?"

"Some, but not nearly as much as before they started in with the hit squads. The shortwave transmitters are still sending out broadcasts, but only because it's harder to geolocate high-frequency signals. I suspect that the HAMs still broadcasting are staying mobile, setting up, broadcasting, and then moving again after every transmission. This keeps the government signal vans on the move and unable to get an accurate pinpoint of the rebel stations. Either that, or they have multiple shortwave stealth antennas spread out in different areas and they randomize which ones they tap into. Either way, they're practicing good COMSEC. Quick, concise transmissions, then off the air."

I thought about that for a bit. The brave souls that take a chance on getting burned out by goons, just to lay down real news. Real data, real facts. It didn't matter which side of the gun debate anyone fell on. Free speech was sacrosanct. Stripping it from existence wouldn't earn a high approval rating from either side of the political paradigm, if that mattered anymore or ever would again. Because the grid went down, the remnants of the government systematically took control. First by trading food for guns, and after the guns were gone, the pressure of the jackboot ripped the First Amendment from the pages of the Constitution. I guess Mao really was right when he said political power grows out of the barrel of a gun. Now everyone that's left is hungry, eager to use their phones as digital informants directly to those in control of both the power and info grids.

This is all on me. I'm no better than a Nazi; the Nuremberg defense will never hold much water in the court of my mind. Even the Nazi guards at the camps were prosecuted, and most of them never pulled a lever or fired a shot. They damn sure helped the genocidal maniacs do their job, though. Was I any better? Maggie let me in on enough that I should have at least asked more questions . . . probed deeper into what the true nature of our mission might be. I could have refused to help, refused to go. Being thrown in jail for a few decades for the sake of mankind would have been preferable to this. At least I could have slept at night; I could have looked at myself in the mirror. I owed the world my life.

I weighed my question carefully before asking Rich. "They're treating us like terrorists, hunting us, killing us like rabid dogs. I never thought I'd suggest this, but . . . let's hit them back. Hard."

"I was waiting for you to say that," Rich said. "But I want you to get some rest. You're operating off pure emotion right now. Just rest. I'll wake you up before it gets dark so we can move boxcars."

Rich's comment brought the fire and charred bodies back to the forefront of my thoughts, sucker punching me in that dark recess of soul only heartbreak can reach. "That sounds good."

"Here, drink a few swallows of this and get a few winks," Rich said, handing me a milk jug half full of white lightning.

After taking a few pulls from the jug, I felt the warmth of ninety-proof descend into my stomach, relieving the sucker punch momentarily. That was how this horrible day ended over a week ago. It didn't take long for me to fall asleep on the floor of that train car that morning.

The day after the great purge, we began to make preparations. I risked multiple round-trip flights under the cover of night to retrieve kit from my property. What I couldn't bring with me I hid deeper in the woods under camo netting. The Reaper's EO sensors would have a hard time seeing anything under the IR reflective material; it would just look like the surrounding foliage. I moved and concealed my truck as well as repositioned netting over the shelter.

Inspecting the crater where my house was, I noticed that concrete barricades were placed at the end of my drive.

A sign was erected facing the road that said:

U.S. GOVERNMENT PROPERTY. NO TRESPASSING.

I wish I had a copy of the deed to staple to the sign in defiance. I owned the property free and clear. I suppose repelling thugs from trespassing on private property after shooting at you makes someone persona non grata in these times. It didn't matter. The toasted MRAP that remained in my front yard was a tribute to resistance, just like the Russian tank hulks that remained in the mountains of Afghanistan.

I loaded up the ultralight to capacity and headed back to the transmission line landing strip. I was heavy with explosives, caps, and wire, the ingredients of today's dissidence, it would seem. Rich and I decided to base out of the train cars, spreading out our supplies to increase their survivability. Using some heavy plastic sheeting and duct tape, I buried the extra carbines and some ammo in the woods near the transmission lines. It wouldn't be a long-term cache, but it would last long enough to keep them safe from seizure if it came to that.

In our sleeping car, we hid only our two pistols for protection from two-legged predators. Our rifles were hidden separately either in the ground or in other train cars. Rich showed me where to toss our pistols if the authorities surprised us. He'd fashioned a hidden drop for our contraband that dumped into a small toolbox under the boxcar floor. Just pull the cabinet fitting, drop the guns, and replace the fitting. If Peterson's thugs found us, we'd dump the guns and radios and submit to search. If asked why we were here, we made up the cover story that we were railway workers and that our engines were malfunctioning, stranding us here. Rich had the lingo, uniform, and keys to back us up. I'd pose as his apprentice.

After rebasing was complete, Rich and I started our discussion of advantages and disadvantages. Right now, Peterson had the people, and their freebie informant phones. As we were guerrillas up against a superior force, we had to compensate our disadvantage with tactics. We had to walk the balance between the information war and kinetics. They were nothing short of the occupying force, and they had numbers, technology, and superior resources.

We were only two guys with guns and explosives, but we were damn sure going to use them.

We departed the boxcar at 2300, fully kitted up. Rich was wearing his hobo garb and looked like any drifter one might see on the side of the road. We headed south along the tracks in the direction of Drake Airfield. The night was cold; the moisture in the air brought the wind chill down to bone-chilling levels. We figured this to be an advantage, as Peterson's foot soldiers would all be indoors staying warm. Our feet crunched in the gravel beside the tracks, which glowed in the moonlight. Both of our packs were full, but not too heavy. I loaned Rich a suppressed M4.

When I started to explain to him how to use it, he stopped me mid-sentence. "I'm familiar," he said.

I didn't probe any further, as I wasn't quite ready for my skeletons to be examined, even if it was Rich doing the examining. The only thing I needed to show him was how to turn on the micro red dot optic. Guess those were a bit before his time. Reaching the railroad crossing light near Southgate, we got low as we heard some people shouting. Motorcycle engines roared, and I could hear tires burning on pavement in the direction of the shopping center. We lay flat on the ground when we saw the headlights. Strangely, the lights seemed to spin like a lighthouse beacon, but we figured it out soon enough: the bikers were doing burnout circles in a vacant lot. Just some hell-raisers out past curfew. None of my business.

We stayed low and crossed the road and continued along the tracks. With the train far behind us, this was an unfamiliar section of track for me. Rich walked confidently south, so I wasn't too concerned.

"How far do you think we have?" I asked.

"Forty-five minutes or so. Then we will spill out near the armory."

"National Guard armory?"

"Yeah, that's the one," he replied.

"Shit, I know where we are. I flew over it a while back. It was crawling with black uniforms."

"Well, that makes sense, I suppose. The armory has all that surplus desert hardware. Tanks, MRAPs, artillery. We'll steer clear, even if it costs us some distance."

We continued for about an hour down the track, when Rich signaled our exit through a clearing on our left. After scraping my arms on some good ol' Arkansas thorns, we emerged in a cow pasture.

"Okay, I know where we are," I said. "We're pretty damn close to the county sheriff's office. We're gonna need to cross the road as soon as we can. We need to make some distance from here."

"Agreed. Let's cross there," Rich said, pointing to half a dozen cars dragged to the side of the road.

I nodded and we increased our stride to the crossing. At the road, we again got low. I went first, sprinting to the nearest abandoned vehicle. Rich followed behind me, and I noticed that he could be very quick when he wanted. His ancient canvas seabag bounced behind him, but I couldn't see it slow him down.

When we reached the Drake Airfield perimeter fence, we skirted the north side, heading for a dark area of the perimeter. I had no idea if the tower was manned at the moment, and if it was, I didn't know if the controllers had night vision spotting scopes to look for wildlife on the runway. It didn't matter at this point. We were committed. Rich and I set up an observation post on a low hillside adjacent to the perimeter fence that surrounded the airfield. Work lights running on generators illuminated the aircraft parking spots, and I could see guards standing around the Reaper remotely piloted aircraft they were prepping for launch. Passing our binoculars back and forth, we watched as M4-wielding guards watched over the shoulders of the Reaper maintenance team while they completed their final cross-checks of the unmanned systems.

We both got damn cold as we observed the activity on the airfield below. So cold that Rich left the post for a few minutes, returning with kindling. Using the rail spike knife I gave him, he dug a hole about six inches deep between us and arranged the firewood inside the hole. Around the outside of the hole, he stacked oval rocks. Within five minutes, Rich's economical hobo fire was stealthily warming our observation post. The fire was subsurface; the stacked rocks hid any flames that might reach out of the ground. The rocks absorbed a lot of heat, releasing it omnidirectionally. We were far enough away for the smoke to disperse by the time any wind carried it to the runway.

With the Reaper sitting on the tarmac, I felt somewhat better knowing that Rich and I wouldn't be getting a bomb dropped up our asses. The maintenance folks cleared out to allow the tractor driver to maneuver the Reaper to starting position. I didn't want to take a shot at the Reaper until it was on takeoff. If I damaged it now, the maintainers would just fix it. If I hit it hard on takeoff, I might get lucky and destroy it.

Tonight, I was running a Trijicon AccuPoint dialed to max magnification. The glowing tritium crosshair dot stood out in contrast to the gray color theme of the airfield. The generator floodlights washed the field with an industrial glow.

"Rich, need you to start spotting."

"You're shooting at the damn aircraft—tough to miss," he said sarcastically.

"Yeah, I know, but I can't be checking over my shoulder or the peripherals for foot patrols. Keep that M4 handy."

I watched as the tractor detached from the Reaper and drove away. The propeller started to spin, cutting the dense winter air, and the navigation lights illuminated on the wingtips. Through my low-magnification scope, I watched the camera turret initiate a diagnostic spin and hoped that the operator wouldn't choose to calibrate the optic on our position. After the turret stopped gyrating, it turned backwards and the aircraft started to taxi to the hold short line of the airfield.

I watched through the chain-link fence as the aircraft turned onto the hold short and then onto the active runway. I trained my crosshairs on the Reaper's empennage directly forward of the propeller casing. If I could hit there, I might damage the engine.

We waited for ten minutes before we heard the propeller spin up to takeoff RPMs. The Reaper lurched forward and began its takeoff. It appeared to move slowly at first, but that was due to my look aspect to the runway. As it passed the distance marker boards, I kept my crosshairs on it, aiming a little in front to compensate for the increasing speed. The Reaper started to rotate as I began to fire suppressed shots. Sparks flew when some of my rounds impacted the chain-link fence in front of us. I kept pumping rounds into the Reaper's engine as fast as I could reacquire and pull the trigger. At first, I thought I was missing. When the aircraft neared the departure end of the runway, I heard the unmistakable sound of metal on metal accompanied by loud popping noises. The Reaper leaned to its left as its nose shot up. With the nose up in a no-power solution, I knew what was next. The Reaper stalled at about a hundred feet and went nose over like a lawn dart. It crashed into the trees at the north end of the runway in a fireball of jet fuel, aluminum, copper, and composites.

With our ingress path on fire, Rich and I began our exfiltration into the woods. Before departing, Rich took a few digital snapshots of the airfield, including the burning Reaper.

"Propaganda," he said.

We departed to the sounds of fire trucks frantically scramming to the emergency. As we went deeper into the woods, the siren sounds faded and were replaced by a whippoorwill.

We were under a decent winter canopy of evergreens when we decided that a break was in order. I sat on a fallen log and took some water as Rich unshouldered his pack and leaned his carbine against a tree. He removed his radio and sat it on the ground, and took out a length of what I thought was cordage tied to a sock. He slung the sock around and released it straight up into the air. It caught on a high pine branch above, just enough to keep the cordage suspended. Rich wrapped the other end around the pine once and tied it off for later. I then realized that it wasn't cordage he'd thrown into the trees; it was an antenna.

He pulled out a set of earbuds and powered up his handheld system as he attached a smaller UHF antenna to his transceiver. He began to spin the spectrum and listen. A few moments went by before he called me over to listen.

Two unidentified voices bantered back and forth about what had just occurred.

"... crashed at the end of the runway, sir."

"What do you mean, crashed? What did the pilots tell you?"

"They say that the engine malfunctioned. They lost control on takeoff."

"Well, then get your fucking asses out there and inspect the aircraft. I'm on my way. You better have something for me when I get there."

"Yes sir, we're on it."

"Major Peterson out."

So *that* was Peterson's voice. That was the man who was organizing the chaos. If we'd let that armed Reaper take off, there was no telling what havoc would have been released tonight. Maybe those bikers would have gotten a taste of airpower, or maybe that mother I ran into at the food line, out after curfew, trying to gather food for her baby.

We listened to the radio chatter long enough to determine what patrols were on what roads before switching to shortwave. Rich attached his long wire antenna to the radio, along with what looked like Morse keys. Sure enough, he started clicking out Morse on his lap. The expression on his face went blank while he keyed away at speeds impossible for me to copy using my Boy Scout training. He must have tapped out code for a full five minutes before he stopped and dismantled his system.

"Well, what was that all about?" I asked.

"We're the resistance, Max. People need to know about what we did tonight. If we die tomorrow, the HAMs on the other end operating printing presses will get the word out. Two men brought down a multimillion-dollar death machine tonight. We're just men, but the idea of what we did can move mountains. You and I can't begin to know what effect this news might have on other cities and towns far outside Peterson's control."

"I'm picking up what you're putting down. Who were you communicating with?"

"A consortium of HAMs that are part of this resistance, and probably what's left of the NSA. I'm just a node in the Washington County resistance cell, and you're the kinetic part of that cell. I know that there are at least twelve other cells, but we don't say where we are when we talk to each other. That way if we get captured, we only know how many others are out there, listening on the night air. We can't be forced to tell them who we talk to or where they're located. It's best not to know, don't you think?"

"Yeah, it is. Trust me, I know."

"Don't think I can't smell something spooky about you, and I know you think the same about me. That's neither here nor there, though."

"Understand completely," I said. "Trust me, I don't want to go down that road, either. You might not like where it ends up."

"Fair enough."

Rich made another hobo fire near our sitting log. I watched him work with my night vision monocular this time. Again he dug a hole with his knife. I watched him arrange the kindling like bicycle spokes around the edge of the hole. He stacked the small rocks he'd gathered in a circle around the hole like an old well from way back when. The rocks served as a barrier so anyone out here in the woods couldn't see our fire, and it also helped with lighting the fire by blocking the wind. He worked quickly, taking no more than five minutes from when his knife stabbed the ground to the fire warming the area. I stood up and walked ten feet from the finished product; I couldn't see the flames at all. Handy tradecraft I didn't learn in school.

We sat around the blazing rocks, warming our bodies and cooking our chicken noodle soup. The road back was going to be arduous with all the increased patrols, so we needed all the rest, food, and drink we could get before moving out.

"Do you think that train will run?" I asked Rich.

"Yeah, it'll run. It's got enough fuel to get on down the road a stretch. Take half a day to prep it and two men to crew it, but it'll move."

"That's good to know. Seems like we're hiding in plain sight. A third of our train is in the city, and the other half is in the woods between the city and the industrial park. Might be worth thinking about, you know, moving somewhere more remote."

"You make a good point, but there are a lot of things to think about before moving a train that size. For one, it's gonna make a shit ton of noise. I'll also bet that the track hasn't been surveyed in a long damn time. No telling how many cars or even HAZMAT trucks are parked across the tracks. We'd be moving slow, stopping often. We'd have every Jesse James in the Ozarks trying to rob us. Then you have to think about the feds. If they stop a moving train, they'll need more than a thin cover story to convince them. They'd be making some radio calls, verifying names and such."

"I guess we're stuck here on the tracks, then. I'm just worried that this good deal we have going will dry up. We can handle the bandits, but we can't survive a hundred oath-breaking lunatic agents of the state putting us under siege. I still don't know how they convinced so many to turncoat."

"I don't think they did," Rich said cryptically. "I think most feds are honest and patriotic, and unfortunately, I think most of the good ones are dead or defending their families right now."

"So who the hell is driving those MRAPs around and talking on the radio?" I said skeptically.

"Don't get me wrong—the guys at the airfield were military, but they were doing compartmentalized work. What's the harm in maintaining and towing an aircraft? They're just doing their jobs. Now, Peterson's crew is different. I don't think they're feds—I think they're contractors, or something different. I could be wrong, but like you, I have a hard time believing that a straitlaced FBI or BATFE agent would agree to execute the atrocities of recent times."

"That's pretty idealistic of you, Rich. You threaten a man's family or take away his food, you'd be surprised what he might do. Put the burning pine knots to his feet, and a man will do just about anything. Even a decent person will do bad things under the pretense of good intentions."

"Oh, I agree. I would just like to think that the men in black are hired guns, not sworn federal officers. If they're hired guns . . . hired by who? That's the big question, isn't it?"

Our soup was ready, as the cans were gurgling through the slits I cut, signaling that they were at a boil. I held the can in my gloved hands, warming them quickly. After the can released enough heat into my gloves, I held it between my wrists, letting my blood carry the warmth throughout my entire body. I was comfortable, even though it was about twenty degrees at the moment.

I cut the rest of the lid from the soup with my folding knife, inspecting it via red headlamp. Elmax super steel, titanium frame lock, 3D machined G10 scale. The staff and milling machines it took to make this blade would probably never work together again. I could almost envision the future when blacksmiths will be jacking up ancient and derelict cars to remove their leaf springs. One day they might scavenge the very coal from our train to forge horseshoes and knives. Thinking about a future like that was a little depressing, so I tried not to.

Rich and I drank soup in silence. Afterwards, I urinated on the fire, and we broke camp for the train.

Every now and again we could here sirens carried on the wind, mixed with intermittent gunshots. I prayed that the shots were the good guys, giving some raiders what for.

We punched through the woods into a cow pasture at about three in the morning. As we crossed the field, I noticed that there were no cows. Plenty of hay and a pond full of water, but nothing to eat or drink it. Slaughtered, no doubt. Since most grocery stores only kept about three days' worth of food stock, I wondered how long it took for the butchers to come for the cattle. If this keeps up, I'm wondering how long before the butchers come for me.

As we helped each other through the barbed wire fence on the far side of the field, we saw headlights coming from the direction we needed to go. We ran across the road, and slid under a lifted 4×4 sitting on the shoulder up on a jack. The noises got louder— motorcycles. The pack of bikers rode on by the 4×4 at a normal speed, seemingly unafraid of patrols or armed agents.

We let the bikers' taillights fade before crawling out from under the truck. With the engine noise gone, we started moving for the train crossing that led to our salvation. We passed Southgate without incident. The area still smelled like burned flesh, reminding me of my family.

Within a hundred meters of the crossing, we heard the motorcycles again. We sprinted as fast as Rich could move, reaching the tracks as the headlight beams illuminated the crossing sign. They were searching for something, someone. No other reason to burn gas like that. We waited and let the pack move on.

When the taillights and sounds faded completely, we started to move. On our feet, we were unexpectedly bathed in headlights from the lot across from what was a car dealership adjacent to the crossing. Motorcycle engines revved and tires squealed as the bikers gave pursuit. There were only two of them, but more would follow.

I heard one of them scream, "Make the call!"

Rich and I turned and ran north along the tracks. The bikers turned off the road and gave chase, catching up quickly.

"Run! I got this!" I yelled out to Rich.

Swinging my rifle around from my back, I flipped the safety off with my thumb, simultaneously pulling the trigger. I couldn't see the rider, but the bike dumped over, spun around in the gravel, and skidded along the tracks. Sparks flew, momentarily illuminating the rider, who lay bleeding on the ground. I switched targets to the left biker, but before I could get a round out of the barrel, I was struck in the shoulder by what felt like an aluminum baseball bat.

The impact knocked me to the ground. In pain, I lay there, nearly passed out from the blow. I managed to get on my feet as the biker threw gravel from his back wheel turning around to come at me again. I raised my carbine and started pulling the trigger. I could hear my rounds impact the bike, and one shot caused a yelp from the rider as the bike fell over and skidded towards me. When it came to a stop at my feet, the rider was gone. I flipped my carbine light on with my thumb, but before I could raise it to high ready, the biker came at me with a big fucking bowie knife. Polished like a mirror, the large blade came at me from above as my attacker attempted to slash my neck.

I instinctively raised my gun to block the blade. When the large steel knife slammed into my aluminum carbine receiver, it felt like it might cut my gun in half. It held. I did my best to give the son of a bitch a good butt stroke to the face, but he blocked it with his clenched fist. I was too close to get a shot off with my carbine, so I stepped back from the knife, which was slashing wildly at my face, and drew my Glock. I squeezed off three rounds at center mass and he went down, still clutching the knife. I got a little closer, but not enough to get my Achilles tendon cut. I stood over him and we shared stares. His hatred for me was measurable by his eyes, and mine by my bared teeth. I felt warmth on my gun hand, so I put it in front of my carbine light. Blood. The fucker cut my hand pretty good with that Arkansas toothpick. As we both bled out, him a little faster than me, I heard gravel crunch behind me.

Expecting to see Rich, I spun around. The other biker was coming at me fast with a baseball bat raised above his head. I leveled my gun to his chest and pumped three rounds into him before he stopped advancing. The only thing I could think of as the second biker fell at my feet was *How high is the body count now?* I knew I hadn't forgotten how many; I just didn't want to face the number. I could smell alcohol and weed from the man that lay dead at my feet.

My ears were ringing from the 9mm shots, but I managed to hear another footfall coming at me. I spun around with my finger on the trigger. This time it *was* Rich.

"I had to do it. They attacked us first," I said with guilt.

"I know what happened; I turned around after I heard your shots. Those guys were waiting on us. They used the other bikers as a decoy. They waited for the others to move out so they could catch us moving. We fell for the trap."

"Yeah, I guess we did." I said, bleeding and shaking in the cold. "Let's get those hogs off the tracks and into the trees. Same with the bodies," I suggested.

I used the last bit of bandage I had in my blowout kit to wrap my hand so we could work. We picked the bikes up and rolled them up the tracks, hiding them deep beyond the tree line. Before moving the bodies, I examined the massive bowie that cut me. Returning the knife to its sheath, I saw the intricate work pressed into the leather. *1%er* was surrounded by a diamond on the front.

"Bad mofos, Max. I know what that mark means, and we don't want to be around when their gang comes rolling back through here."

We dragged the bodies back to the intersection, putting them just off the road. Right before leaving them, I heard a ring coming from one of the bodies. Reaching inside the biker's leather into his vest pocket, I retrieved a phone. The caller ID indicated "Flak."

"Turn that off—let's bring it with us. I have some pictures I want to text to Peterson," Rich said, laughing.

"Turning it off won't do any good, man. These things can remotely be put in a maintenance mode. Even if you pull the battery, most phones have a secondary that powers the bios and other low-order functions of the phone. They can ping its location with the battery removed."

"How the hell do you know all that?" Rich asked.

"Read about it online. I'll turn the phone off and put it in the saddlebag of one of those hogs. We can take an ammo can with us and retrieve it later. Acts like a Faraday cage. We can't be tracked if it's stored in a metal box."

"Smart. What are you gonna do with that sword?"

"This thing?" I said, holding the twelve-inch bowie in front of me. "It did a pretty good number on me—might as well keep it. Close encounters and all."

I squeezed the bandage tight around my hand while we walked to the boxcar. Arriving, Rich retrieved the keys from his hiding spot and unlocked the "house." A coal fire was burning hot within Rich's standard five minutes. He put some water on the stove for my hand. After cleaning it up, we both agreed that stitches might do more harm than good, so I boiled the dirty bandage and rewrapped my hand.

It was early in the a.m. when my head hit the coffee bean pillow. I was haunted by the sounds of revving motorcycle engines before my mind finally relented and shut down.

My head throbbed when I opened my eyes to early morning. With so much going on, I was granted a temporary reprieve from the grief of losing my aunt and cousins. I swung my legs over and sat up, inviting another sharp pain in my head and injured hand. It felt warm. Fighting infection. Rich was not in the boxcar when I woke, so I put a can full of water on the coal stove and tossed in a few more chunks to get more heat. The sun wasn't up, so I didn't worry about anyone seeing the coal smoke. With the water to a boil, I waited for it to cool a few degrees before washing my wound out and boiling my bandage again. Antibiotics would be nice, but keeping a cut clean was 90 percent of avoiding any infection.

Remembering the half bar of soap I had in my pack, I took off my dirty clothes and washed up with more coal-heated water. Rich had a laundry bucket near the door, so I filled that up with some bottled water and eventually brought it to a boil. I shaved a few pieces of soap into the boiling water with my folding knife and dropped my clothes in. I was buck naked when the door slid open.

"That's no way to greet a man in the morning," Rich said, laughing.

"Sorry, my clothes were starting to walk me around. Need to stay clean with this cut."

Rich walked past me and leaned over the bed on his side of the boxcar. After shuffling around back there, he pulled out a scrap of corrugated steel.

"Here, I use this. Better than just swishing them around in the water."

The piece of metal was small enough to fit inside the bucket alongside my clothes. I spent thirty minutes or so scrubbing and hanging them up all around the stove. By this time, the sun began to peek over the horizon, beaming marble-sized orange dots through holes on the eastern boxcar walls. My skivvies dried fastest as I laid them directly on the stove and listened to them sizzle. Felt good putting on warm clothes.

"You know," I said, "I've been thinking about our next move."

The coal fire was dying as daybreak was upon us.

Rich placed his can of soup directly in the stove and said, "Go on."

"If we can rig my radio up somewhere we can watch, we might be able to do something better than just blowing up a toy airplane."

"Set a trap for them? Make them come to the radio? Then what?"

"We use the explosives in my pack to blow their asses back to where they came from."

Rich's grin signaled his support for the plan.

We schemed most of the day after moving boxcars. I didn't quite understand Rich's ways, but I respected them. In the afternoon, we kitted up and did some reconnoitering to check on the ultralight. After being satisfied it was just as I left it, Rich helped me pull it deeper into the woods, away from the transmission-line clearing.

Walking down the hill from the ultralight to the train, I saw a rabbit emerge from the trees. Before I could react, Rich had already plugged it with a suppressed shot from his M4. I took some cordage and tied the game to my pack. We were both tired of chicken noodle soup, but chicken rabbit noodle soup? That was a different story.

After reaching the train, we decided to head for the overpass to get a vantage point of south Fayetteville. We climbed the cars and headed north, jumping the gaps all the way. After a few minutes I could see Rich's panel collecting electricity ten cars ahead. Passing our night car, we moved on until the bridge was in sight. There were no cars passing by underneath, not even police patrols. When we made our final jump to the car that spanned most of the bridge, we viewed nothing but a ghost town in both directions.

We set up shop on top of the train, and I lit a can of Sterno for water boiling. A few minutes later, we were drinking hot pine needle tea. Rich set up his radio for UHF/VHF police comms collection, and we began conducting a proper stakeout of the major road artery running perpendicular to the train below us. Rich lay prone with a notepad in one hand, tuning his radio with the other. When he found a frequency he liked, he began to copy. Satisfied with his collect, he passed his notepad over to me. I was getting pretty good at reading his shorthand, but didn't understand the way he serialized his report. KL01, KL02, KL03, etc.

"What does 'KL' mean?" I asked.

"It means klieg light, something from an old job. Anyway, check out KL02 and tell me if you see anything strange."

I read through Rich's serialized KLs:

KL01 BOLO for armed saboteurs connected with Drake attack remains active. 5.56 shell casings discovered at suspected overwatch area.

KL02 Agents recovered at West Fifteenth on night of Drake attack were shot with a nine millimeter Glock handgun.

"They can't be talking about those one percenter bikers I killed, right?"

"Two men dead, shot by a nine-millimeter Glock handgun last

night, and found on West Fifteenth? Come on, Max, work with me here."

"You're right, I just don't want to—"

"Me neither. I don't want to think about a kangaroo government using a one percenter biker gang to do their dirty work," Rich said, finishing my thought.

"This sort of expands our enemies list. We should probably agree that any one percenter that sees us out in the open is going to try to kill or capture us. If that's the case, we might want to shoot first, because that's what they're going to do."

Rich thought about what I said for a moment before weighing in. "If we shoot first, unprovoked, what does that make us?"

"Survivors."

Engine noises coming from the east forced us to stop our discussion and get flat on the boxcar. The vehicles passed quickly under our overpass; the wind vortices vibrated the bridge and boxcar slightly. An MRAP was the lead vehicle, followed by two white buses. As the buses passed, I caught a glimpse through the back window of someone in leg irons. Prisoner transport. The last vehicle was another MRAP, and signified the end of the convoy. I watched them speed west to the grassy knoll area before turning right onto Razorback road.

"Those buses are going the wrong way if they're headed for Washington County Jail," I said to Rich.

We packed up our camp, satisfied with the observations we'd made, and headed back to base, fifty or so boxcars south. A few cars shy of our destination, Rich stopped in his tracks and turned around, facing me. He whispered to himself for a bit before letting his mind focus on the here and now.

"I have a plan. We'll need that ammo can and that biker's cell phone."

It took about an hour to gather our supplies in one spot. I'd made a point to spread out our kit for security reasons, but that also meant that getting at what I needed was a chore, especially if it needed to be done quickly. I went alone to recover the biker's cell phone. Rich stayed behind to prepare the rabbit stew. The trip was largely uneventful, except for one detail. Returning to the spot where I shot the bikers, I saw none of my spent 9mm shell casings. I knew from Rich's report that they dug 9mm balls from the bodies of those bikers, but someone had recovered the brass, too.

Backtracking to the motorcycles, I saw no evidence of tampering, or that anyone had been here since we hid them in the woods. The only boot print I noticed was mine, and I promptly scuffed it out. I recovered the phone from the saddlebag and immediately dropped it into the metal ammo can and sealed the lid.

I decided to search the rest of the saddlebags for anything useful. My hand throbbed a little while trying to unbuckle the heavy leather straps, but I eventually got in. One of the bags held a ziplock bag full of cocaine, and another with marijuana. There were half a dozen bottles of prescription meds in with the drugs, all with different names on the bottle. I grabbed all the meds and was very happy to see codeine and doxycycline. I had no idea what the other bottles were, but took them with me anyway. Affixed to the handlebars of one of the bikes was a garden hose, probably the biker's gas card.

I opened the final saddlebag and suddenly dropped to my knees, releasing all the pine needle tea and morning soup I had in my stomach. Inside the saddlebag was a severed human head, a female. It pains me to write what I'm about to, as it's disgusting and sad beyond belief . . . but a jar of Vaseline sat near the head inside the bag, and the woman's mouth was smeared with it. Sick fucking bastards. I'll never unsee that.

I heaved a few more times, sending pain shooting through my hand. Finally I found the strength to get back on my feet. I stuffed the drugs and meds in my pack and headed back to Rich. I decided not to share what I'd seen in the contents of the saddlebag. No use ruining someone else's day.

Back at the planning boxcar, with all our incriminating shit, we piled all our mission items in one spot and started going over the plan. That was part of the beauty of having access to so many boxcars. We could keep our incriminating kit spread out and sleep knowing that if we're captured, we won't be found alongside rifles, stacks of ammo, explosives, and other dirty things.

"Got the phone?" Rich asked.

"Yeah, it's in the can."

"Find anything else on the bikes?"

"Yeah, this," I said, tossing the Baggie full of cocaine into Rich's lap.

"Damn, is that what I think it is?"

"I guess so. I'm not really into that sort of thing."

"Me either, but this could come in handy. Drop a little on the trail if dogs are tracking us, or maybe snort a little to stay up at night when we need to."

"Yeah, if you say so. More importantly, I also have some prescription meds. Painkillers and antibiotics. I can really use those right now. My hand is killing me."

I rubbed my wound, feeling the radiating warmth of the battle against infection being fought under the skin.

"Prep the charges Max, but we can't mess with the phone here. We'll have to set it up on-site."

"Yeah, we wouldn't want to be broadcasting our position right now. I'm on the charges; just have the phone ready."

As I shaped explosives, placed caps, and measured copper wire, my mind entered a calm period. I thought of avenging my losses through high-order detonations. Not very healthy to think that way, I know, but anger was better than sadness, so I grasped on. Catalyzed by the ghastly image of what I saw inside the motorcycle saddlebag, I was able to shape the explosives quickly. With eight grenade-sized charges prepped, I began looking for shrapnel. Rich had an old coffee can full of pennies, so I used those to pack the charges with. One of the pennies was dated 1981. Ancient. Rich tells me that any pre-1982 pennies were near-solid copper. Copper. I couldn't stop thinking about it after sifting my hands through so many pennies. Most of the time my brain has a reason for locking onto things, and most of the time it's too late when I find out why. Copper.

I had eight charges positioned inside of soup cans packed in with pennies as a shrapnel medium. The caps extended out the open ends. I placed them carefully in my pack along with several lengths of copper wire and a clacker.

"I'm ready when you are."

"Okay, let's talk targets," said Rich. "We have two logical choices. We can follow the road and turn right where those white buses went and activate the decoy there, or we can do it near the sheriff's office."

We departed at sunset.

We took the tracks most of the way, only hearing motorcycle engines one time. After reaching the field adjacent to the sheriff's office, we began to pick out targets. I knew that the area close to the buildings would have cameras, and the bright perimeter lights indicated that they had power. There were four MRAPs and several squad cars parked out front. Across the road and down a bit was an old house with the front porch caved in and no lights. I scouted ahead to check it out. Sure enough, it was condemned two years ago, according to the faded plastic sign stapled to the front door.

After going back for Rich, we set up shop inside the house. It didn't take much to get inside. The back door was unlocked. The smell of moldy wallpaper and mothballs permeated the air inside the old place. Rich immediately went for the fireplace and looked up the chimney. I laughed at him.

"What's so funny?"

"I don't know, maybe seeing a Santa look-alike at the chimney."

"You won't be laughing when I warm the place up thirty degrees."

Rich worked his hobo magic. Before I knew it, he had old furniture legs and fallen limbs from the backyard filling up the fireplace. A master fire starter, he had a blaze going inside of five minutes.

We worked quickly. I unlocked the front door and wired a charge just inside. I wired another charge at the back door and ran both wires across the yard into the trees on the other side of the fence. I wired a third and fourth charge in the living room near the fireplace, careful to conceal the wires until I had them out the cracked window on the other side of the room. I labeled the charges by tying knots in the ends of the wire. Charges one and two had that many knots, and three and four the same. I wired my special gift and final charge in the mailbox by the driveway, and concealed the wire by running it through the culvert to the trees where the other four wires were located. I had at least fifty yards of distance between the house and myself.

Back inside, Rich had the phone out of the ammo can and was plugging an SD card into it. He turned it on and a bright splash screen momentarily overtook the fireplace as the brightest light in the room.

"You've got to be kidding me. *DHS*? They named the damn cell network DHS. How original! Okay, just let me send a hot tip to Peterson and we're good. Just a second."

I saw Rich thumbing away on the touch screen before he placed the phone near my fireplace charge, facedown.

"Let's get the fuck out of here. We don't have much time."

We sprinted as fast as we could to the trees where my five leads sat under the weight of a rock. I had the clacker in my hand at the ready. I could see the firelight from the living room spill out of the bare window, casting a faint amber trapezoid on the ground outside.

I think I held my breath for a full minute before speaking. "What did you send?"

"I sent Peterson what he asked for. If you see something, say something. I sent the sonofabitch a photo of the burning Reaper and the circus that started after it crashed."

"Wow. That's gonna get their attention."

Sure enough, it did. According to my watch, just over nine minutes had passed when two MRAPs pulled up near the mailbox. I could have detonated the mailbox charge, but it would only scratch the paint of those behemoths. Oddly, no one got out. They just sat there, engines running for five minutes, before we heard the thunder approaching. Behind me, over my right shoulder, I could see dozens of headlights speeding down the road to our location.

"Max, that's too many. We need to abort."

"You go ahead if you have to. I'm staying right here," I said, fixated on visions of the severed head I saw in the dead biker's saddlebag.

The fleet of bikers pulled in beside the MRAPs, revving their engines, shaking the damn ground they were thundering so hard. I could hear them yelling and screaming over the sounds of their motorcycles. They made enough noise to tip off anyone that would have been inside that old house. I didn't think it was very smart until the moonlight revealed a platoon of bikers emerging from the field across from us into the overgrown backyard. They already had a pincer attack set up and I wondered how long the backyard bikers had been lurking in that field before the thunder showed up. Yeah, these guys were sneaky. This was the second time they set a trap using their main force as a decoy.

With my night vision optic, the moonlight was magnified and I could see the glint of their bowie knives and pistols as they advanced on the house. They held the knives blade down in their left hands and a pistol on top in their right—Harries technique. The bikers came like a pride of lions, quietly and surefooted.

Ten feet from the back door, the lead biker held up his fist, signaling the others to stand fast. Then I saw the screen of a phone through my night vision monocular as he made a call.

I took this time to connect the leads from the front and back door into the clacker. From our vantage point fifty meters from the side of the house, I could see both doors. The biker in the backyard was calling his counterpart in the front. I saw movement from one of the breachers in the front as he tossed something through the window. I instinctively tucked my face into the grass before the small explosion rang out—a flash bang.

"Fuck, I'm blinded!" Rich whispered loudly. There were multiple kicks as both doors swung inward and the bikers funneled into the house.

I squeezed the clacker.

The windows in the back kitchen and the front room

disintegrated outward and the house walls flexed, absorbing the concussion from the blast. Then came the screams.

I quickly yanked the entry det wires from the clacker and attached the fireplace wires. The shrieks of suffering and death continued to blast from the old house of pain. It took some determination, but we waited . . .

After a few minutes, the back doors opened on one of the MRAPs and three men in black fatigues spilled out. One of them barked orders at the remaining bikers, but I couldn't hear what he said.

"There. Him. That's Peterson," said Rich.

"How do you know?"

"I've heard his voice on the radio enough to recognize it."

Whatever Peterson said to the bikers, it worked. They started their march towards the house to recover their buddies' corpses. Perfect. I'd learned a thing or two overseas.

Ten bikers entered the front door and I waited for a few seconds before detonating the fireplace charge.

Ka-blam, you fuckers.

Another gigantic explosion, this time shooting embers out the windows. New screams. Even though Peterson was out of range of the mailbox charge, I detonated it anyway. The blast knocked over about twenty bikes, peppering them with pennies. The supersonic pocket change sparked against the MRAP armor but had no real effect. *Copper, MRAP.* I could hear gearboxes click into first gear and they lumbered forward down the street, away from the action.

Peterson continued to holler orders, but followed the slow MRAPs as if they were his lifeline. I didn't even know I was doing it, but I had my carbine unshouldered and was tracking Peterson through my scope.

I was about to take the shot when I heard the rotors of a helicopter approaching. Rich and I took off then, running through the field and into the woods as the massive spotlight beam from the chopper illuminated the house and surrounding area.

Rich gasped for air and said, "Shit. I thought we killed their air support."

"Doesn't look that way."

We wasted no time in finding the tracks and moving along them. I jogged, counting rail ties as I went, checking on Rich. He didn't get too far behind me, to his credit. I was carrying all the heavy kit, though. We made it to the crossing sign and increased our pace until we could see the locomotives. We stowed our kit in our designated supply car and took only pistols back to our sleep car.

Safely in for the night, Rich lit a coal fire and began copying klieg light intelligence from his radio. I cleaned my wound, sipped some pine needle tea, and took a quarter pill of codeine to take the edge off the pain. I doused the lights but was again haunted by the sound of machines; this time, helicopter rotor blades.

The following is Rich's transcript of radio traffic intercepted last night:

KL05-Police Comms (PC): patrolling area in vicinity of (IVO), fifteenth street and seventy one. No sign of insurgent activity.

Biker Comms (BC): Roger, we'll keep our patrols going up and down MLK. You hear or see anything and call us first. It's personal for us, law dog. Got it?

PC: Affirm, all yours.

KL06-Peterson: All stations, we're looking for at least two males at this point. We'll have air support for the rest of the night, unless Benton needs the bird more than we do.

KL07-PC: Curfew violators reported by citizen via phone on seventy-one and Dixon.

BC: Okay, law dog, my boys are rollin'. Finders keepers.

The heat and swelling in my hand had gone down. The pain meds really helped me get some sleep last night, too. This morning before daybreak, Rich and I did our routine, pine needle tea and soup. I used the leftover tea to pour over my wound and boil my dressings. Just to make sure I could kick an infection, I started a regimen of antibiotics. At this point, Peterson probably required a chip be implanted in everyone's butt for them to be authorized for medical care, or something equally absurd.

After our morning move to a different boxcar, I brought up the prospect of aerial reconnaissance to Rich. He agreed to monitor police comms while I flew overhead and to transmit to me immediately if he heard anything about a helicopter being scrambled. I took my M4 along. If I had no other choice but to be downed by a door gunner of a helicopter, I might get a lucky shot off from the ultralight.

At about noon, we split ways and I headed south along the tracks to the transmission line, and Rich headed north to the overpass. If he had to transmit, it would be better if they triangulated the signal there.

I moved slowly up the tracks with my M4, sidearm, new bowie, and the two-way. I wore the large trophy knife on the left side of my belt, hoping that it wasn't used to behead that poor woman. My

Glock sat securely in my Bravo Concealment holster on my right hip. I couldn't decide which tugged my pants the most, as the combined weight caused me to tighten my belt a notch to keep my pants up. That might be attributed to my current economic collapse diet of soup, soup, and more soup. At least the rabbit Rich shot mixed it up a little.

I could see the clearing up ahead to the left, but the hair on the back of my neck bristled and I got low, below the tracks. I controlled my breathing and listened. No engines, no talking. There was absolutely no sound except the slight wind at my back blowing dead leaves south in my direction of travel. I didn't move, as movement and contrast leads to detection. My only camouflage was my coal soiled clothing and patchy bearded face. I stared up the tracks, searching.

Although I couldn't be certain, I suspected that I was being watched.

I slowly picked myself off the ground started to get on my feet when I was tackled from the trees by a large dog. The creature slammed me against a boxcar wheel, bursting stars into my vision before it took hold of my jacketed arm. I knew at that split second that I couldn't shoot the dog, as I'd risk shooting myself in the scuffle. I drew the bowie as fast as I could and started to stab and slash at the vicious animal. One of my slashes cut across its muzzle, resulting in a yelp, and it stepped back, giving me a better view. It wasn't a dog. Before that moment I wouldn't have believed anyone telling tall tales of wolves in northwest Arkansas, but there it was.

The creature was injured but didn't retreat. Its gray jowls disappeared, revealing every one of its menacing teeth. My shoulder was bruised but I didn't think the teeth cut through all the layers of clothing I had on for the flight. The beast got low and it looked as if it were going to pounce, so I drew my sidearm and shot at the ground in front of it. The round threw rocks into the creature and it yelped and ran back to the tree line. This gave me enough time to make it to the boxcar ladder. I climbed one-handed so I could shoot the wolf if it tried to jump me on the ladder—and sure enough, it did. I was just out of the animal's reach when I heard its body slam against the train car and its teeth snap at the air like a steel trap. The animal growled and then howled loudly, seemingly angry that it lost its lunch. I holstered my pistol and readied my carbine. I didn't want to shoot the creature—it didn't know any better—but I would if I had to. I jumped to the next car and the enraged animal followed, howling again.

Four more wolves emerged from the trees and paced the ground below. They looked up at me hungrily, their faces stuck in perpetual snarls. I was literally one step away from being ripped apart.

I jumped to the next boxcar to see if they would follow, and they did. The alpha was injured, but I think this only made him angrier, more determined. On my next jump, the alpha got between the trains and jumped on the linkage, trying to get to me. He slipped and fell to the other side of the track, thrashing in anger. I was at least a hundred meters from the transmission clearing and another two hundred meters to the ultralight. There was literally no way to make it without dealing with the wolf pack below.

The alpha returned to the pack and grabbed one of the smaller wolves by the neck, tossing it to the ground and barking. The smaller wolf stepped to the rear of the pack and then they all continued to snarl and snap at me from below. Reluctantly, I put the crosshairs on the alpha's heart, but intentionally shot the ground in front of it again. The other four retreated to the tree line, but the alpha kept growling and jumping halfway up the boxcar at me.

I didn't really want the associated bad karma, but I had no choice. I put the crosshairs on the alpha once more and took two shots to make sure the creature didn't feel pain. One in the chest, and one in the head. The alpha didn't even yelp before his large body hit the rocks near the track. I placed a few warning shots at the ground in front of the rest of the pack, and they scattered into the adjacent forest, barking as they went.

I waited for a few moments, examining my shoulder to gauge how bad it was. Blood blisters were already forming where the fangs pinched my arm; a hard-core bruise would soon follow. My right hand still suffered from the cut, and my left shoulder throbbed from the dead alpha wolf, which apparently possessed the jaw pressure of a T-Rex. I tested my upper body range of motion to make sure I could manipulate the ultralight controls.

With the wolf barks gone, I moved down the ladder and headed for the transmission clearing. Instead of hugging the tree line up the path to the ultralight, I gave it about fifteen feet of buffer in case one of those land sharks decided to pounce on me again.

I cut into the forest and located the ultralight. I did a quick walk around the airframe, checking the oil, fuel levels, and coolant. It needed some gas, but it would keep me airborne for forty-five minutes with what it had in the tank, not including the battery.

I pulled the nose off the ground and dragged the airframe behind me to the clearing. When the main gear snapped a twig, I dropped the nose and pulled my gun. Damn wolves in my head. I eventually got the ultralight into the clearing facing the takeoff direction. After a quick preflight focusing on the wing pins, wing material, and other failure points, I started the engine. With the temps and RPMs looking good, I commenced takeoff and rotated early in the cold winter air with no cargo. Avoiding the lines above, I banked to the right and climbed over the train and the surrounding forest. I offset the train a few hundred meters and flew north so that I could visually let Rich know I was okay. I was afraid that he might have heard my unsuppressed pistol shot.

Keeping one eye on the terrain and the other on the train, I spotted the lone solar panel that was the visual marker that I was passing our sleep boxcar. A few seconds later, moving at a good clip, I could see Rich laying prone on top of the overpass. I rocked my wings and caught him waving. I turned back southwest away from the train for a few minutes before risking a call. Good luck to Peterson with geolocating a moving aircraft.

"Pontiac, Toyota, wildlife delay. Hope you need a coat. On mission. Risk no response. Toyota out," I transmitted to Rich from a safe distance.

I could only imagine what the radio chatter sounded like on his end when he switched over to police comms.

I climbed in a corkscrew pattern over the forest. This reduced my exposure to anyone on the streets below. I was high enough to avoid engine noise detection and radio towers, but low enough to see the detail on the ground. Although I didn't tell Rich, my main focus was to track where the buses might have gone that day we observed them speeding under our train.

I flew west to I-49 before turning back east down MLK and left on Razorback. I wanted to approach from the opposite direction of the train, just in case. Overhead MLK, I dropped down to a thousand feet and slowed the aircraft. I was barely able to maintain altitude at this speed, but I wanted a good look at the stadium.

Heavy concentration of tents on the football field; I could see people walking around inside. I kicked the engine over to electric and got low over the field, flying in circles. Some people took notice and started pointing. After the first uniformed agent took a shot at me with his rifle, I kicked back over the internal combustion and went full throttle north out of there.

Clearing the stadium to avoid gunfire, I almost missed it. Below my main gear mounts, I saw a massive parking lot with one large tent in the center and at least ten thousand people outside. A ten-foot-high double-layer razor wire fence circled the parking lot and part of the field to the north. I saw two men with a dog patrolling between the two razor wire fences. Three white buses were parked on the street adjacent to the fences. Once again, I could see the people pointing up at me, and the guards taking aim. I started to climb higher, taking notice of my chronometer. I'd been airborne for thirty minutes.

With my wool watch cap and a bandanna holding my two-way in place on my left ear, I heard a ringing sound.

"Go for Toyota," I transmitted.

"RTB, dragonfly inbound. Pontiac out."

I yanked the controls and banked the ultralight southeast in the direction of the train. There was a helicopter inbound, so I had to get high and fast. From Rich's intercepts, I assumed the chopper was coming from Benton, the adjacent county. If they were airborne, that meant that they could be here in ten minutes, and probably triple my airspeed. Although it was only as useful as a child's teddy bear in my current situation, I verified my M4 was still strapped to the seat on my right. It was, and it made me feel a little better. Over the train, I got spooked.

What if someone on the ground spots me descend, or if I was some-how being tracked by radar? I thought.

I then made the decision to push for Black Oak, to the safety of my shelter.

"Pontiac, Toyota, do not wait up on me. Do not respond. Out," I said, hoping Rich copied.

Over Highway 16, my tank ran out and the prop began to act as a barn door. I began to fall from the sky.

The drag from the prop threw me forward in my seat against the five-point harness. I switched to electrics and began to maintain altitude. I was at seven thousand feet, well over a mile high, so I could conserve power by cutting the electric RPM to accept a slow descent. At this altitude, I couldn't see much detail below, just the winding road and familiar buildings.

Overhead Black Oak Baptist Church, I again corkscrewed, but this time in the other direction. Losing about a thousand feet per turn, I cut the throttles on my sixth revolution and touched down, kicking up frozen cow patties on home pasture.

I taxied the ultralight to the edge of the field, away from the county road. I could see the evergreen branches that I piled on top of my ATV. They were beginning to turn brown. As soon as I shut down the aircraft, I gassed her up with the reserves cached on the cargo rack of my ATV. No use leaving the tank empty; might have to leave in a hurry. After camouflaging the aircraft, I hoofed it to the shelter, not wanting to risk starting up an engine. I didn't have enough situational awareness to know who was in the woods these days.

My shoulder throbbed where the wolf chomped me. I didn't take any pain medicine before leaving, as I didn't want my flying affected. I was pretty sure I had some ibuprofen in the shelter, and dammit, I needed it.

The walk in was quiet, but I wasn't getting surprised again. My carbine was at high ready; neither wolves, government agents, nor Bigfoot were going to get the drop on me again. Fortunately, I arrived at the shelter anticlimactically. It looked like rain was coming.

After checking my caches and truck, I entered the shelter. The air inside smelled stale, prompting me to check the battery banks and turn on the ventilation. The charge was sitting at 90 percent. There was substantially more room inside now; I'd previously moved a third of my supplies to the train. A quiet sound on the hatch outside prompted me to again reach for a gun, but it was only the rain.

Thirsty, I took an empty water bottle from the bedside and went topside to collect some rainfall from a nearby tarp cover. I drank two full bottles and headed back inside to escape the biting cold. I stripped naked and hung my clothes under the inlet vent and lay on the bunk, thinking of what I had witnessed today.

The people inside that fence were prisoners—there could be no question about that. I saw men, women, and small children down there. I had to get them out, or at least give them a chance.

This was all my fault to begin with.

Maggie knew; she knew in her heart and could have stopped this. Thinking of that made me feel angry, guilty, and ashamed all at the same time. Why would we do this to ourselves? What could have possibly been the goal? These were the questions I asked myself a hundred times a day but could never find so much as a even a path to the answers.

I rested until the rain relented, and the sun was low in the sky. It wasn't any use heading back tonight; the sky remained gray and unwelcoming. Getting caught in high winds in an ultralight was a death sentence.

Leaving the shelter with my carbine and bowie, I decided to hike up to where the house used to stand. I hadn't even cleared the trees near my house and I could see the hulk of the disabled MRAP in my front yard. The barriers were still up at the top of my drive, but there wasn't any sign of activity. This place was forgotten by everyone but me. All the memories, all the times Jim and I had our grand adventures in our own Hundred Acre Wood—those were what was important. Not the house that once stood here.

Back at the shelter, I fired up the propane stove and prepared some rice and canned chicken. A bottle of hot sauce would have been nice, but the meal suited me fine. I wondered what most of the town's population were eating tonight, especially the people inside the razor wire of that gulag. I planned to bring a few bags of rice back with me to mix with the soup; I had the surplus payload.

I'm tired and sore from the wolf attack, so I was happy to find a bottle of ibuprofen with the kit I had stored here underground. My alarm is set for three in the morning; hopefully I can be airborne before sunup.

My watch alarm went off but I ignored it for a few minutes, halfway between consciousness. I lay there in that limbo, running scenarios in my head, asking myself how much daylight I'd need to see the power lines when I landed at the clearing. At the same time, for some reason, I thought about time travel. In my mind I wondered why the movies never accounted for the sun's helical orbit around the Milky Way, or our galaxy's movement in the cosmos. Send a DeLorean back in time, and it would end up somewhere in deep space, waiting years for the Earth to catch up. Perhaps this was my subconscious wishing for a do-over, a second chance to go back before everything went to shit.

Forcing myself to sit up, I hit the overhead lights. I felt a shallow breeze from the top of the shelter. Shit, I'd left the ventilation fan on. Battery banks were now down to 83 percent. But my clothes were dry, thanks to my ventilation oversight, so I got dressed and kitted up for the hump back to the ultralight.

On my first trip, I carried one bag of rice. The second round trip, I risked using the ATV so I could transport more supplies.

With a full five-gallon gas can strapped to the ultralight, along with a few bags of rice and other odds and ends, I was ready for takeoff. I had some time to spare, as I wanted to arrive on top of the LZ at five so that I could see the power lines—I'd left my night vision monocular on the train. I picked a better hiding spot for the ATV and cut some fresh branches with the new bowie to cover it. The quarter-inch-thick blade chopped branches like an axe; it only took five minutes to completely conceal the ATV with fresh foliage.

On preflight, I noticed a hole in my starboard wing the size of a 5.56 round. One of the guards from yesterday. I covered the hole on both sides with Band-Aids until I could get some duct tape to effect a better repair.

Preflight complete, aircraft gassed and ready, and cargo strapped. I pulled the nose around on a departure heading, strapped in, and tightened the goggles over my watch cap. By the time I took off, I noticed the faint glow of beginning light in the east. I climbed to three thousand and followed the road to the tracks, descended to two thousand and flew north along them. I established an orbit over the LZ for ten minutes until certain of the location of the power lines. Confident, I timed my entry into the corkscrew and shacked the landing fairly well.

I folded the wings and dragged the aircraft into the trees, cutting some more foliage for camouflage. I hid the fuel in a separate location not far from the ultralight and used the heavy tarp I'd brought back with me to form a makeshift pack using some cordage. I managed to fit three bags of rice in my expedient homemade backpack; the rest could wait until later.

Exiting the woods, a beeping sound fought through several

layers of clothing from somewhere inside. I took a knee, startled by the noise. It was five in the morning; there was no wind. The beeping sound seemed louder than those shoplifting alarms that always went off because the clerk forgot to deactivate something.

Locating the radio, I reluctantly keyed the microphone. "Go."

The response was immediate. "Toyota, Pontiac, status Railfan."

"Damn it, Rich, I didn't bring the book—it was only supposed to be a quick scout," I said aloud.

I couldn't acknowledge him for fear of signal triangulation near the ultralight, and I didn't want Rich to transmit the meaning of the code word for the same reason. I dropped my makeshift pack full of rice near one of the transmission line poles and headed down the hill, greeted by the rising sun. Carbine ready, I spilled out onto the railway clearing and hugged the train north to the sleep car. I thought it strange that the wolf carcass was missing, but kept moving.

As I crept north, I heard a loud metal clanging sound ahead. With the train sitting on a slight curve in the tracks, I could only see twenty cars ahead from where I was. Passing another car, I discovered the source of the noise. At least ten people were taking turns trying to pry the lock from one of the boxcars up ahead.

I ducked under the train to approach from the other side. As I slowly passed another boxcar, I heard a loud thumping sound, different from the metallic clanging. Reaching another car I heard it again: *thump*. I passed another gap between boxcars: *thump*.

This time the sound was right above my head. Dammit, I should have known. Someone was jumping roof to roof between boxcars.

"Franky, get your fuckin' ass back here! It's your turn to work the fuckin' lock!" I heard coming from up ahead.

I sat down with my back to the boxcar wheel. *Thump*.

I felt the energy from Franky's jump as it traveled from the roof to the boxcar walls to the wheel I braced against. He was on my car. I could hear his boots as they struck the rungs of the ladder and again when they landed on the gravel rail bed.

Peeking past the boxcar wheel, I saw combat boots and camo pant legs move up the tracks in the direction of the others who struggled with the boxcar lock. I waited until Franky opened up some distance before I shadowed him from the other side of the train, walking from rail tie to rail tie to remain quiet. Five cars away, I decided to crawl under the train and take a peek at what I was dealing with.

With my optic dialed in at 4×, I counted eight men armed with blunt weapons and fixed-blade knives. One was brandishing a shotgun, practically begging to shoot the lock. I watched as comedy ensued. I heard something like "Go ahead" right before the man aimed his shotgun at the hardened metal lock attached to the metal boxcar and pulled the trigger.

The ear-shattering loud report from the shotgun was followed by at least three different screams of "You shot me!" in unison. It turns out lead buckshot will ricochet off hardened steel. The shooter was cupping his balls and the other idiots applied pressure to wounds on their legs and stomachs.

"I need a fuckin' doctor!" the shooter exclaimed to whomever would listen.

"Quit whining before I snap a picture of you with that shotgun and send it in," one of the men threatened. "I could use a month's worth of food right about now." The other men nodded their heads in agreement.

Hearing that, things went from comedy hour to serious business. Knowing that they had phones and wouldn't hesitate to burn me with them meant that I'd have to kill them all if I were discovered.

The leader began tapping something on his phone.

"We'll wait on the Hub," I heard him say.

As I pondered my best course of action, I heard multiple text alerts from the gang of eight. Just like before all this went down, the Pavlovian scavengers instantly drew their phones like Old West six-shooters and began gazing at the screens.

"Food!" I heard the leader yell as they all ran for the bridge.

The three injured men tried to keep up, eventually disappearing north behind the curvature of the train. With the scavengers now gone, I emerged on the familiar side of the boxcar. The sleeping car was locked up tight when I arrived—no sign of Rich.

After waiting nearby on Rich for an hour, I decided to look for a spot to make camp. With wolves, feral dogs, and other animals likely on the loose, I didn't feel good about sleeping on the ground. From the feel of the air, I guessed it would drop below freezing tonight. Before heading into the trees, I backtracked to the coal cars. I filled my cargo pants and jacket with as much coal as I could fit and headed back to the cover of the woods. This was much faster than making a lot of noise looking for good firewood, and it would burn longer and hotter.

The spot I chose was a hundred meters from both the power lines and the train tracks. I wanted to be able to hear the scavengers. I don't use my knife to dig like Rich does. In fact, it makes me cringe a bit when he does it, knowing how rocky the ground is here in the Ozarks. Also, it would be an awkward task with a twelve-inch bowie; instead, I fashioned a decent shovel from a piece of dry wood and used it to dig a hole for the coal. After that, I shaved a good bit of wood from the shovel and topped it off with some old-man's beard from a nearby tree. Coal was particular, and could be an ass kicker to start compared to a plain wood campfire. Of course, if Rich were here, he'd already have it started without any kindling. Hobo skills.

There were enough rocks out here on the forest floor to build a castle, and if I had the time, that's exactly what I'd do. I settled with a decent fire ring stacked a foot high to absorb a lot of heat. With the fire prepped for tonight, I went back to the power pole to recover my pack full of rice. With the food safely cached back at my expedient campsite, I used the tarp pack to get more coal. I returned with about fifty pounds of it. Of course, my lighter was locked inside the train, but I always keep a fire steel in my coat and there was five gallons of gasoline cached fifty meters away from camp.

I was armed but cut off from my supplies; Rich had the keys to the kingdom sitting on his belt. I had nearly a full Glock mag, plus two fifteen-round backups, but only one spare M4 mag if things went kinetic.

Rifle>pistol>knife>fisticuffs.

I wasn't night vision capable right now either, so tonight was going to be interesting. My only flashlights were mounted to my firearms, and my spare 123 batteries were also locked up tight in the supply car. I dumped the fifty pounds of coal into a pile near my fire ring and unraveled the heavy tarp. Repurposing the 550 cordage I used to construct the pack, I wrapped tarp material from each end around a small rock and tied them off, forming two rock anchors. With this new, expedient hammock now at my disposal, I placed it six feet up between two trees near the fire ring. Testing it out, it wasn't exactly comfortable, but it would keep me off the cold ground and allow me to absorb the radiant heat from the coal fire.

By the time I had a proper camp set up I was fairly hungry, so I recovered one of the cans of chicken I'd stashed on the ultralight. I didn't want to risk a fire in the middle of the day, so I enjoyed it cold and was damn happy to have it. I sat on a rock bench I'd rolled into the camp and listened for any two-way traffic. There was none. Just to be thorough, I scouted both the sleeping car and our tactics and supply car with no joy. The locks were securely fastened. Walking past the boxcar that those men shot, I saw only cosmetic damage. I wondered why the scavengers picked this boxcar until I noticed the spray-painted graffiti cheeseburger painted on the door. Morons.

With no communications from Rich and the train locked up tight, I headed back to camp. At three p.m. the temperature dropped to around forty, leaving me shivering as I waited on the darkness to come.

The unmistakable sound of helicopter rotors cut through the air to the north. The rotors got louder before fading, over and over again signifying that the helicopter was on an orbit. I heard it until the sun dipped behind the trees at four.

I couldn't wait any longer. My core temperature was dropping, the heat robbed by the rock I rested upon. Using the spine of my blade, I struck bright sparks into the kindling for a long while before it took, encircling the coal in flame. Once the coal took, it began to billow heavy smoke. As the fire spread through the coal, intense heat radiated, warming the camp in all directions. The rocks surrounding the coal fire absorbed the intense heat; the expanding gases trapped inside escaped as the rocks popped and snapped like firewood.

With the fire raging, I placed two more handfuls of coal in the center before climbing up into the tarp hammock with my M4 and radio. Sleep came in waves; the coal smoke shifted with the wind, sometimes waking me up, sometimes sparing me for an hour.

Somewhere in REM sleep, dreaming of talking cheeseburgers, I heard a whispering voice: "Max, wake up."

My gloved hand indexed my carbine when I heard it again; this time I was awake: "Psst. Max!"

Peeling the tarp away from my face, I looked out at the camp. "Rich?"

"Yeah, it's me. I can see you, but you can't see me. Using your handy gadget. Found you by the smell. Can't keep a hobo away from a coal fire, you know."

"What the hell happened?"

"Talk about it in the morning. I brought my bag—we should stay here tonight. Give the train a rest," Rich said, laying his bedroll out next to the fire.

"You know, I'm sleeping up here because there's wolves about."

"My meat is too old and tough for any wolf," he said dismissively.

Rich put another handful of coal in the fire and was asleep before I could climb out of my hammock for a bathroom break. It was a lot warmer on the ground near the fire; Rich's bravado made me rethink climbing back up into the colder hammock. Like wolves, we were pack animals. I boiled some bottled water from Rich's seabag in my empty chicken can and made some pine needle tea. I could hear dogs barking far away between the metronome of snores.

———

I stayed up late at the campsite, sitting by the fire, drinking my tea. After racking out an hour before sunup, Rich took his shift, putting handfuls of coal on the fire every once in a while. Snow started falling hard after I turned in—I woke up with two inches on the ground. The fire warded off the worst of it for us; still, it was a miserable night. Remembering World War One history and how those men slept in freezing foxholes half full of water made me buck up.

I woke up at about seven with the sun already a few fists up the eastern sky. Rich had found the rice and was cooking breakfast—soup and rice.

"Mornin', Max," he said gruffly.

"Morning. So tell me, why did we sleep out here on the ground instead of in the train?"

"Well, after I warned you about the helo and copied your last radio call, I thought I might not see you again for a bit. I left the train and disappeared into the woods until the chopper was done looking for you. It eventually called bingo fuel and headed back north to Benton County."

"So why lock the train on me?" I said, the pain in my back from sleeping on the ground reminding me of the night before.

"I set up shop out here in the woods and kept listening. I overheard Peterson say on the radio that he was sending a text to his peon distro asking for some recon around the train overpass at MLK. He wanted his MRAP strike team on alert until the recon was complete. He didn't specifically order the informers to search the train, but he did say to search around the bridge."

"What did he tell them to do if they found anything?"

"Pictures . . . he wanted them to text pictures to what he's calling 'the Hub.' His orders were to follow suspects and update the Hub with any changes until backup arrived. You see, Peterson has created thousands of full-time spies, paying them with pennies in government-stockpiled food. He doesn't need an army of black-uniform-wearing goons driving MRAPs when he has thousands of hungry people killing one another to work for him. The irony is that the informers paid in advance for their own Big

Brother smartphones and had been behaviorally programmed to carry them their whole lives."

"Oh God. We're in trouble," I said, shaking my head in despair.

"Especially when these devices are tracked in real time, pictures geotagged, and have the potential to be activated as a remote video device anytime Peterson wants. He's even enabling less restricted phone capability as payment for services rendered. Want outgoing calls? Complete a mission. These people have been slaves to the machine so long, they'll kill another human being for it."

"Let's break camp and regroup at the tactics car," I suggested.

We doused the fire and slogged through the snow, carrying our supplies to the train.

"Oh, by the way, I skinned your wolf. The pelt is hanging in a tree at my cold camp closer to the bridge. I had to flesh and brain it in near dark. Funny how nature always gives you enough brain to tan the hide of its owner, 'cept some people I know."

I had no idea what he was talking about, but didn't want to sound ignorant about the wolf-tanning process, naturally. "That thing almost killed me, along with a few of its buddies."

"I was hoping that was the case. Beautiful animal. Shame you had to do that."

"Yes, it was."

"Well, it's your skin. We'll go back for it later. Might need to brain it again."

At the bottom of the transmission line hill, Rich recovered his key ring from a hiding spot at the base of an H pole. The coast appeared clear, so we leapfrogged to our destination, covering each other along the way.

Once inside the train, we unloaded our kit and strategized. From the way I looked at the problem, it was all about centers of gravity, links, and nodes. The bad guys were using the cellular network as a force multiplier, enabling full-spectrum dominance of Washington County. Rich and I couldn't walk down the street without one of our friendly neighbors snapping a picture of us because we might look suspicious. I'm sure Peterson's crew didn't have the manpower to investigate all the leads, but if enough of the same people kept showing up in his "Hub" database . . .

Rich and I were outcasts; we'd been unplugged from the grid too long. We couldn't fit in at this point. We were not integrated with the system. Walking down the street, it wouldn't take long for one of the thousands of citizen sensor operators to inform on us. Wearing a backpack? Terrorist. Slicing an apple with a pocketknife? Terrorist. Not in possession of a slavephone? Terrorist. Hell, maybe we really *are* terrorists . . . or is it freedom fighters? How about just survivors?

Best I could figure, the main center of gravity was Peterson's spy grid. We couldn't just disable it; we had to destroy it. Simply put, this meant that high explosives needed to find their way to cell tower and network nodes. Peterson's critical capabilities were his men and his armored MRAPs. We couldn't fight those unless we took out the supply chain that fueled them, and we just didn't have the intel to make that happen at this point. What we did have was a working aircraft to spot the cell towers and mark them on a map. I explained to Rich that the best effect would be to spot the targets by day, and destroy them under the cover of darkness.

———

Finding targets was the easy part: Look for high terrain, see a cell tower. The day after the snow, I repaired the bullet hole in the ultralight's wing fabric and took off after the helicopter went bingo fuel and returned to its home base in Benton County. At six thousand

feet, I was high enough to avoid ground detection, but it was no-
ticeably colder than at two thousand. Rich ran protection on the
radio in case the helo got word to scramble back to Washington
County to intercept me after refueling.

Cruising at altitude over Fayetteville, I headed for Mount
Sequoyah, the tallest peak in the area. After two passes, I spotted something that didn't look right—a perfectly symmetrical
two-hundred-foot evergreen. As an Arkansan, I've never seen a
two-hundred-foot tree in my life. The faux pine was inside of a
square fence adjacent to a small building. Obviously a disguised
cell tower designed to not be an eyesore. The whole micro telecom facility was surrounded by forest with nice houses sprinkled
in the vicinity. Lowering my altitude and switching my angle of
observation, I saw a MRAP parked outside the fence. I snapped
as many one-handed pictures as I could before heading back to
the train.

There were no private cars or trucks on the road. I did see a
wolf pack of motorcycles heading down 71, but the night we set a
trap for them confirmed they were working for Peterson; they were
willing wards of the superstate.

After landing and debriefing Rich, we started to analyze the
pictures via the three-inch screen of his camera. Not ideal, but we
didn't have anything else to work with. At least we had an indefinite
trickle of electricity coming down from the boxcar roof to power it.
We couldn't operate with impunity with the existing civilian command-and-control structure working against us.

Rich paused on one of the pictures and zoomed in. "There's
a MRAP sitting there next to the cell tower fence. That's, what, a
fifty-cal on top?"

"Yeah, most likely."

"We can't go up against that. We'll get mowed in half."

"I thought about that on the flight back. There are ways to take out an MRAP. The insurgents did it in Iraq on a regular basis. The problem is it involves specific materials and some backyard ingenuity."

"What materials, exactly?" asked Rich.

I didn't really want to go into it with Rich, but he seemed very interested. Constructing what he was asking about was no small task.

"It's called an EFP, or explosively formed penetrator. We need explosives, which we have, but that won't punch through MRAP armor alone. We'll need to make a modern-day cannon, but not like you think. For starters, a housing cylinder for the explosives, and the most important part of the weapon is the 'lid.' Copper is best. It needs to be a quarter-inch thick, disk shaped and slightly concave, like a dinner plate. We match the copper 'dinner plate' diameter to our explosives housing cylinder, concave side out. When we detonate the charge, it forms the copper into a hypersonic, armor-busting, semi-cylindrical projectile. If built correctly, it will go through just about anything."

"Why didn't you say so?" Rich said. "We're sitting on a mountain of coal, have electricity for a blower, and all the parts to make my famous ten-dollar forge. We have a train car full of inch-coiled copper, and it's softer and easier to forge than steel. Making your dinner plates won't be hard. How many we need?"

I don't know why I kept underestimating Rich; perhaps I'm still looking at him through an old lens, judging him based on his age and lifestyle.

"Only one. A MRAP gets hit with this, and everything inside is dead from the heat and over pressure. You can make the copper plates from wire? How long will it take?"

"They won't be as good as if they were machined or came from a foundry, but they'll work, I'm sure."

"But how long?" I asked again.

"As I said, they won't possess perfect symmetry, but I can make the first prototypes within a few hours."

I drew up the plans on some scrap paper, including measurements based on the estimated thickness of the MRAP armor. The EFP device would need to be housed in eight-inch sections of cylindrical steel. One side solid steel, drilled for a detonator, and the other side Rich's forged copper dinner plates, held in place by two one-inch steel brackets after the explosives are packed. The steel brackets had two functions. One, to hold the copper penetrator tightly in place, and two, to help shape the copper as the explosive material blasts it from the steel housing at the MRAP.

After the plans were in place and Rich understood them, I began helping him construct his forge. We went from boxcar to boxcar acquiring pieces and parts and ended up constructing the basic forge in the doorway of the empty boxcar right next to our sleeping quarters. In the end, Rich's forge was made with nothing more than a small coal barbecue grill and a hair dryer. For an anvil he used the rails themselves; they were constructed from steel just as hard.

I've never seen so much copper, an entire boxcar full of massive coils that must have weighed tons each. Using a piece of firewood as a hammer, I started cutting long sections of wire by slamming the log down on my bowie knife. The spring steel was much harder than the pure copper and made short work of the task.

After harvesting the copper, I stood on top of Rich's forge car wearing night vision, keeping my M4 ready as the sun began to fade. Rich worked by headlamp, forging the red-hot copper on the cold steel rails. He employed the hardware that connected boxcars to hammer-forge the concave shape that was needed. I thought it would be louder, but Rich's hammer struck true most of the time. When it didn't, a dull pinging sound was the only indicator. As the dead of night came upon us, Rich finished three plates fitted to the housings he'd improvised. They looked pretty good. I could see the individual hammer strike marks in the bright, freshly forged copper. As I examined it by blue LED light, it reminded me of armor plates worn before the world revered iron and steel.

We shut down the forge at about one in the morning and moved the EFP hardware to our tactics car. Tomorrow, bright and early, I'd pack the charges and finalize the incursion into the city.

It didn't take long to shape the explosives inside Rich's EFP housings and affix the detonator caps. I formed the stuff as tight as I could get it, stuffing wood spacers into the cylinder around the C4 to eliminate any shifting. If the explosives favored one side of the cylinder over the other, it could skew the projectile. Each device weighed about twenty-five pounds once constructed. I couldn't use the ultralight—it was much too dangerous to risk landing near the target in the city, and the terrain was too uneven to allow it anyway. I'd be going alone; Rich would move operations to the camp, where I would meet him after the mission was complete. I used the remaining hours of daylight to organize my kit.

Loadout:

EFP
Demo explosives
Wire
Clacker
Duct tape
Two-way radio

NVD
Batteries
Suppressed M4 w/ 3 spare mags
Glock w/ 2 spare mags
Bowie w/ fire striker
ZT folder
Three cans of soup
Can of rice
Water
Sterno
Lighter
Hank of 550
Sixty pounds of kit, seven miles

I made my final comms coordination with Rich, going over the code words likely to be used before jumping down from the boxcar.

Rich swung my pack to me, saying, "Godspeed with this heavy thing."

Instead of moving north toward the bridge in the direction of the target, I had a thought. I went south, prompting Rich to shout from the boxcar down the tracks, "Wrong way, ain't it?"

"I don't know yet—tell you in a few minutes," I said as I disappeared behind the curvature of the train.

The pack was heavy, but endurable. The only problem was that I'd need to ditch it if I had to get away in a hurry, and that wasn't an option. Without the contents of the pack, the mission was a failure. I didn't want to be self-imprisoned on that train for the rest of my life until Peterson's goons brought up our number, like they did with my family.

Thinking of them caused me to move a little faster, stand a little taller, but I knew that edge would wear off at about the five-mile mark, or the first time I had to jump in a muddy ditch at the sight of headlights. I kept moving in the opposite direction toward the railroad crossing. I had about twenty minutes of usable light remaining.

Not long after passing the lead locomotive engine, I saw a group of people crossing the tracks ahead a few hundred meters. I dropped prone and placed them inside my carbine optic. In the fading light at 4×, I could see that they were just kids, probably heading home to beat curfew; I would bet they had phones. Everyone in this new system was a threat until proven otherwise.

I reached my destination as the sun disappeared. The motorcycles were exactly where Rich and I last saw them. I went over both bikes. They'd been shot up, but only one had critical damage to the radiator. The other hog had only cosmetic pings on its gaudy chrome. Unfortunately the bike that worked was the one with a human head still sitting in its saddlebag. I removed the bag and slung it over a branch so the animals couldn't get at it, and put the other saddlebag from the dead bike onto the good one. Noticing the garden hose on the handlebars, I siphoned gasoline from the other bike until it began to overflow the tank and spill down the sides of the custom-painted gas tank. With my breath and hands reeking of gasoline, I pushed the ride out into the open, near the tracks. I detached the headlight electrical connection and placed duct tape over all the reflectors, turn signals, and taillight.

The bikes had been abandoned for a while, so I was relieved when I turned the gas tank switch position to accessory, illuminating the console. I kicked the hog down into neutral, blasting my eyes with another console light. Using the duct tape, I covered anything that would wash out my night vision monocular. I mounted the bike and squeezed the clutch before turning the switch over two clicks to ignition. I had to push the start button twice to cycle the engine enough to start. I revved it up a few thousand RPMs and it sounded great, confidence inspiring. The speedometer read one twenty, but I seriously doubted I'd ever see that. Much of the snow would be melted on the roads, but there would be patches of ice here and there.

I kicked it down into first and revved the engine, letting go of the clutch. The back wheel threw rocks as I drifted the bike around in a one-eighty, heading north along the tracks.

Through my night vision monocular over my right eye, I could see light spilling out of a crack in the door of a boxcar up ahead. I saw only faint starlight through my unassisted left eye.

I stopped next to the door. "Found a ride."

Rich's white beard was visible before the rest of his face. "Wow. Giddy-up!"

He jumped down from the train and locked the door, heading south to the campsite with his hobo roll, radio, and rifle. I sped north on the uneven terrain, constantly fighting the motorcycle until I reached the bridge. After a brief scare brought on by the unexpected steepness of the hill leading to the main road below the train, I was on my way. I easily but carefully cut through all the wrecks and abandoned cars up and down Highway 71. Parts were slickened by icy patches between cars that saw less sunlight. If I was in my truck, I could have never navigated the road. When I reached the old courthouse that my great-grandfather helped build, I turned right, leaving 71 business.

Through my right eye, I could see some light spillage from the motorcycle console, but not much. I could also see the Milky Way clearly in the sky, its light magnified by technology. Looking down at my hip, lights from the tritium rear sight on my Glock were amazingly bright. I saw two different worlds, one in each eye. I was on the road that went past the projects, if that's what they could even be qualified as. Just a few state-run apartment buildings, nothing like the squalor of some major cities.

I saw the reflection of a stop sign ahead, and for reasons I can't explain, even now, I slowed down in preparation to stop. As I did this, I was temporarily blinded by a flash of white light. At first I thought someone was shooting at me, but there was no sound. As soon as my optic recovered from the whiteout, I saw a man standing there in the darkness, his phone pointed right at me—now a weapon more powerful than a gun.

I hit the gas and the bike began to growl, speeding me through the four-way stop, leaving the informer behind. The Hub would have my picture in a few seconds, and the MRAPs and swarm of bikers would soon follow. I cranked back on the gas, moving at breakneck speed down the back roads, turning and turning like a Tron Light Cycle. My two-way radio vibrated inside my jacket. Rich already knew, and was trying to warn me.

I cut into the entrance of an overgrown cemetery, switched off, and dumped the bike behind a large tombstone covered in thick moss and snow. I used the dead and artificial flowers from the nearby graves to cover any exposed motorcycle chrome.

Escaping the cemetery for a row of nearby homes, I prayed that no one would find the bike. I didn't have the key needed to lock the ignition. Moving slowly under the cumbersome weight of my pack, I went house to house, looking for any that might be suitable. None of them were occupied. They didn't have garages, and no vehicles sat in the driveways I knew I took at least half a dozen turns before stumbling upon the cemetery, and it was one I'd never seen. The incoming force couldn't know I was here.

I chose the house with a view overlooking the cemetery and

set up observation in the kitchen. I didn't risk transmitting, but left my radio within earshot in case Rich heard something worthy from his end. After an intense two hours of waiting, I heard the two-way beep.

"Bahama."

It was Rich's voice, and that was the code word for all clear. I shouldered my pack and shuffled back to the graveyard, noticing the arching metal sign over the entrance that read "CONFEDER-ATE CEMETERY." This explained why most of the gravestones were just large sandstone rocks, their markings long erased by time and neglect. I felt the surface of a stone and could almost make out the grooves of a letter; it was the last remnant of whoever lay below.

After nearly throwing out my back to upright the bike, I was on my way again. Although I didn't see it with my own eyes, I hoped that all the motorcycle activity in response to my presence would mask mine. I wasn't far from where I needed to travel the rest on foot. Looking for a place to hide the bike, I found a burned-down house, its garage also mostly burned and caved on one side. I rolled down the driveway and was able to walk the bike backwards under the fallen structure and inside what remained of the garage.

I sat down, smelling charred timber and plastic. I again went through my kit, thinking ahead to what I would need next and in what order. I made sure my two-way was set to vibrate before I duct taped it to the shoulder strap of my pack, as well as placing the EFP and duct tape on top before closing my pack, satisfied with its organization.

Through my night vision monocular, I could see the faux tree half-hidden by terrain, including a steep grade hill I'd need to summit. I moved as fast as I could up the hill, but winded myself quickly and had to slow my pace about halfway up.

After peaking the hill, I had a clear line of sight to the facility. The MRAP, adjacent to the building, and the tower base were all illuminated by bright lights. This meant that they weren't using night vision, and I had a pretty good advantage if I remained in the shadows.

I closed to within fifty meters of the facility, but still well out of its light radius. Dropping my pack on the snow-covered grass, I removed the EFP, clacker, and tape. Using the chunk of charcoal I brought, I then blackened my face and pulled my watch cap down over my ears. I press checked my carbine to ensure a round was in the chamber, checked the safety, and slung it across my back.

I crept in slow and low around the bright arc of light that protected this command-and-control node. If the tower was the center of a clock, I was at nine o'clock but needed to move to three o'clock without setting foot in the light. I crept along, passing high noon and then one.

Movement. Two guards left the small building, walked through the open gate, and went to the MRAP, where one of them rapped on the driver's window. I couldn't hear what they were saying but it looked like a watch turnover. The man in the driver's seat got out and was replaced by the new guard. The offgoing gunner didn't leave the MRAP until his shift replacement closed his door. Smart. The entire MRAP crew was never exposed during watch turnover. The offgoing guards then disappeared inside the small building. I noted the time: 2200 hours.

The fresh gunner briefly got behind the fifty-cal on top of the MRAP. I could hear him check the action on the slide, verifying the status of his crew-served weapon. After checking the gun, he disappeared inside the bowels of the armored steel beast.

Keeping a close eye on the MRAP, I began the placement and wiring of the EFP. I chose a tree barely outside the light radius to attach the device. This thing was homemade, not Iranian precision machined. The closer I could get, the higher my probability of a kill. This wasn't the type of explosive you could just tape to a telephone pole and forget about; its copper "dinner plate" had to be aimed, food side out, directly at the target prior to detonation. The employment resembled that of a cannon more than anything else. Place explosives behind your projectile, aim, and hope you don't miss.

Now only twenty meters from the MRAP, I worked quickly, motivated to return to the darkness. The longer I remained in the gray area between the two light extremes, the higher the chance of receiving fifty-caliber incoming. I knew the turret on top of the MRAP was open to the interior, so I had to be quiet with the explosive work. But, God almighty, I'd never heard duct tape this loud as I wrapped the roll around the tree and the EFP.

When I was finished, I stepped back to admire my own handiwork. All good. I was satisfied with the device azimuth and elevation; it should impact the driver's side and pass through part of the engine. I began running the wire counterclockwise to midnight around the light radius of the facility. The detonation wire could reach no farther—I simply didn't have enough to get me back to the nine o'clock position. I then attached one lead to the clacker. Twenty-three hundred hours.

I returned to my pack and reorganized everything again for the next phase. My plan was to wait for the next watch turnover and detonate the EFP while both sets of guards were potentially in the line of fire. At best, this was a sinister act of preemptive aggression, but I had to remind myself that I was dealing with scum, plain and simple; these were people that hired murderous criminals to help with their dirty work as they gunned down college kids or slaughtered families in their sleep. The system may have made me what I am today, but now they had to deal with the end result.

Back at the twelve o'clock position, I lay waiting in the grass and snow, weapon trained on the target area. This was the first time I noticed the extreme cold. Up to this point, I'd been so concentrated on the EFP and how I was going to bring down the Hub node after I neutralized the MRAP. At five minutes to midnight, light from the small building spilled out of the open door. I attached the final wire to the clacker and held it in my support hand.

As the two men passed through the open gate, only ten feet from the MRAP, I forced myself to think about Jim, Matt, my aunt, the college kids at the knoll, the body in the trunk, the severed head in the saddlebag, the mother and her hungry child, and, lastly, my mission to Syria, which started this whole shit in the first place. My blood ran cold as the men rounded the back of the MRAP. Just like before, the offgoing driver exited first and was quickly replaced by someone new. As soon as the rear door opened, I squeezed the clacker.

The explosion rocked the area, evident by the blast concussion and how it simultaneously threw snow and bent every blade of grass away from its epicenter. At the precise moment of detonation, a bright flash noted the impact of the copper projectile, no doubt now blast forged into a long, skinny piece of copper moving at six thousand miles per hour. The concussion didn't hurt me lying in the prone position, but it ripped the watch cap off my head.

A few milliseconds after the EFP impacted the MRAP between the driver and passenger doors, a secondary explosion sent the MRAP spinning a meter off the ground. The large vehicle landed on its side, the impact tremor shaking the area as it went up in flames. I looked up, thanking God for sparing me more screams.

I jumped to my feet and reached down for my pack. It wasn't where I left it, as the concussion rolled it a few feet away. I grabbed it and began recovering the wire I'd just used to detonate the EFP. Heading for the burning MRAP, my weapon was trained on two things, the approach road and the adjacent building. My first order of business was to destroy the electronics inside the building.

I wired three small charges to the equipment racks with most of the explosives that remained, saving the rest for the tower itself. The blinking equipment lights and sounds inside the telecom building brought me back to Damascus for a moment . . . and to Maggie. That seemed like a different life, so long ago. I wondered where she was now.

Enough. Need to focus. I shut the door and paid the wire out behind me all the way to the street. When I detonated the charge to the building, the door flew off and disappeared into the sky, impacting somewhere very distant. The charges weren't big enough to level the building, and that suited me just fine. Flames licked out of the top of the doorway when I raced past with the last bit of wire and explosives.

Half past midnight.

My ears were ringing from explosions, but I managed to push through and duct tape the remaining charge to the base of the tower. My two-way vibrated, indicating an incoming call.

I leaned my chin down to the shoulder strap and keyed the mic. "Go."

"Kitchen sink."

Running out of time. I strung the wire behind me and ran for the sturdiest thing I could get behind—the burning MRAP. I think I stepped on an ear as I hid behind the flaming wreck. The smell of burned flesh was pungent and I could actually see a skeleton forming inside, lumps of muscle falling from the bone due to the intense heat. Gagging, I squeezed the clacker, bringing about the final explosion. The concussion tossed debris against the vehicle, blowing the fire in my direction. The skin on my hands burned for a second or two until the pressure equalized and the fire retreated back to the vehicle, licking the corpses inside.

A great creaking sound followed and time slowed for a moment, giving me a second to regret the charge placement. I placed enough explosives to do the job, but mistakenly ran straight out from the charge. The falling tower bent at me. I rolled into the far side of the MRAP for cover, burning my clothes and the side of my face. When I didn't think I could take the heat any longer, the tower slammed into the MRAP. Fake branches and parts from the tower's emitter farm broke off from the fall, shattering against the ground and all around me. It was a miracle that I was still alive. I jumped away from the intense heat of the burning vehicle and held my face and hands to the freezing concrete, scraping some nearby snow against the burn to relieve the searing pain.

Forcing myself off the ground, I grabbed my pack, making sure my carbine and pistol were still with me, and headed for the cover of darkness beyond the clock of light. My burns would blister, but I'd survive. As I pressed forward to the burned garage, I knew I was in for a night of intense pain, but managed to reach shelter before that happened.

With the fire fading at my back, I risked a quick transmission. "Miller Time."

I received no response, as expected. I must have lain on my back for twenty shivering minutes before I could hear the cavalry pass by. I listened with the right side of my face pressed firmly against the cold concrete that provided a temporary reprieve from the searing pain. My hands fared better, but not by much. I took them off the concrete long enough to grab a few bottles of water. My skin was going to need it. I was about half a mile from the fallen tower, but could hear a lot of activity—at least one helicopter, multiple passing motorcycles, and MRAPs.

The last thing I wanted to do was be near an open flame, but I lit my Sterno can anyway. I hadn't eaten in hours. I lay on the concrete garage floor listening to the vehicles go back and forth, cooking my rice and soup on the blue flame. It would be suicide to get on the road now.

My night on the concrete slab was miserable, measured in cycles of what most would consider torture. In order to minimize the pain, I had to keep my face and hands on the concrete, but this drained my body heat. When I could feel hypothermia start to set in, I got on my feet and jogged in place, but this brought renewed agony from the burns. Back and forth: concrete, jogging, concrete, jogging, each round achieving its own special level of hell. More than once during this rhythm of madness I nearly broke down and started a fire. Only the constant sounds of motorcycle engines and the faint side spill of headlights into the garage kept me from risking it. As sunrise approached, the vehicles disappeared, but I was left to the solitude of endless pain and suffering. I'd left the codeine back at the train.

With the morning upon me, I now had to get off the ground and start improving my situation. One lone MRAP passed by on the road after sunup, likely dispatched to survey the damage in daylight. It wouldn't do them much good, as I had obliterated the tower for keeps. Once they saw the EFP damage to the flipped MRAP, they'd be shitting their pants. I took pleasure in knowing that they'd now have to manually show Peterson the photo. Can you hear me now, asshole?

On my feet, I rummaged through the third of the house that

remained standing, most of it the garage. The part of the kitchen that had survived the fire offered nothing that would help soothe my burns. Under the sink was a wastebasket full of rotting trash. It told the story of a different time. A discarded peanut butter jar revealed that the house burned a while back, in the beginning of all this before people began starving. Under the jar's tight lid I discovered a perfectly good teaspoon of peanut butter at the bottom. I indulged from the edge of my folding knife. It had been ages since I'd had any peanut butter. This wastebasket time capsule gave me the strength to carry on.

I moved to the next house, from back yard to back yard, lumbering over a six-foot-tall wooden privacy fence. Coming down the other side of the fence, the wood scraped the side of my face. Pure agony. I couldn't risk entering from the front, as I would be completely visible from the road. The back door was locked. Through the split curtains of an adjacent window, I could see furniture and chairs piled up behind the front door. To my right, the door leading from the kitchen to the dark garage was also open, as were most of the kitchen cabinets.

Satisfied that the house was abandoned, I started to breach the door. With the bowie, I chopped away some of the door trim, allowing me to wedge the quarter-inch-thick blade into the doorframe. I put my weight laterally into the blade, flexing the doorframe from the bolt. Eventually the door gave and I was inside. As I stepped into the kitchen, a noxious odor hit my face. It was an effort to keep from doubling over the sink to give up my precious teaspoon of peanut butter. Smelled like roadkill. The house might be home to a rabid attic skunk or raccoon since the collapse, so I held my carbine ready, illuminating the light mounted to the rails.

A half-full propane tank, some tools, and a kayak were the only things of value, but all were too cumbersome to deal with. I glanced at the kitchen, but was certain it was empty. As I moved down the hall, I ducked at the distinct engine sound of the approaching MRAP. Risking a glance through the curtains as it sped by, I hoped to see rage on the driver's face, courtesy of my handiwork. Unlike last night's ball-cap-wearing MRAP crew, this driver wore full body armor. The gunner on the roof was also ready for action; his fully armored torso rotated the gun back and forth, scanning for targets. If they thought for a second I was inside this house, they'd light it up, Swiss cheesing the whole structure to the ground, rabid skunks and all.

The burning pain in my face and hands reminded me of why I was in the house. In the first bedroom on the right I found the source of the smell. As I nudged the door open with the barrel of my carbine, the smell intensified. A male corpse hung motionless from an orange extension cord secured to a ceiling fan in the center of the room. Underneath the body was a stepladder kicked on its side. Aluminum gallows. I couldn't help but stare. The man's shriveled lips curled up to reveal yellow teeth. A prune-like tongue hung from the corner of his mouth.

"Keep your peanut butter, Max," I said aloud.

I noticed a wheel gun tucked into his pants and took it. The body swayed eerily back and forth, and the fan creaked. I feared the corpse would fall and crash on top of me, licking me with that dry tongue. I stepped back with the dead man's short-barrel .44 Magnum in hand. My fingers were coated in slime from the Hogue grip and cylinder. One full-speed loader sat on the bed, twelve rounds total. Using a nearby comforter, I wiped the slime from the gun and tucked it into my waistband. Poor bastard. I wondered why he didn't use the gun instead. With no suicide note in sight, I'd never know.

The other bedrooms yielded nothing that would be worth strapping to the motorcycle for the return trip. In the bathroom, I took two rolls of toilet paper and some dental floss before I checked under the sink. Bingo! Lotion with aloe.

Trying the sink, I heard only air being sucked into the pipes. I flung the lid from the toilet reservoir and, after skimming the stagnant water, I cleaned my face and hands. The pain reached a crescendo from the washing, so I began applying the lotion, not waiting for my skin to dry. The effect was immediate, but whether psychological or not, I didn't know. From peanut butter to aloe, the day was looking up.

I decided to barricade the back door with a dining room chair and get some shut-eye in the bedroom farthest from the corpse. This time, I only woke up every hour or so to come out from under my acquired mountain of blankets and occasionally tend the burns. When nightfall arrived, I said good-bye to the house and went back to the garage where my motorcycle waited. I changed out the batteries in the two-way and reorganized the pack before starting up the bike. The engine's growl was amplified by the enclosed space. I ducked under a half-charred two-by-four and motored off into the darkness ahead.

—————

As I again light-cycled like in *Tron* through the grid of back roads, I was forced to lay my motorcycle down in a shower of chrome sparks. An inch-thick steel cable was strung across the road at neck height. The NOD-amplified glint of starlight bouncing off the twisted steel cable warned me at the last possible moment. If I hadn't seen it, I'd have slammed into it at fifty miles per hour, taking my head off. As the bike skidded, I felt the asphalt grinding through my jeans and into my skin before the bike came to rest. Seeing flashlights approach, I leg pressed the bike upright and sped away as blood ran down my shredded jeans.

It was eight o'clock when I arrived back at the camp, burned, beaten, scraped, and exhausted.

"You look like hell, Max," said Rich. "I honestly thought I'd never see you again, but I'm damn glad you made it!"

"Me too. It was a rough one. How'd we do?"

"You didn't hear?"

"No, how could I? I barely made it back alive," I responded wearily.

"I sent out a two-way transmission in the blind—you must have missed it. You brought them to their *damn knees*, Max."

"I don't understand, I only destroyed the tower. We figured it would degrade their ability to hunt us, but—" I said before Rich interrupted.

"Listen to me—it started the morning after you destroyed the tower. Peterson relied heavily on the Hub to supplement his agents, but he horribly underestimated its vulnerability. I was listening to everything fall apart, in real time on the radio. The population was accustomed to their weather, news, and food pickup locations being delivered digitally. When the information stopped flowing downstream from Peterson, a few thousand angry citizens marched on the sheriff's office, demanding they be told where all the food was being stored. Peterson refused."

"And?"

"He gunned down a hundred of them," Rich said coldly, not making eye contact.

"How the fuck does that mean we brought them to their knees, Rich? Now you're telling me I'm responsible for a hundred more deaths—on top of untold millions!" I blurted, wishing I hadn't as the words left my mouth.

"Okay . . . first thing. Peterson's goons may have killed a hundred, and that is tragic, but don't kid yourself; the people got their hits in too. Many of the protesters had Molotov cocktails tucked inside their coats; they lobbed them at those storm troopers after the shots started coming in their direction. They got lucky; some of their Molotovs made it inside the turrets, burning the crews out of three vehicles. It didn't stop there. A few courageous men captured the abandoned turrets and started sending fifty-cal rounds into enemy vehicles and even the sheriff's office."

"That's . . . that's great. Geez. Sorry. I didn't mean to snap. My burns," I said, holding my hands up.

"It's all right, I understand. But . . . can you run that by me again? That part about 'untold millions'?"

Reluctantly, I spent the next hour explaining everything to Rich from start to finish, sparing no detail. Either I was a patsy used to bring everything down, or the government unknowingly opened Pandora's box. Evil? Incompetence? Did either matter anymore?

"So that's why I do what I do. This is why I fight," I said to Rich, tears of guilt streaming down my face, salt irritating the burns.

Rich was like a human supercomputer, processing chunks of data. After a long silence, he finally spoke. "Max . . . it's not your fault. It may seem that way right now from your vantage point, but it's really not. There are too many variables at play. Do you really think they'd trust a junior operative to pull something like that off? Yeah, okay, you had a partner, sure . . . but there are more moving parts to this that neither of us know. You can't be sure that *yours* was the only team sent in. Want to know something? I heard the Eurozone fall with my own ears on shortwave BBC, *before* Syria. What you did over there isn't what's important; it's what you do *today*. We're only two guys with guns, remember when you said that?"

"Yeah, I remember. That's still true."

"No, Max, it's not," Rich said, wearing a conspiratorial grin. "I made radio contact with the three stolen MRAPs."

After washing up for the night and applying some burn ointment Rich had in his trunk, I passed out. The pain was intense, beaten only by extreme exhaustion. I slept for nine hours solid before waking up in a panic, seeing the sunlight scattered throughout the boxcar. Rich sat on his rack on the other side with his carbine across his legs.

"Thought you might have needed the recovery time."

I was thankful. Rich poured us some Sterno-boiled pine needle tea. I was getting tired of the hobo lifestyle, but it sure beat living under an overpass somewhere, waiting to get murdered for my boots.

The road rash on my leg throbbed when I swung my legs off the bed. All the blisters on my face and hands had formed, and the pain dropped a notch below unbearable. Between the road rash and the blisters, it honestly hurt to do just about anything. A half pill of codeine helped some.

"We're meeting them tonight," Rich told me nonchalantly, between sips.

"Who?"

"INKY, BLINKY, and CLYDE, the code names I've given to the rebel MRAP crews. Just like a cell, they won't know where we sleep at night, and we won't know where they hang their hats. Protects everyone. Meeting is set for midnight behind where Southgate used to be."

"I'll be there."

I procured a set of blue railroad coveralls from Rich. They fit a little loose, but my jeans were trashed from dumping the bike. I cut my old jeans into strips, boiled them, and put them aside for extra bandages. Feeling better around lunchtime, I had some rice and helped Rich with a new project he was working on a few cars down. With a black fifty-five-gallon drum, a garden hose, and a soup can as a shower head, Rich cobbled together a decent solar shower.

An hour before midnight, we started moving for Southgate. Since we were early, we stopped at the locomotive engines to check their status. He gave the engines what looked to me like a thirty-point inspection by flashlight.

"Half full of fuel, fluids are good, battery on number one could use a charge, but it's serviceable."

"How long would it take to get them moving?"

"I'd need a few hours to make sure it was done right. There's a couple cars I'd cut in the back. Don't think I'd want to spend fuel pulling three boxcars full of Magic 8 Balls."

"How far could you get?"

"With that amount of fuel, probably a few hundred miles, assuming I couldn't find more along the way."

We broke off from the train and headed south to the crossing. The cold was brutal but welcomed by my blistered skin. Rich seemed to move without a care, but I worried about night things, like headhunting bikers and wolves. Up until now, it was Rich and me versus the world. The prospect of meeting new people that shared our disdain for this sudden tyranny raised my spirits, and I was already forming plans in my head on how to utilize them.

Approaching Southgate, I could see a late-model Ford truck parked behind one of the looted shops. As we got closer I noticed it was not your typical good-old-boy pickup. A fifty-caliber crew-served machine gun sat mounted on a tripod in the bed.

Rich cupped his hand next to his mouth and said, "Elkins."

"Elks!" responded from the darkness.

The three rebel MRAP drivers were present, two sitting in their modified technical with the third on gun duty. Smart—no point wasting the MRAP's precious diesel for a simple midnight meeting. We made introductions using only code names, reiterating the ground rules of not revealing more than absolutely necessary. INKY was a former marine and Enduring Freedom veteran. CLYDE was National Guard, and BLINKY was just a cubicle worker that saw his wife get mowed down in front of him by Peterson's thugs.

We shared intel for an hour before Rich and I deemed the group vetted enough to receive a code book and a separate frequency schedule. At the end of that exchange, the civilian asked one simple question:

"What do we do now?"

Simple enough, but when I thought for sure that Rich was about to answer, Rich pivoted to me instead. I didn't hesitate—these were men and could smell weakness. They'd already been through a lot, and now it seemed all eyes were on me to make a decision.

"We execute an attack in one week," I said. "Make no mistake, we're going kinetic, and people will die. It's up to us to make sure we take enough of them with us. With me?"

All four men, including Rich, nodded in unison.

"I won't reveal the target until the night before we attack. That way, if your cell gets rolled up, the target is still viable. It's hardened, but that's what you guys are for. We'll meet back here in six days, the night before we attack. I'd like you to alter your MRAPs a little, but it won't make a lot of sense right now. You have any paint?"

INKY nodded. "We can get some, not a problem."

"Good," I said, scribbling instructions on a piece of scrap paper from my journal. "This, exactly as indicated, okay?"

The three men huddled over the paper smiling. I suspected they understood more than I gave them credit for. After shaking hands, we parted ways. As Rich and I departed the company of our new friends, the white Ford truck turned out of Southgate and headed east.

"You think they'll show?" I asked.

"They'll do whatever you tell them to, but I have a question."

"Shoot."

"When were you gonna to tell me this plan of yours?"

"When were you going to tell me that I'd be calling the shots?"

"You always knew that, Max."

He was right—I did.

In the days after our meeting with the ghosts, as Rich calls them, we made some pretty decent quality-of-life improvements at the train. The shower collected enough rainwater for a test run, and I took advantage. Not the coldest shower I've ever taken, but close. My wounds seemed to improve after they were washed with something better than toilet tank water. I'd been popping antibiotics regularly, but was more conservative with the codeine. Even taking quarter doses of prescription pain meds made me crave it more and more each day. The people that needed it full-time before all this were now dead, mean, or had gone mad.

Rich's recent eavesdropping has been interesting. Peterson was truly reeling from the losses at his headquarters, hanging hastily painted signs that offered desperate rewards for information leading to the killing or capture of those involved in the recent rioting and theft of government property. There were still some rats out there in the populace; the ghosts' names were being passed up the echelon as Peterson begged his handlers for reinforcements. Rich couldn't hear the distant end of the conversation on his portable radio, but Peterson's response told both sides of the story. What was left of the central government could not even spare one asset for Arkansas. Little Rock was much larger and had been denied federal reinforcements already.

"How can you expect me to crush this rebellion without logistics support?" Peterson's voice inquired, presumably to some distant bureaucrat.

Meanwhile, I took this downtime to coordinate a plan complex enough to meet my end state, but not overly optimistic. Even with three rebel MRAPs, we couldn't go head to head against Peterson and survive. In thinking through the philosophy of the situation, our small resistance cell could be represented as a school of fish. We could not survive without the population, the water. Peterson was doing a good job at removing the water from the metaphorical pond by disappearing anyone he deemed a political prisoner. The scales were tipped in his favor, but he was starting to panic.

Rich and I looked over the EFPs that remained, double-checking that the explosives were properly packed inside and that the solid copper plates were aligned. Logistically we were set. Our tactics boxcar was packed with ammunition, explosives, and everything else we needed for our unfortunate lifestyle of dirty tricks. According to Rich, we hadn't even dented a percentage point of the train's food stores. Yesterday, when Rich and I checked some of the more distant boxcars, we almost wept with joy upon finding one stacked to the ceiling with cases of canned meat. Last night's dinner was gourmet, with chopped mystery meat and cooked rice—a true luxury.

I hiked up to the campsite and pulled the tarp out of the trees. Using the Bowie, I sliced a large rectangle from the heavy brown material and laid it on the flattest ground I could find nearby. I'd already cut the stencils from scrap cardboard, so it didn't take long to spray-paint what I wanted on both sides of the tarp. I chopped the straightest stick I could find and wrapped the width of one end of tarp around it, securing it with paracord and duct tape. After letting the letters dry, I rolled up the banner and took it to the ultralight for later.

Yesterday, Rich forged a U-shaped gun rest out of a rail spike with his forge; I installed it on the ultralight with a liberal amount of duct tape. After gassing up the ultralight, I chopped some new foliage to conceal it and headed back to the train for the next preparation.

Rich was waiting on me when I got back. We grabbed the remaining EFPs and headed down the tracks to the bridge that spanned over the main road leading to the university. Upon arrival, we remained concealed as a group of vagrant teens approached, and would be walking under the bridge momentarily. I could hear them cursing and carrying on while they passed by, but they seemed relatively harmless. With the cell tower destroyed, I was relieved that I had other options besides killing them if Rich and I were discovered. With the mob then safely up the street, Rich and I got to work.

On both sides of the span facing west, we attached our EFPs to the bridge.

"Aim at that pothole, the one next to the sign," I said, pointing.

With both EFPs directed to a single focal point, it wouldn't be difficult to take a cheap shot as a target passed over the pothole. Using some of the spray paint I salvaged from the shelter, I put a quick coat over both devices, concealing the shiny copper projectiles. We ran the EFP wires to the top of the boxcar we'd been using for observation and taped them to the roof for easy access.

"Hold on to this," I said to Rich, handing him the clacker.

"These gadgets will work at that distance?" Rich asked skeptically.

"They'll work as far as the eye can see, if they're aimed right. That copper will be moving at five or six thousand meters per second when you detonate the charge. To the human eye, it's instantaneous."

"What will it do to them?"

"You'll see. It won't be pretty."

Rich didn't seem too keen on using them. After what I'd seen at the cell tower, I can't fault him. It's a terrible weapon designed for uncivilized times. The day of our meeting with the three ghosts is fast approaching; I need to get back to the shelter one last time before we go hot.

I took off this morning just before sunup. Tomorrow night we'd be meeting with the ghosts, and I'd be revealing the target and plans. We haven't made contact with them since our meeting, but that was expected.

I climbed up from under the transmission line runway on a full tank, turning southeast for home. Below me on the roadways, there was no activity, not even military vehicles. Peterson's agents were typically out around that time, but with his tipper Hub network shut down, I suppose business was slow.

After landing and concealing the aircraft, I finessed the choke on my ATV long enough to get it running even after all the cold weather. I visited each of my various caches around the property, taking from some, improving camouflage on others. Down in the shelter, my batteries hovered between 99 and 100 percent charge. I grabbed the ultralight engine oil and filters and my toolbox and stacked them on the ATV, along with some food and extra ammunition.

With the ATV packed, I needed some time to recompile and think, so I hiked to my truck and recovered my keys from a plastic bag under a nearby rock. I closed my eyes and clicked my fob, unlocking the truck. With my eyes still closed, I imagined a time before this. I was just a man, walking to my truck, about to go on a road trip. When I opened my eyes again, the dusty film and layer of acorn shells that covered the netting over my truck was a stark visual reminder of the exact opposite. I pulled the netting from the cab, piling it up on the tonneau cover. Inside the truck, I honestly thought that these were the most comfortable seats I'd ever experienced. I was getting far too used to case lot furniture and coffee bean pillows. Although my brain was screaming for me to stop, I couldn't control my hand as it inserted the key into the ignition and turned. The engine sputtered for a second from abandonment, but soon roared to life.

The screen illuminated on my dash, with all the familiar colors and hues of technology. It told me that it couldn't find my Bluetooth device, so I tapped the screen over to maps. No GPS signal.

"Are you indoors?" it asked.

With no phone, no satellites, and no CDs, I had no music, which was the real reason I came to the truck, if I was being honest with myself. At least I had seat warmers for a while. If only I could wire these up in the ultralight. I had a full tank of stabilized gas, and could be back at the train inside of twenty minutes, but it didn't fit the plan. I needed the ultralight. Besides, if Peterson's MRAPs caught me on the road, I'd be shredded to pieces in short order at the barrel of those fifty-cals.

In desperation, I started scanning through the AM spectrum. Like CDs, AM was a dinosaur unless you were the type to listen to conservative talk radio or Hispanic music; I couldn't understand one of those, and didn't like the other. The radio scanned through nearly every available frequency before it stopped and words began to spill from my advanced, now worthless sound system.

I grabbed a pen and paper from my center console and began copying.

". . . Abraham from Radio Free Oklahoma, where the candle is in the window! Know that there are people out there that don't like what's been going on and have been doing a little something about it. We're looking at you, Arkansas! That's right, the word is out, Arkansas has . . ."

A thirty-second interruption cut in at this point, but was obviously automated.

"The time is zero nine fifty central. This is a Homeland Security update. More food is on the way. Recent terrorist activities have prevented longer utility availabilities and food distribution, as well as cellular and data services. A reward of two months' rations is offered for information leading to the capture of terrorists or the prevention of terrorist activities. If you have information, wave a white flag at any security vehicle, and an agent will stop to assist you."

The transmission faded, yielding to the first station.

". . . way to destroy them is on the ground, before they take off. Radio Free Oklahoma is gathering a list of known airports where these machines are based, all across America, or what's left of it. Anyone that knows of a way to bring down their armor, send it in, and we'll broadcast it . . ."

The Homeland Security transmission interrupted again, broadcasting the same message. I noted the time and AM frequency for

Rich before shutting down my truck, maybe for good. We weren't the only ones hitting back, and that was something that people needed to know.

Back at the shelter, I made preps to shut it down for long-term abandonment. I disconnected and hauled the full propane bottle down into the shelter, along with any other stores I could fit. It was better to have valuables locked away underground than sitting in a tarp covered hole somewhere else. I had the room, so I stacked a few cartons of cigarettes on the ATV for Rich. All packed up, I made a final sweep, heading for the clay ground near the pond. If anything were moving around here, the clay would tell me. I could see the deep impressions even before I got close. I had never seen a wolf track at Black Oak, but the imprint in the clay was much larger than the coyote common to these parts. The track made my heart race a little faster. The pain in my shoulder was gone, except when I put my arms above my head, but the memories were permanent. I wasn't far from the salt lick my cousins placed last year, so I decided to move in a little farther.

As I ducked branches, avoiding thorns and craggy landscapes, I knew what this walk was really about: I might be saying good-bye to the woods where I grew up.

The clearing was up ahead. As I broke through the last brush, I could clearly see the deer stand Jim put in years earlier. Rust broke through its flat-black paint, making it easy to spot among the surrounding trees. I half expected to see a dead man rotting in the stand, with a ravenous pack of wolves circling below. Approaching the stand, the salt lick came into view, and the familiar buck. I got low and watched him as his head bobbed back and forth between the salt and the attentive scan of its surroundings. His broad chest faced me like a barn door; I could easily drop him from where I crouched on the damp, mossy ground.

He lived.

Once again, I hit the winding trail on the ATV, convinced I could do it blindfolded, and probably really could.

Back at the cow field, I started up the ultralight for a few minutes before shutting it down and removing the oil plug. Filthy black oil spilled out onto the grass; I was pushing it with the engine. I quickly changed the filter and estimated the torque on the plug before replacing the black sludge with new oil. Once that was complete, I was airborne again.

I looked forward to finally being able to pass Rich information he didn't have.

———

It snowed last night, concealing any tracks I'd made after my flight back to the train. Rich is in his corner, going over communications frequencies, smoking the cigarettes I brought back for him. Every night for the past week, I could hear him hammering the rail like an anvil, heating the cable steel with the intensity of his ten-dollar forge. Today we braved the snow, slogging through the three-inch powder to get to the bridge for some practice. We lay in wait on top of the boxcar for the regular patrol, and froze for about forty-five minutes before we heard anything approach. Rich held the disconnected clacker like I showed him. When we felt the vibration of the passing MRAPs underneath, I knew less than a second remained. The front wheels of the lead MRAP rolled over the pothole aim point when I slapped Rich on the back.

"Did you squeeze before or after I hit you?" I asked.

"Before, way too soon."

"Better now than tomorrow, eh?" I said to him.

Now it's closing on midnight. There is a tangible feeling of hope, mixed with some dread, at least in our microcosm aboard this crazy train. We met with the ghosts tonight and I put it all on the table. INKY, the leader, was the first to ask the obvious question.

"What's the target?"

I pulled a page from a road atlas in my kit, turning on my red headlamp so everyone could see. I traced their ingress route with my finger, straight down MLK, under our train where Rich would be laying prone above. Rich would have his carbine at his side, EFP detonator in one hand, radio in another. Overwatch. If anyone happened to be tailing them, Rich would engage with the EFPs. I continued to trace the route so they could start memorizing it.

"Make a right here, half a mile, you'll start to see the target on the right. You can't miss it," I said to the ghosts.

"What is it?"

"It's a detainment facility. I flew over it a while back and nearly got shot out of the sky." I pointed to a circled spot on the map. "Here are two pillboxes. You'll need to take care of those."

"Okay, what about after that? What's the big picture?" INKY inquired nervously.

"We're assisting a prison break—the largest in United States history."

I briefed details to the ghosts well into the night, pointing out estimated guard strength, what likely reactions might be, etc., etc. Before Rich and I left the meeting, I reminded the ghosts that it was very likely that not all of us would make it back.

"I took an oath to the Constitution of the United States, as did most of you. Right now, the entire state, maybe even country, is effectively a Constitution-free zone. It started with airports, and then it was highways, then it was our e-mail and phones, and then it was shopping centers and sporting events. Now it's everywhere. Just an idea can make a difference. We brought down their drone, destroyed their Hub grid communications, and disrupted their criminal contractor network. That was when we were only two guys with guns; now we're five, with bigger guns."

The raw energy of resistance that flowed between us was palpable. The ghosts would head back east to pick up the MRAPs and convoy in before sunup, where they would lay in wait at an agreed rally point. Their signal to roll would be my flyover after sunup. From this point on, they'd be going in hot, shooting anything with wheels along the ingress.

Before saying our good-byes, Rich asked that we all bow our heads. I never saw the harm in asking for a little help from above. After a few short words, we all said our amens and shook hands. Rich and I left the ghosts and disappeared under the moon like so many times before. It's time to blow out the candle with the hopes to write again soon.

Click, clack, click, clack, click, clack.

I didn't really sleep well the night before, waiting restlessly for my watch alarm to begin beeping. When it finally did, I got up and stoked the coal fire for breakfast. Afterward, Rich and I went over the plan once more. Rich would remain at his observation post over the bridge, copying communication intelligence from the police frequencies and sending radio warnings out over two-way. I'd be flying with earbuds under my watch cap so that I could listen and transmit regular updates from the air. Although the ghost's MRAPs would be relying on their powerful fifty-cal machine guns to punch through the detention facility's defenses, I was carrying an even more powerful weapon. To complement that, I had a box full of gifts from above that Rich had been busy forging the past week.

Rich shook my hand and said, "Godspeed" before I jumped down from the train, strapped on my cargo, and walked south in the direction of the transmission lines. My surroundings began to glow in vibrant colors from the golden daybreak light, but maybe it was something more. I was seeing clearly for the first time since I could remember; a sort of brain fog lifted from my consciousness. Walking along the tracks through the snow, I remember catching a glimpse of a fox trotting down the hill from the transmission lines. It saw me but paid no attention as it nimbly hopped over the tracks in two short bounds and disappeared into the tall grass beyond. I hoped that it wouldn't encounter the wolves I saw somewhere out there.

At the ultralight cache, I uncovered and pulled it into the opening, checking the tarp I'd cut and painted previously. After folding the wings out and locking them into place, I conducted a thorough preflight. I buckled my cargo box in the passenger seat and rolled up the tarp after attaching it to the rear of the aircraft below the propeller. I tied a shoestring knot around the roll so that I could pull one end from the cockpit, unfurling the rectangular-shaped tarp behind me at the right time. With everything as it should be, I started the engine and waited for it to warm up. Strapped in, I had a clear backlit view west, down the transmission line beyond the tracks and to the mountains in the distance. I taped my two-way to my arm and ran the earbuds under my wool cap. I hit the throttle, commencing my takeoff roll down the clearing, crunching over frozen and snow-covered grass. My face was numb with cold before my back wheels left the ground, but I was airborne and climbing.

Small clumps of snow and ice fell from the aircraft as I climbed to a thousand feet, following the meandering train north. I dropped to five hundred before reaching the bridge so I could check on Rich. Far below, he lay prone on the boxcar above MLK, a snow angel around him from where he cleared last night's precipitation. I dove a little lower, rocked my wings, and waved at him. I had enough time to see him salute before I climbed back to a thousand feet.

I flew the roads to the rally point, a large barn near Shoffner's corner at the western border of Elkins. I dove down to two hundred feet and established an orbit as close as I could get without clipping the barn with my wings. The doors flew open and three black MRAPs pulled out with gunners manned up on top. I climbed back up to a thousand and flew slowly along our route, just ahead of the convoy. As I flew west, I could see a dot formation of small vehicles closing fast on my convoy.

"INKY, Horsefly, company inbound, bikers."

"Roger."

From high above, I watched the ghosts' fifty-cals arc forward. The bikers slowed at the sight of the approaching vehicles, likely thinking they were fellow criminals. I could tell the difference between the MRAPs by the extra markings the ghosts applied to the roofs: *I, B, C.* BLINKY broke off and pulled up beside INKY in an insane chicken maneuver with the bikers; both gunners opened fire. Their fifty-caliber rounds minced the bikers to pieces. From my vantage point, I saw body parts fall off, some of them thrown a distance by the overwhelming firepower. BLINKY, the cubicle worker, was the most aggressive of the three. After shooting one of the bikes over onto its side, he kept firing at the underside, pushing it into a guardrail with the rider still on. There were no motorcycles standing after the ghosts were done—only red chunks of meat wrapped in denim and leather, and twisted chrome. I guess the ghosts didn't enjoy my saddlebag severed head story any more than I liked living through it.

I was getting too far ahead, so I did a quick three-sixty turn, putting me back on top the MRAPs. The convoy moved quickly, only slowing once to navigate around a gaggle of abandoned cars. Close to Rich's observation post, I lowered altitude again. MLK was directly below as I cruised at forty knots, skimming above the power lines.

"Funnel spider, horsefly, ghosts inbound."

Rich's single transmitter click acknowledged the message.

I was first to reach the bridge, buzzing only ten feet over Rich's head. I rocked my wings again and climbed. The ghosts arrived within a few minutes and passed under Rich.

Back at a thousand feet, I headed straight for the facility. Checking my watch, I had thirty minutes of fuel remaining just as the massive rectangle of double razor wire fence appeared in the distance. I flew the route the ghosts would be driving, directly over the defenses of sandbagged sentries that manned crew-served guns. Looking down, I could see them reacting to the overflight, slewing their guns to me.

"They're about to fire at me," I said calmly to the ghosts over the battering wind at a thousand feet.

"We're on it," INKY's voice responded, just as calm.

I could hear the ghosts' fifty-cals bursting at the sentries, but didn't have time to watch them work. I was overhead the facility now. Thousands of prisoners split their attention between me and the distant sounds of gunfire. I started my descent, spiraling downward in great arcs, above so many faces and hands gesturing upwards to the morning sky.

Reaching the end of my arcing dive, I pulled the shoestring knot on my homemade tarp banner, allowing it to unfurl behind the aircraft. As it extended out and began to wave in the wind behind me, a great boom of voices screamed out from below. The cheering sounds of rebellion.

When I decided what to put on the banner, I had to be brief, to strike a chord with as many people as possible, with as few characters as possible. I imagined being imprisoned, starving down there; what would have been the one word to wake me up, to make me fight?

#RESIST

The ants below had just realized that they outnumbered the grasshoppers a hundred to one.

I watched the ghost MRAPs speed up the hill to the prison. On the radio, I could hear them take coordinated shots. Two enemy MRAPs started firing back at the ghosts, but one of their gunners was overrun by ten prisoners and pulled out of his turret onto the ground. As the ghosts peaked the hill in front of thousands of prisoners, another booming war cry filled the air.

The ghost's block-letter paint jobs were clear and vibrant in the morning sun:

#FIGHT

I continued my low orbit of the prison, picking a spot to airdrop the box, the contents of which Rich had worked so hard to complete. A riot was forming below the aircraft; the guards began to fire at the approaching horde of prisoners, some of them taking the time to shoot at me. I felt the shots impact the frame of the ultralight, instantaneously bringing the backup electrical system down to zero charge. Flying with one hand, I tipped the heavy cardboard box over the side of the aircraft, dropping it between the mobs of prisoners and guards below. I watched it fall, eventually impacting the ground and busting open, its contents skidding in all directions. There were fifty ten-inch steel shivs in the box, forged from rail spikes. The prisoners picked them up out of the snow like they were gold bars and began charging. Women, men, all fighting like tigers for their freedom.

As I continued to circle above the prison yard, I noticed a pair of guards firing at a group of people taking shelter behind large pots of flowers.

They were shooting at children.

I dove at them, drawing their fire away. The two guards attempted to empty their M4 magazines into me, succeeding. One of the rounds went through the meat of my left bicep, and several struck the aircraft and engine, causing immediate mechanical failure. As my right wing bent upward from frame damage, I lost control of the airframe and spun out of control towards the firing guards.

The last thing I remembered before I crashed was pummeling the armed men like rag dolls into the inner chain-link fence. The impact caused me to black out, not sure how long.

My vision was only a single pinpoint of light when I came to. Barely conscious, I reached for my carbine, pulling it by feel from its rack behind the seat.

I could feel something shake the ultralight; I was still strapped in, but nearly upside down. Hearing dangerously close gunshots, I aimed my carbine at the noise and pulled the trigger ten times, sweeping the suppressed barrel horizontally in front of me. The eight-pound weapon felt like a forty-five-pound weight as my brain began to check out. I heard my gun clang against the ultralight frame and hit the ground before I blacked out again.

I faded in and out of consciousness, but I can't be sure when or how often. I remember my boot heels scraping while I was being dragged by my injured arm across some concrete. I remember the screech of duct tape being wrapped around my bicep, I remember being in the back of a vehicle.

But most of all, I remember Jim's voice.

Jim. He was alive.

In this new unconscious realm, I was gifted with overwhelming happiness alongside incapacitating rediscovered grief.

I woke up dehydrated in the dark. As I came to, my eyes began to focus on the candlelight.

Click, clack, click, clack, click, clack.

I was on a moving train, hooked to a swinging IV bag full of clear liquid. I reached over to touch my injured arm, wincing in pain. It was tightly wrapped in bandages.

"Hello?" I asked blindly, too weak to sit up.

"Don't move, Max," Rich responded.

"How long?"

"Four days. You had surgery yesterday. Doctor says you won't lose your spankin' arm, so don't worry."

I laughed, causing strain on my stitches, which made me cry, canceling them both out.

"Jim," I said weakly.

"Yeah, he's fine. Three cars back, sleeping. It's two in the morning."

"Where we headed?"

"Away from here."

Nearly a month has passed since the assault on the detention facility.

After crashing the ultralight during the assault, I remembered Jim's voice and being pulled from the wreckage as I blacked out. In the days leading up to the attack, Jim suspected that Rich and I had been planning something; he'd spotted my ultralight overhead. He could trust no one with what he knew; there were rumors among the detainees of informers imbedded inside the prison wires. These bootlickers likely hoped to earn the food and favoritism of the authorities in the region by turning coat on any prisoner that whispered of rebellious things.

Shorty after sunup on the day I became conscious, the train made an impromptu stop to push an abandoned vehicle off the rail crossing down the tracks. My smile must have stretched from cheek to cheek when I saw my cousin climb into the boxcar. I hadn't slept since Rich told me he was alive.

My reunion with Jim was rough on both of us. Painfully, I watched my cousin break down as he confirmed my worst fears, having never discussed it before that moment. It killed me to hear the confirmation that my aunt and cousin Matt had been killed after the night assault on their home. Sometime during the raid, Matt defensively shot and killed three federal agents that were attempting to firebomb the house. After capture, he was summarily executed on the spot alongside his mother; she was killed for possessing a two-way radio and the hunting rifle she had slung across her back. Jim was sleeping when the gunfight started. He was forced to his knees to watch his mother and brother be murdered by the light of his burning home.

With flowing tears and a clenched jaw, Jim proclaimed that if the raid were just one hour later, he would have been the one with the radio and bolt-action deer rifle when the agents came. It was to be his turn to take the next watch.

After the raid, Jim was hooded and transported to the detention facility for "interrogation." The endless nights of torture, incarceration, and rage that followed the raid affected him in ways only he could fully understand. Daily, he was herded with a handful of other prisoners to what the guards referred to as the Conversation

Room. Bright lights, sleep deprivation, and threats of life imprisonment were the first interrogation techniques used against him. These initial tactics soon yielded to noise torture, waterboarding, and eventually old-fashioned beatings. The heinous slaughter of his mother and brother, coupled with Jim's treatment inside the wires, transfused his typical jovial demeanor, replacing it with cold hate. This easily explained the uncharacteristic aggressiveness I kept hearing about. The other prisoners that fought alongside Jim testified to his unchecked rage during the attack. After the crash, he gave everything, risking his life for both of us. They say he killed one guard with his bare hands before liberating his gun and killing five more. That was before he carried me out of there on his back, returning fire, shadowing the friendly MRAPs for cover.

Since that day, progress has been slow.

We hadn't moved far, maybe thirty miles down the tracks. Frequent stops to clear the path slowed our progress to a crawl. We were well outside of Alma when the conductor on duty spotted that a good portion of the tracks up ahead had been washed out. Stopping wasn't out of the ordinary. We'd hit the brakes countless times before to move a random vehicle from the tracks, or to pick up groups of survivors. This time would prove to be different. People on the train initially devised a plan to remove a section of track behind us to repair the section in front. Doesn't really matter anymore, though—we can't get much farther south even with good track now.

After we stopped the train in the mountains on the north side of the washed -out area, Rich set up the antennas to do a radio scan for intel. According to him, the train sat on a section of track near the top of the Boston Mountains, perfect for reception. When he powered up the radio, he quickly began tuning through the frequencies he'd archived inside his Velcro binder. Homing in on something, he pressed a headphone tightly against his ear and began feverishly writing. Although I couldn't hear the audio at that time, I could tell by Rich's body language and the corrections he was making on paper that he was copying a recorded loop. Rich matter-of-factly handed me his shorthand and moved on along the spectrum as if nothing was wrong.

Arkansas Nuclear One reactor had melted down following a failed emergency shutdown. A fifty-mile exclusion zone extended in all directions from the stricken plant. If the washed-out tracks hadn't stopped our advance, we'd be glowing in the dark by now and probably dead before the end of the week.

We decided to set up camp here outside the exclusion zone to catch our breath and regroup. We'd be safer here for now, utilizing the radiated territory as a buffer shield from whatever approached from the south.

In the days that followed, Rich copied local line-of-sight chatter about the radiation and wind patterns. It wasn't but a few days before he intercepted a bombshell shortwave transmission loop, apparently originating from the Joint Chiefs of Staff.

The U.S. capital had been temporarily relocated to an undisclosed location. A military coup was currently under way and the United States nuclear arsenal was now under the launch authority of the chairman of the Joint Chiefs of Staff. All non-military personnel to include police, federal agents, and civilians were to disarm and cease hostilities immediately. There was now a nationwide sunset-to-sunrise military curfew in effect. Fighters, gunships, and drones would be patrolling the skies over the major cities to quell hostilities.

Here, deep in the Boston Mountains, not much has been changed by the news. Although the way south is blocked by the washed-out tracks and fallout radiation, the tracks luckily go both ways. Rich's radio has brought fuel trains, tractors, and track repair equipment to rendezvous here in the Boston Mountains. They have been arriving steadily over the past week, forming the longest railway consortium in history. To hell with the system's never-ending struggle for control. We won't live in fear; we won't submit. We may stay, or we may trek north, down the forgotten tracks, listening to the click-clacking echoes of America's prosperous past. Her future is up to us.

Once just two guys with guns.

The previous record is classified as a historical document, transcribed from petabytes of text, audio, and video recovered from various sensors that were located in the territory formerly known as the United States of America. Hub records indicate that there are nearly five hundred fragmented personal accounts of the Rebellion of 2021. The Max ▬▬▬▬▬▬▬▬ account stands out from the rest, as it is widely considered by historians to be the most accurate and complete depiction of how, where, and when the rebellion began. This fifty-third edition includes old government voice transcripts recently robotically excavated from the radioactive zones in and around the former District of Columbia. Although the redacted digital portions of the record outlining the early days of the rebellion survived the nuclear/EMP exchange of 2025, not until 2093, when the yellowed pages of the handwritten volume was discovered at an estate sale in the Arkansas territory, was the rest of the account made available. The identity of Max ▬▬▬▬▬▬▬▬ remains unknown as of this imprinting.

<<<< >>>>

ACKNOWLEDGMENTS

This novel would not be possible without the caring support of my wonderful wife, the candid feedback of my editor, the confidence of my publisher, the career helmsmanship of my agent, and of course you, the reader. For my daughter, I pray that by the time you are old enough to read this you'll find nothing familiar within these pages, and that we'll share a laugh about your eccentric old dad, who worried too much during these times of turmoil and uncertainty. For my readers, thank you for joining me once again down another bleak path to oblivion that hopefully remains in the fiction section where it belongs. Finally, I must thank the United States Navy for the crucible fire spanning twenty years that forged who I am today, both in life and on paper.